MOM'S THE WORD

MOM'S THE WORD

CASE FILES OF AN URBAN WITCH™ BOOK FIVE

MARTHA CARR

MICHAEL ANDERLE

DISRUPTIVE IMAGINATION®

LMBPN Publishing
PMB 196, 2540 South Maryland Pkwy
Las Vegas, NV 89109

Version 1.00, June, 2021
ebook ISBN: 978-1-64971-827-3
Print ISBN: 978-1-64971-828-0

THE MOM'S THE WORD TEAM

Thanks to the JIT Readers

Jeff Goode
Dave Hicks
Diane L. Smith

If we've missed anyone, please let us know!

Editor
Skyhunter Editing Team

CHAPTER ONE

Lucy Heron stepped off the Silver Griffins' private magical subway car, with its steaming engine and its gleaming blue carriage, and into the station hidden in the hillside beneath Griffith Observatory. There was seldom a crush of people on this line. It didn't cater to the broader magical population, never mind the mundane humans who filled the streets of L.A., oblivious to the society of witches and wizards, elves, dwarves, gnomes, and other magical creatures hidden within their city. Still, every commuter line was going to see some extra bustle on a Monday morning, and she let a small crowd of wizards, witches, and administrative gnomes flow past her before heading across the platform to the station keeper's office.

Normandy the gnome sat behind his counter, peaked cap sitting jauntily on his head and buttons gleaming on his uniform. He smiled and raised the window as Lucy approached. "Good morning, Agent Heron. Did you have a good weekend?"

"It was lovely, thank you." Lucy's northern English

accent added roundness to the vowels. "Charlie and I took the kids for a walk in the country, then to the archaeological site Dylan's going to help at."

"He must be very excited."

"Him and all his friends. They think they're going to be the next Indiana Jones. I hope they're not too disappointed when it's all dust and tiny trowels." Lucy set down her Wonder Woman travel cup with steam curling off the top of her tea and opened her Batman backpack. "I managed to do some baking with Eddie too, so these are for you."

She handed Normandy a paper bag full of chocolate and peanut cookies. The gnome beamed.

"They smell delicious. Thank you, Agent Heron."

"Thank you for keeping this place so well for us." Lucy zipped her bag shut and picked up her tea. "Looks like the crowd's gone, so I'll head on up. See you later, lad."

"And you, Agent."

A short walk along a tunnel, then a climb up a steeply spiraling set of stairs took Lucy to a secret door into the Griffith Observatory, close to the planetarium. The whole place was quiet this early in the day, so she didn't have to worry about dodging tourists as she made her way past the planetarium and the pendulum, down an exhibition hall, and through a secret doorway opened by a tap of her wand.

In the reception of the Silver Griffins' L.A. base, the last few agents from the morning rush were still in line to pass security procedures.

"This is ridiculous," a gray-haired wizard said indignantly. "I've been working here for decades. You know who I am."

"That's exactly what a doppelgänger would say," the receptionist said curtly. "So if you want to come in, you'll need to get your wand out."

"This is outrageous, a jumped-up nobody getting ideas above his station."

"Wand, please." The receptionist's smile was brittle.

"You can't talk to me like this."

"That works both ways. Now please, your wand."

With a derisive snort, the wizard placed his pine wand on a box on the reception desk. A light on the box flashed red. Behind the wizard, Lucy drew her short, knobby wand, just in case.

"Damn thing's clearly broken." The wizard slapped the box. "You should get that looked at."

"Actually, we had it tested this weekend." The receptionist slowly reached under his desk. "Why don't you give it another try?"

"Fine." The wizard made as if to place his wand on the box again, then let go of it and grabbed the receptionist's wrist before he could press the alarm button. "Oh no, you don't!"

The receptionist tried to jerk back, but the wizard gripped tight and yanked him forward, slamming his forehead into the receptionist's face. For a moment, the wizard's wrinkled features turned into something blank and pale.

"Stupefacio." Lucy waved her wand. The spell hit the wizard, who went limp and fell to the floor, stunned. His face rippled, and the wrinkles vanished, along with the sharpness of his nose, the jutting chin, and the piercing brightness of his eyes. They left behind a face as blank and featureless as a mannequin in a department store window.

"This is why we need security checks." The receptionist rubbed his nose. He picked up his desk phone. "Security to reception, please. We have a doppelgänger again." He sighed as he put the phone down. "Probably hired by one of the criminal gangs, trying to get in and find out about security for the crown."

"What crown?"

The receptionist blinked, then put on another brittle smile. "Nothing. I probably misspoke, and if I didn't, it'll be somebody else's job to tell you." He pointed firmly at the box on his desk. "Once you pass security, that is."

Lucy tapped her wand on the box. This time the green light came on, and the receptionist waved her into the office as a pair of security witches appeared to take the doppelgänger away.

Jackie Kowal was already sitting at the desk opposite Lucy's, a big mug of coffee steaming in front of her as she stabbed furiously at her keyboard.

"Something annoying in the inbox?" Lucy asked.

"Always," Jackie said. "How am I supposed to get any work done when people want me to go to endless meetings and fill in stupid forms? Because I got people's asses into gear for the cleanup after Mr. No, I have to waste my time on messages from the director of this or the head of that."

"Senior management is talking to you?" Kelly Petrie asked through the sneer on her perfectly made-up face as she walked past. "Are you sure they haven't got your email address mixed up with someone else?"

"Very funny. You can have all these emails if you want. I only want to go chase some rogue magicals."

At that moment, a pigeon landed on top of Jackie's monitor with a message wrapped around its leg.

"Not another one!" Jackie glared from the bird to two others pecking at worms near her wastepaper bin. "Bureaucracy is going to be the death of me."

"Excuse me, Agent Heron?" Sam, the regional manager's PA, had appeared silently by Lucy's desk. "Mr. Applegate would like to see you in his office."

"Ha!" Jackie said. "This time it's for you. Have fun!"

"Thanks, Sam." Lucy took a paper bag out of her backpack, picked up her tea, and headed for Applegate's office. Through the glass wall and open shutters, she saw two other people sitting inside, talking to the boss.

She knocked, then walked in, and placed the paper bag on Applegate's desk.

"Some biscuits for you, sir." She smiled. "I hear that you're still recovering your strength, and chocolate chips are medicinal."

Roger Applegate gave a jovial laugh and patted his belly. The buttons of his three-piece suit looked a little strained.

"My wife's been taking a similar approach to my recovery," he said. "I keep telling her it was my mind not my body that got attacked, but I have to admit, I don't mind this sort of medicine. Thank you very much." He took a cookie, then offered the bag to his guests while nodding toward Lucy. "This is the agent I was telling you about, number 485, Lucy Heron. Lucy, this is Margaret Sunder, head of security for North America."

A short, gray-haired witch with a narrow face and piercing eyes gave Lucy a sharp nod. "Agent Heron."

"I believe you know Agent 399, Ellis Ellis?"

A lanky wizard in a charcoal gray suit and red sneakers smiled at her from behind his neatly kept blond beard. "Howdy, Lucy. How's tricks?"

"Pretty good, lad. And you?"

"Back in L.A., so I can't complain."

Lucy knew what that meant, but she didn't think that Ellis would want her to ask about his dating life in front of their bosses.

"Roger tells me that you're one of his best agents." Margaret Sunder studied Lucy as she spoke. "And that you also have some knowledge of art and galleries?"

"Mr. Applegate is too kind," Lucy said. "There are lots of agents here as good as me. Yes, I do have some art knowledge. I worked in a gallery in Leeds in my teens, back when I wanted to be a curator, and I still get to exhibits when I can."

"Excellent. Then I have a project for you." Sunder waved her wand, a slender strip of birch with a velvet grip, and an image appeared in the air. It consisted of a dozen different objects, most of them made from silver or gold, several decorated with gemstones. They included candlesticks, a bowl, a dagger, and a crown. "This is part of the Trakai Hoard, a collection of medieval metalwork discovered in Lithuania at the turn of the millennium. It includes several magical artifacts, which we were unable to secure before details of the hoard went public. Artifacts that, in an ideal world, mundane humans would never see.

"Because of its historical and financial value, the Hoard

became instantly famous, and we were unable to take control of it. Instead, the Silver Griffins have been covertly providing magical security around the items for over twenty years. During that time, we've built up a robust network of security magics around the Hoard's usual home. There have been multiple attempts to steal all or part of the Hoard, none successful.

"Now, part of the Hoard is leaving Lithuania for the first time since its discovery. For the next six months, this part will form an exhibit at the Los Angeles County Museum of Art. It's a matter of absolute certainty that one or more magicals will try to steal parts of the exhibit. We need someone who understands both magic and museums to arrange suitable covert security for as long as these items are in L.A. Are you up to the task?"

"Yes, ma'am." The items shown in the images were beautiful. Lucy couldn't wait to see them up close, as well as to have an excuse to hang out in the art museum. This was going to be the best assignment ever. "I'll make sure they're secure."

"Excellent. Agent Ellis will stay in town to provide a liaison from my office. If you need anything from me, let him know, and I'll ensure it gets immediate attention."

Sunder stood and headed for the door.

"Roger, I'll speak to you later." She nodded a curt goodbye and headed out, followed by Ellis.

Left alone with Applegate, Lucy turned to her boss with a grin. "Thank you so much, sir. This is going to be brilliant."

"You've earned a chance to do something you'll enjoy." Applegate brushed crumbs from his vest. "Not only for the cookies but for all the times recently that you've saved us from disaster. I'll send you details of the assignment, but for now, perhaps you should spend the day scoping out the gallery, really get a sense of the place." He grinned. "Have fun, Agent Heron."

CHAPTER TWO

A mile away from the Observatory, a subway train stopped in a station on the main magical line. Elves and dwarves, gnomes and Willen, witches and wizards all poured out. Some of them were commuting into town from the edges of L.A., but others had traveled across the country to do business. Some had come even farther.

As the rush-hour crowd dissipated, a dozen witches and wizards gathered together on the platform. They spoke to each other in nearly as many languages as there were travelers, though with a skew toward German and Eastern European tongues. All of them wore comfortable clothes and carried suitcases as well as backpacks and long, slender bags that hung from their shoulders.

Gruffbar the dwarf stroked his neatly trimmed beard as he watched the travelers from the side of the platform. This would be the first time he met these clients in person, and he liked to get an idea of who he was dealing with before he approached. They were what he had expected from an ancient order of magical warriors: muscled, alert, with the same sort of bright, confident energy as professional athletes. Not that Gruffbar's law work involved many sports people, but he'd seen them on TV, and he was a decent judge of what made a person distinctive. The Knights of the Hinterland were certainly that.

He raised a hand in greeting as he approached. "I'm Gruffbar Steelstrike. Is one of you Klara Schulz?"

A witch in her late forties stepped out of the small crowd. She was an imposing figure, six feet tall in her flat-soled sneakers and with the sort of sternness that said she wouldn't tolerate any nonsense. Her handshake was intimidatingly firm and left Gruffbar confident that there were plenty of muscles underneath her loose sports clothes.

"*Guten Morgen*. I'm Schulz, the Chancellor of the Knights of the Hinterland. This is my deputy, Oskar von Konigsberg."

The young man standing next to her gave a curt nod. He was a fraction taller than Schulz, blond-haired and blue-eyed, and wore an expensive designer t-shirt that flattered his ridiculously muscled body. While Schulz's sternness created the impression that she was waiting for the world to disappoint her, Konigsberg looked as though he had already passed judgment and whoever he was looking at, his sneer was specifically for them. Gruffbar had worked for far worse people, morally speaking, but none had created such an instant sense of loathing as this puffed-up young man.

"Pleased to meet you." Gruffbar didn't allow a hint of his feelings to show. "Shall we go straight to the safe house?"

"*Ja*, that would be good," Schulz agreed.

Gruffbar led them out of the station, through a magically hidden door in the back of a Starbucks, and into the street. The group inevitably drew some attention as they passed through the coffee shop, and he heard someone speculating on whether they were a sports team. The number of admiring looks sent Konigsberg's way only made Gruffbar dislike the man more.

Several rental cars were waiting outside, all driven by trusted mechanics from the garage where Gruffbar had his office. The Knights of the Hinterland piled in. Gruffbar, Schulz, and Konigsberg all got into the same car, and the small convoy headed out through the streets.

"It's not far away," Gruffbar said, "but I thought this was the easiest way to get you all there the first time, without losing anyone or having to worry about luggage."

"I would expect nothing less for what we have paid you," Schulz said.

"Of course. The safe house itself is a set of apartments above a Chinese restaurant. It was the best I could arrange on short notice, given the specifics you provided."

"I'm sure it will be fine."

Gruffbar raised an eyebrow. "You're putting a lot of faith in someone you've never met."

Schulz turned from watching the street go by to look at him.

"Faith is for God, *Herr* Gruffbar. Where creatures like you are concerned, I rely on your greed."

"Creatures like me?" Gruffbar tensed. "You have a problem with dwarves?"

"Not dwarves, lawyers. Few of you people are anything but mercenaries, and if there is one thing that our order has learned down the centuries, it is the limit on how far we can trust a mercenary."

Gruffbar laughed. "That's fair. As your current sword for hire, is there anything else you want from me?"

"*Nein*. Our business is our own. If we need you, we will find you."

"You make it sound like you'll hunt me down. You know you have my number, right?"

"I know, but if I need to, I will hunt."

They pulled up in a back street beside a set of dumpsters. The Knights got out, and Gruffbar led them inside, up the stairs to their apartments.

"There's some basic food and drink supplied, in case you're hungry after your journey," he said. "Though by the looks of you, I guess you'll want protein powder more than coffee and croissants."

"We can shop once you're gone." Schulz put her bag down in the corner of the first apartment. "Thank you, *Herr* Gruffbar."

She shook his hand. To Gruffbar's surprise, so did Konigsberg. To his even greater surprise, the guy smoothly and discreetly slipped him a fifty in that handshake. The kid might carry himself like he was God's gift to God, but he certainly knew how to tip.

"I'll get out of your hair," Gruffbar said. "If you need anything…" he made sure to catch Konigsberg's eye, "call me."

Once Gruffbar was gone, Klara Schulz gathered her men and women in the living room of one of the apartments. Space was limited, but it would do. Once she got rid of the sofa and brought in a suitable table, this could be their command and control room.

She set a crystal on top of the TV set and tapped it with her wand, a dagger made from a tough alloy of star metal and silver. There was a *crackle* like static as anti-surveillance magic spread out through the room. That wasn't only for the dwarf's sake, though she knew what sort of clients he usually worked for and therefore how little they could trust him. More important was keeping anything said here from the ears of the Silver Griffins. If they knew what the group planned, it would put every-thing in jeopardy.

She surveyed her companions, eleven of the best and brightest that the Order of the Knights of the Hinterland had to offer. Therefore, the best and brightest in the world. Strong, smart, skilled, and committed to their cause.

"There will be many distractions in this city." Centuries ago, when the Order had ridden into battle alongside the Teutonic Knights and the Swordbrothers, their leader would have addressed his troops in German, the language of the Order's founders. These days, English had become the universal language, the one spoken by recruits from all over the world, so she used it now. In two hundred years, her successors would probably use Chinese, but that was for them to deal with: her view was long, her concerns immedi-ate. "Amid these distractions, it is more important than ever that you remember who you are and what binds you together. We have a mission, one we have labored at unflinchingly for over eight hundred years. What is that mission?"

"Drive back the darkness," the Knights chanted in

unison. "Lift the light. Hunt down the monsters. For the glory of God and a better world."

"Good. If you ever find yourselves uncertain, if you need something to bring you back to the path, remember those principles and choose your actions in their service. God and the ghosts of the Order will light your way.

"Now, to our mission here."

She waved her dagger wand, and an image appeared in the air. It was a crown, crafted from intricately intertwining strands of gold, with red gemstones like droplets of blood around the outside and sharp points gouging the air above.

"The Grand Master's Crown, stolen from the Order by a heathen Samlander sorcerer during the Secret Crusade, hidden away for centuries. Without it, we have been unable to appoint a Grand Master or access the full magic of that post. For centuries, chancellors such as myself have guided the Order, but we have been without a true leader.

"The time has come to end our long period of deprivation. We have found the crown, and we must reclaim it. No one will simply give back what is rightfully ours. We must earn it once more by force of arms, of wits, and magic."

"For the glory of God and a better world," the Knights chanted.

"Indeed. The crown is on its way to Los Angeles. Where better for us to retrieve God's gift to us than in the City of Angels?"

"What is the plan?" Oskar von Konigsberg asked.

"The crown will arrive in the city within the next few days. We will seize it during the journey to the museum and leave using the magical subway."

"What if that first attempt fails?"

Some leaders would have resented a subordinate questioning the infallibility of their plan. Schulz was not that sort of leader. She was too smart, too experienced, too well-versed in the history of the Order to believe that every fight would end in victory, no matter how well they planned. It was important to have contingencies and valuable to have a deputy who understood this. His question in front of the others did not undermine her. It showed his faith in her ability to lead.

"Then we will have to take it from the museum. For that reason, we will start staking out the place today, in the guise of tourists. Better to be over-prepared than to be dragged down by ignorance." She looked around the group. "You have an hour to pick your rooms, unpack, and freshen up, then be back here ready to receive your orders. For the glory of God."

"For the glory of God," they chanted, then hurried away.

CHAPTER THREE

Lucy sat on the sofa with a sketch pad in her lap and a pencil in her hand. After a day surrounded by art, she felt inspired to have a go again.

Not that she'd spent the whole time looking at the exhibits. Applegate had sent her to LACMA to assess the layout and consider the best options for magical security, and that was exactly what she had done. She'd poked her head into every corner of every corridor, gone along every public hallway, and used her wand to get into the places where the public wasn't supposed to go. She had thoroughly assessed the layout and the challenges it offered, and tomorrow she would start work on a plan to keep the artifacts secure in a building like that.

Still, you couldn't spend all day in an art gallery and not take in the wonders around you. She had taken the opportunity to see paintings, drawings, and sculptures, to take her time with the art. Normally, she only got to visit on her lunchtime or with the kids in tow, and either way led to a rushed experience. This time she had slowed down and enjoyed herself.

Although she had been thinking about art again recently, this was the first time she had felt truly creative. Seeing the amazing things that others did was inspiring. She wouldn't be able to imitate their achievements, but she could at least draw inspiration from them. Once she got through dinner and settling the kids down for the evening, she'd grabbed her old notebook and pencil and sat, fizzing with creative energy.

The problem, she now realized, was that after so long without setting pencil to paper, she didn't know where to start. It wasn't like going to a drink and draw class with Charlie, where they'd been given a focus for their work. It wasn't like when she had done this regularly, and each time she drew, she was working on something left in the air from the time before. With a potentially infinite range of options to choose from and without the grit in the oyster that would turn into a pearl, she didn't know where to start.

Buddy the dachshund wandered into the room, hopped onto the sofa, and flopped his head down in her lap.

"Hey there, lad. Are you looking for some attention?"

She ruffled his ears and stroked his head. He let out a low, satisfied grumble and dribbled slightly on her jeans.

"Bless you, you soft thing. Should I draw a portrait of you?"

Buddy didn't say no, so she set to work putting his image down on paper. It was fun, and the results were fine, but it wasn't quite the moment of excitement she had been looking for. She hurriedly finished the sketch and set it aside.

"Sorry, lad, but I need something more."

She reached down the side of the sofa and picked up her laptop. A quick internet search led her to more drawing exercises than she could ever possibly need, but once again, the problem was knowing where to start. A YouTube video on how to sketch a landscape? A guide to structuring a portrait like Da Vinci? A blog post on how to draw like Jack Kirby? There were so many options.

"Draw your family," she read. "That sounds like the one for us, doesn't it?"

Buddy drooled in what she took as agreement.

"All right then, let's have a look."

The link took her to a website crammed full of ideas and inspiration. There was an art history section showing how the depiction of families had changed down the centuries. There were technical sections on how to portray bodies, faces, and clothes. An advice section listed what approaches to art would create what sorts of atmosphere in a family picture, from charcoal sketches to grand oil paintings. There was even a part on collage and photo editing to make the most of digital images. What caught her attention was a section labeled "Exercises for inspiration," which suggested a load of different approaches to engage creative imagination. Most of them started with family photos and the memories they evoked.

Lucy went from the browser to a folder holding her photos. She was vaguely aware that it wasn't really a file on her computer, but something Charlie had set up on the cloud, probably backed up to the magical internet, to ensure that their photos remained secure. He was a wizard in more than one sense when it came to technical things. For Lucy's purposes, there were photos on her computer, and that was all that mattered.

She opened an album of pictures from a holiday they had taken a couple of years before when Eddie was still a baby. It was the last time they'd been to visit her folks in England, and they'd made the most of it, taking Dylan around all the historical sites a ten-year old boy could want. There were photos of them walking along an ancient earth mound and climbing the ruined remnants of castles. Others showed them gaping in awe at castles and cathedrals built nearly a thousand years before, without aid from any modern machinery—although Lucy wondered if a little sly magic had gone into making those grand buildings possible.

Every image made Lucy smile. There were her parents, with Ashley riding on Lucy's dad's shoulders, the little girl using her grandfather as an improvised steed. Tiny Eddie stood on the medieval walls of York, holding himself up with one hand on Charlie and the other on the worn stones. There was Dylan, overexcited in every single photo, until one near the end of the trip where he had fallen asleep at the dinner table. Lucy laughed out loud at that one.

"Up to something fun?" Charlie walked in with a programming manual in his hand.

"Family photos. You want to join me?" She patted the sofa on the opposite side from Buddy.

"Sure. Shall we maybe open a bottle of wine to go with it?"

"That would be lovely."

Charlie disappeared into the kitchen. There was a *thud* of cupboard doors, a *pop*, and he returned with an open bottle and two glasses, which he filled before taking the seat next to her.

"Oh, wow," he said when he saw what she was looking at. "Your homecoming trip. Like *Spiderman* without the supervillains."

"There was some magic and mayhem, though," Lucy recalled. "Remember when Eddie first saw Mum's cat, and he wanted to be just like it?"

Charlie laughed. "He wasn't used to transforming yet, was he?"

"Nope. He got so confused when he found that he had paws and ginger fur. I've never seen a kitten with an expression like that on its face before."

"In fairness, the cat was pretty baffled too. One moment it was tolerating the clumsy attentions of a tiny human. The next, there was a kitten on its back, and we were all panicking over what would happen next."

"If only we'd known what lay ahead."

"He sure got the hang of things quickly though, didn't he?"

"Did he?"

Charlie chuckled and brought a picture up on the screen.

"Don't you remember this?"

Lucy looked at the picture in confusion. It showed a small dog running around her parents' back garden, chasing a butterfly. The dog looked familiar, but she couldn't think whose it was.

"You'll get it in a second." Charlie grinned at her.

Then a memory rushed back. They'd been at a place called Brimham Rocks, a cluster of strangely eroded stones in North Yorkshire. Eddie, who had been confused by turning into a cat a week earlier, was fast getting a grip on his powers. He had seen a dog and decided he wanted to be like it. Fortunately, no one outside the family was looking as he changed shape, but it had meant that he didn't fit his harness anymore and could run free. For a kid who could barely toddle twenty steps on his own, he'd proved remarkably fast on four legs, and they'd chased him all around the rocks before getting hold of him. Of course, he didn't understand that he shouldn't change in front of other people, so they'd bundled him into the car in dog form and hurried him home, where he'd eventually worn himself out running around the garden.

"It's one of those special memories, isn't it?" Lucy said. "At the time, it was a complete nightmare, but in hindsight, it seems so fun."

"Your dad thought it was funny at the time. Don't you remember him laughing and throwing sticks while we chased Eddie through those ferns?"

"Oh yes! I was about ready to kill him by the end, but it turned out to be a good idea. Chasing sticks tired Eddie out enough so he would sleep in the car."

"Smart man, your dad. I guess that's where you get it." Charlie kissed the top of her head. "More wine?"

"Sure."

They kept browsing through the photos, past that holiday and back to previous ones. Five-year-old Ashley arguing with a creationist museum curator in Utah, Dylan levitating fallen branches in Yosemite, the four of them at the Alamo when Ashley was still a baby. Then back through pictures of Ashley's first steps and her first feats of engineering to ones from before she was born.

"Oh, wow," Lucy said, as an album caught her by surprise. "Our wedding."

There they were, with the sun shining down on them, her in a long white dress, Charlie in a suit with his hair almost tidy, and two-year-old Dylan as ring bearer, wearing the cutest little shirt and vest combo. Confetti littered the ground, and sunshine beamed from their smiles.

"I looked so beautiful." Lucy wiped a happy tear from the corner of her eye.

"You still are." Charlie kissed her.

A few minutes later, Lucy finally found a chance to set aside her wine glass and shut the computer.

"I think it's time for bed." She took Charlie's hand and pulled him to his feet.

"What about your art?" He was an unconvincing picture of innocence.

Lucy snatched up the pad and pencil. "All the great artists draw nudes. I need a model." She waggled her eyebrows.

"I'm not sure I'm ready to be immortalized that way."

"Then you'd better find something else to keep me entertained."

CHAPTER FOUR

It was a lousy morning for traffic, so Jackie was in a bad mood by the time she walked from the Observatory into the Griffins' reception and slapped her wand down on the security box.

"Be careful with that." The receptionist glared. "You might break it."

"Good," Jackie growled. "Then I wouldn't have to go through this every morning."

The light turned green, and she strode through the door into the Griffins' HQ. Her mood didn't get any better when she saw a cluster of Griffins, including field agents and admin gnomes, gathered around her desk.

"What are you lot doing here?" she asked. "Don't you have your own space to clutter up?"

"I do," said a low, genteel voice from the center of the group. "Are you going to make me go back to D.C. so you can sit down?"

"Uncle Harold?" Jackie pushed a wizard aside to get through to her desk. Sure enough, sitting in her swivel

MARTHA CARR & MICHAEL ANDERLE

chair was a gray-haired man in a three-piece suit with a blue pocket square and a watch chain dangling across one side. He smiled and stood to greet her.

"Little Jack-Jack, it's been far too long."

Jackie hugged her uncle, and in the process, glared over her shoulder at the surrounding crowd to try to make clear how bad the consequence would be for anyone who repeated the phrase "Little Jack-Jack." Judging by their smiles, that message wouldn't be as strong as the temptation to amuse themselves at her expense, but she had ways of evening those scores. For now, she was too happy at seeing her uncle to make a fuss.

"Director Kowal was telling us about his work in the seventies," Sam said. "Trying to keep the peace between American and Soviet wizards during the Cold War. Hunting gremlins through the New York disco scene. Trapping unquiet spirits in post-war Vietnam. It sounds amazing."

"You're too kind," Harold said. "I was happy to tell a few old war stories for this young..." He looked at Sam. "Woman? Man? I'm sorry, modern fashions confuse me."

Jackie cringed in horror, but if Sam minded, it didn't show. Instead of outrage, Harold received a smile.

"Young person will do," Sam said.

"Young person, then. Though of course, everyone's a young person compared with me now, and it's kind of anyone to indulge me in my old stories."

"Are you kidding?" This time the excited exclamation came from Jim, one of the office's youngest field agents. "You're an absolute legend, sir. It's fantastic to have you here."

"You're too kind," Harold said. "Now, if you don't mind, I'd like a chance to catch up with my niece."

The crowd reluctantly dispersed and Jackie pulled up a chair next to Harold. "Do you want a coffee?"

"Kind of you to offer, Jack-Jack, but young Applegate got me one already."

"Roger Applegate, our manager, made you a coffee?"

"Oh, yes. He remembers how I like it from back in the day."

"Applegate never even makes coffee!"

"What can I say?" Harold winked. "I don't need to tell people to jump. They know to lift their feet for me."

Jackie laughed and shook her head. "Is that why you're here, to entertain yourself by making senior Griffins nervous? Surely you can get more of that sort of fun in D.C."

"What can I say? Variety is the spice of life." Harold sipped from his cup, then grimaced. "No wonder Roger doesn't make his coffee. He's terrible at it. Where's good around here?"

"There's a place down the hill called Maru, might be a bit hip for you, but they know how to make a brew."

"Hip, I can cope with if it saves me from one more damn cup from Starbucks. Why we made a transport deal with those ridiculous hippies, and their burnt coffee beans is beyond me." Harold closed his eyes. "Ah, yes, Maru, got it."

He opened his eyes, pulled out a well-worn wand, and twitched it in the air. A portal appeared, gold magic glowing around the edge of something darker.

"Uncle Harold, you can't just go opening portals!"

Jackie exclaimed. "We're supposed to stop unregulated magic."

"Young lady, I wrote half the rules. Magic doesn't get more regulated than me. Now come on, we're going for coffee, my treat."

He stepped through the portal and Jackie hurried after him. They emerged onto a building site, concealed from the road by six-foot fences, and when they appeared through those fences, they were only two doors down from Maru.

These were the moments with Uncle Harold that amazed Jackie. She was used to the grand stories of high adventure and historical events. Everyone in her family seemed to have them, thanks to generations of service in the Silver Griffins. She'd grown up with stories about Uncle Harold in Berlin, her mother's battles against djinn in the Saudi desert, and the distant ancestor who had stopped the first two assassination attempts against Lincoln, the magical ones that they were allowed to stop. Those stories might seem remarkable to everyone else in the office, but to her, they had become mundane. Seeing the precision and subtlety of Harold's magic, the ability to target a spell or open a portal at the right place and time, was amazing. It wasn't just history. It was a gift.

They walked up to the coffee shop, placed their order, and found a seat. As usual, the waitstaff seemed charmed by the quaint gray-haired man with his old-fashioned suit and the twinkle in his eyes.

Harold had always seemed old to Jackie. He was the oldest of his generation of Kowals, while her father was the youngest, and she was the youngest of her set. That put more than a simple generation's gap between them, and though he wasn't quite into grandparent territory, he'd always seemed like something from a bygone age: sprightly, forceful, but somehow at odds with the modern world.

"I saw your parents last week," Harold said. "Your mother wants to know whether you have a boyfriend at the moment or even a girlfriend. She's not fussy how the grandkids happen as long as she gets them."

"Mom has the others to give her grandkids, and if she wants to know about my love life, she can ask me directly."

"Sure, she could, but gossiping is far more fun."

"You didn't seem so keen on gossip after I drank you under the table at Grandma's wake."

"I believe that session was a draw."

"Draw, my ass. You fell asleep with a salt lick on the back of your hand and a lemon wedge halfway up your nose."

Harold chuckled. "Ah, fun times."

Their coffee arrived, and they took a moment of comfortable quiet to enjoy the first few sips.

"Seriously, though," Jackie said. "What brings you to town?"

"Partly, I've been looking for an excuse to catch up with you. Don't make that face, Jack-Jack. You know I mean it. Life's always more fun around my favorite niece."

"You said partly?"

"There's this Trakai Hoard exhibit too. Half the wizards in D.C. are talking about it. After twenty years of guarding those objects, parts of the Order of the Silver Griffins have gotten a little obsessed with them. I can't go back to

Lithuania since an incident there in the nineties, so I thought I'd take this opportunity to see what the fuss is about."

Jackie raised an eyebrow. "Is retirement really so boring for you that you'll travel across the country to look at some old candlesticks?"

"Crushingly boring." Harold sighed. "I miss the old days, sneaking across borders, hunting monsters, being chased through the streets by savage shifters. You know how mundane people spend their time after retiring? Coffee mornings and cruises. You either spend three hours over a bad coffee in some lifeless chain coffee store, or you lock yourself up in a floating tin can for weeks on end. That is no way for a person to live."

"It can't be all bad. Surely you and Aunt Adelle are enjoying spending more time together?"

"Oh yes, that part's great, but you can't spend your whole time with a single person. Everyone needs something for themselves, Adelle included. She's been begging me to find a hobby and leave her some time to herself."

"So you came to L.A.?"

"Exactly!" He took another sip of his coffee. "Now come on, I spent half an hour telling my stories to your colleagues. You must have some stories you can tell me. From what I hear, it's all been kicking off in L.A. this year."

They sat there for an hour while other customers wandered in and out, and Jackie told stories about what had happened with the L.A. Griffins in the past few months. They'd defeated Zero, the magical loan shark. They brought down Meredith Womack's crime school. After that, they'd destroyed the smog monster that had tried to choke the city. Most recently, they'd captured the dream stalker Mr. No, who had sapped away part of the vital life force from dozens of people, including Applegate. It was satisfying to tell the stories, to have someone ask about the role she had played, and praise her for her achievements.

However, she was painfully aware of how different the focus was from when Harold told his tales or anyone else in the family, including her siblings. With their grand magical tradition, Kowals were usually the center of the story, while Jackie often found herself on the fringe, a supporting player to Lucy Heron. It wasn't something that had ever bothered her until now, and if she had been talking to anyone else, it still wouldn't have. Still, there was something about talking to a family member, even one as fun as Uncle Harold, that cast things in a different light. The family had a reputation to maintain, and she wasn't contributing.

"You okay there, Jack-Jack?" he asked. "You look a little down."

"I'm fine."

"You know what'll cheer you up?" Harold said. "Get out there and get laid."

"Uncle Harold! You can't say things like that!" She realized it was gross hypocrisy, that she only objected because of who was saying it, but she stood by her words.

"Your face!" Harold laughed and slapped the table. "Your mom bet me I wouldn't say that to you, and now she owes me a steak dinner."

"I'm so glad I'm getting you fed." Jackie rolled her eyes. "Now I definitely am going back to work."

"Dinner later?"

"Sure, but no steaks, and no more talk about that, understood?"

"All right." Uncle Harold stood and hugged her. "It's great to see you, Jack-Jack. You take care."

CHAPTER FIVE

Dylan Heron clutched a trowel in one hand and a brush in the other, squeezing them so tight in excitement that his knuckles went white. To his left, his friend Sofia blew a curly length of hair back from her face, while to his right, his other best friend Lance struck a serious and studious pose, like he'd seen archaeologists do on TV.

"Thank you for coming along today, kids," said Professor Angie Werner, the archaeologist leading the dig. She had a bright smile and dusty hands, as she'd already been working alongside her team while the child volunteers were in school. "This is an exciting experiment for us, giving young people a chance to do some real live archeology, and we hope it'll be equally as exciting for you."

Three different schools had offered their pupils a chance to join in the dig, and Dylan had assumed that would mean that there were masses of kids there, that he would struggle for an opportunity to talk with the archaeologists. He didn't know whether to be disappointed or pleased that so few of his classmates had cared enough to join, meaning that there were fewer than twenty volunteers in total. At least it meant that he had a better chance of learning, and when it came to history, that was a good thing.

"It might not look like much, but this is a very exciting opportunity for us." Professor Angie led them across the site. To one side was a row of half-built houses, while the other side was a wasteland. A mechanical digger sat motionless by a heap of dirt before the archaeologists' trenches. "We're lucky that the company building these houses is run by a man who's interested in history. When he found something he thought might be an old building, he contacted the university right away and rearranged his construction plans so we can do a full dig."

"I thought you said this would be fun," Sofia whispered to Dylan.

"It will be," he replied.

"You mean it had better be. We've given up band for six weeks for this."

Professor Angie pointed down into a trench, where students and professors carefully scraped one layer of earth away from another layer.

"What we're looking at here is a pre-Columbian settlement. Who can tell me what that means?"

Several hands shot up, Dylan's among them. He was pleased to see that he wasn't alone in his enthusiasm.

"Yes, you." Angie pointed at him.

"It means that it's from before Columbus reached America and Europeans started coming here," he said. "Apart from maybe some Vikings and Basque fishermen of Newfoundland."

"Wow, somebody's really done their homework!" Angie smiled widely. "This settlement is from before the Columbian exchange when people and goods started moving regularly back and forth between America and Europe. That means it can help us understand how people lived then in this part of America."

Lance's hand went up.

"Yes?" Angie asked.

"How did they live, then? Were they all, like, out hunting all the time?" Lance mimed throwing a spear. "Or were they, like, planting crops and building houses and all that stuff? Did they have plays and songs and books?"

"Ooh, a curious mind. Normally, I'd be more than happy to tell you, but today, I want you to see what you can work out for yourselves. After all, that's what archeology's about."

Angie led them to a series of heaps of dirt with large sieves sitting next to them.

"This is all soil that came out of the site before they realized there was something to study here. Based on what we've seen, I'm confident that there are artifacts in there, and I'd like you to help find them."

Dylan listened while she gave instructions on what to do. He doubted that she meant artifacts like his mom and the Silver Griffins used the word, meaning magical objects. This time it referred to anything of interest to archaeologists, and that made it more exciting to him. He was about to help people work out what history had looked like. Magic seemed pretty ordinary compared with that.

Soon, he was working with Sofia and Lance, sifting through their heap of dirt, looking for anything of interest.

At the same time, Professor Angie walked between the groups of school children, offering advice and encouragement.

"This is not exciting," Sofia muttered. "I mean, maybe if we were still all five and into making mud pies, but I'm nearly thirteen years old, I am too old for that."

"You're not thirteen for months," Lance said. "I'll be thirteen before you are, and I'm happy doing this."

"I thought you'd want to be back at school already, playing guitar or joining in drama club."

"I mean, like, sure, that would be cool, but not as cool as this!"

Lance held something aloft between his fingers. It was pale and flat and maybe two inches across.

"A stone?" Sofia asked. "Woohoo, thrilling."

"An arrowhead!" Lance frowned and looked at it doubtfully. "I mean, I think it's an arrowhead, right Dylan?"

Dylan looked at the chipped stone. "Yeah, that's totally an arrowhead. You should go show it to Professor Werner."

"Yes, I found something first!" Lance strode proudly off, clutching his arrowhead.

"Right, that's it. I'm gonna find three things before he gets back." Sofia scooped a heap of dirt into her sieve and shook it vigorously.

"Archeology isn't a competition, you know," Dylan said.

"Tell that to Indiana Jones and those Nazis," Sofia said. "You want to be the one who gets their face melted?"

It seemed like an unlikely outcome, but Dylan started working harder anyway to be on the safe side. Soon, he stood beside a growing heap of sifted dirt on the one hand and a clutch of discarded stones on the other. Not everything an archaeologist dug up was of interest. He'd also found a couple more arrowheads and a rock that looked like someone might have shaped it into a tool.

"Check it out!" Sofia said. "This is way more exciting than Lance's stupid arrowhead."

She held up a slender stick a foot long with symbols burned into it down one side and bands of stone wrapped around one end as if someone had melted them on. It had broken nearly in two in the middle, and sparks were jumping out of that break, sparks that Dylan recognized as magic.

"You should put that down." He eyed it with concern.

"Why, so Lance can dig it up again?"

"No, because it's a magic wand, and I think it could be dangerous."

"Oh." Sofia's eyes went wide. She and Lance knew, even though they shouldn't, that Dylan was a wizard from a family of magicals, and she had seen enough to know that a little miscast magic could lead to a lot of harm. "Let me—"

The was a *crackle*, like milk hitting Rice Krispies and a shower of sparks from the wand.

"Seriously, put it down," Dylan said.

Sofia didn't respond. Instead, she stood frozen, only her eyes moving.

"Oh no." Dylan looked around. Fortunately, no one else was watching them. He hastily pulled out his wand. "Subvolo."

At his command, the wand levitated out of Sofia's hand and landed in the dirt. He cast a hasty countermagic, and she started moving again.

"What's that doing here?" she asked, her voice rising in pitch.

"I don't know, but we should get it out of here before—"

There was another shower of sparks. This time, a patch of dirt next to Sofia's foot caught fire. She hastily stamped it out, then stared at Dylan.

"Seriously, dude, how do we get rid of it?" she asked.

As if summoned by the moment of worst possible timing, Lance and Professor Angie walked toward them.

"Well done, Lance," the professor was saying. "Now, let's see what else is in your heap, shall we?"

"Sure, Professor."

Sofia tried to kick the wand out of view, but as her foot hit it, there was another *crackle*, a flash, and the professor froze where she stood.

"Stupefacio!" Dylan exclaimed. Another burst of magic hit the professor with no visible change.

"What's going on?" Lance looked worried.

"What was that?" Sofia hissed. "You haven't done anything!"

"I panicked." Dylan also kept his voice low to avoid drawing the other students' attention. "I thought if I stunned her maybe she wouldn't notice being frozen."

"Whereas being stunned is perfectly normal?"

"Have you got a better plan?"

"No, I'm not the wizard!"

"What's happening?" Lance asked loudly.

"Ssh!" they both hissed.

Dylan inhaled a deep breath and drew on the powerful magic that always flowed through him. It was risky, tapping into it like this, but he needed to get the situation under control. He wrapped his hand in magic and took hold of the broken wand. Its power was trying to spill out, but he held it in.

"Open my backpack, quick," he said.

Sofia did as he asked, and he dropped the wand inside. As it landed, there was one more *crackle*, and flowers bloomed from the side of a different heap of dirt to the bewilderment of the kids working there.

"Oh wow, Australian winter roses." Lance hastily improvised an excuse as he rushed over. "My dad told me about these, apparently they get really confused about when to bloom, so they can suddenly spring up at, like, any time."

While Lance provided a distraction, Sofia zipped the bag shut, and Dylan hurried to Professor Angie. He dispelled the freeze, and she collapsed, staring vacantly into space. Then he dispelled the stun spell and crossed his fingers.

"Are you all right, Professor?" He stuffed his wand out of sight.

"I… Yes, no, I…" Professor Angie looked around. "What happened?"

"I don't know, you were walking over here, and you fell over."

"Oh, dear." She pressed her hand to her forehead. "I don't remember what happened at all. You don't think it's a stroke, do you?"

"Ummmm…" Dylan didn't know much about strokes, except that they were dangerous. "Probably not, but maybe you should go see a doctor, in case?"

"Yes, you're right." She got to her feet. "Sorry, kids, I'm

going to have to miss the rest of your first day. I'll leave one of the others in charge."

Still looking dazed, she stumbled away across the sight.

"Here." Sofia thrust Dylan's backpack into his hands. "No way I'm holding that, with what's inside. You think there's more here like it?"

"Don't know, but we should keep an eye out. I should call my mom, get her to pick this thing up before anything goes wrong. You still think archeology's boring?"

Sofia laughed. "All right, Indie, you win that argument for now."

CHAPTER SIX

Lucy and Ellis stood on Wilshire Boulevard, watching the people and the cars go past. He was leaning against a palm tree, his phone out, while Lucy scrutinized the men in high visibility jackets setting out traffic cones farther down the road.

"Do you think they could be setting up a trap?" she asked.

Ellis glanced up from his screen and shook his head.

"No, that's the power company. They've been planning this work since before the Trakai Hoard's visit was even announced."

"What if criminals sneak someone onto the team doing the work now that it's underway?"

"Then the guy we sneaked onto the team will let us know." Ellis grinned. "This ain't my first rodeo. I've learned to spot the obvious clowns."

Those words reassured Lucy, as did Ellis's relaxed tone. This was the first time she'd been responsible for arranging this sort of security detail, and having help from someone more experienced took away the worry that she might miss something obvious.

"What are we looking for out here?" she asked.

"Anyone scoping out the routes available to bring the Hoard to the museum. The smart criminals will do it without making themselves visible, but this is our chance to weed out the dumber ones, make sure we're not dealing with all of them at once."

"You think there will be more than one group after the Hoard?"

"I'd bet my hat on it."

"You're not wearing a hat."

"All right then, I'd bet my sneakers, and this here is one of my favorite pairs." He raised his foot, showing off the bright red Nikes. "There's a reason we've been guarding the Trakai Hoard so carefully, and this is the best chance there's been to grab it in twenty years. Ain't no way that doesn't draw all sorts of attention."

"So how do we spot people scoping out the route?"

"Look for suspicious behavior, anyone acting in a way that doesn't seem right."

Lucy carefully ran her gaze up and down the street.

"How about that lad?" she asked. "The one sitting on the concrete wall past those palm trees. He's been there for ages."

"He's been stood up, probably by an internet date. Nothing suspicious about that."

"How can you tell?"

"Keeps pulling his phone out and looking at it to see if

there's a message. Only he doesn't want to look desperate, so then he sticks the phone away a second later, looking all embarrassed. If he was waiting for friends, he might call them or play a game on his phone, but he doesn't want to risk running down the battery when it's his only line to her."

"You got all that from just looking at him? Wow."

"What can I say? I have experience, both in security and in being stood up." He smiled, dismissing any hint of bitterness. "Anyone else catch your eye?"

"Not really. What about you?" She pointed at his phone. "Have you been scanning for trouble using your magic app?"

Ellis shook his head and put the phone away.

"No, just messaging Sarah."

"Oh, really?" Lucy grinned. "Going well, is it?"

"She's your best friend, you tell me."

"Sorry, but the bonds of sisterhood forbid me from breaking the sacred seal of the confessional." She waved her hand in a rough imitation of a religious blessing. "I *can* say that she seems very happy at the moment."

"I'll take that as a good sign." Ellis stroked his beard, and a serious expression crossed his face. "All right, reckon I've got one."

"Really?"

"See the little old lady facing that bunch of street lamps?"

"You mean Urban Light?"

"This ain't about the art. It's about the lady. What do you notice?"

"A little old lady knitting in the sunshine. Seems innocent enough to me."

"Except she ain't knitting like a little old lady."

Lucy watched the woman's hands move, trying to work out what Ellis meant, but she couldn't see it. The needles clacked against each other, slowly but steadily using up the wool. It looked like real knitting to her. "I give up. What's wrong?"

"She looks like an old lady, but she's knitting like a hipster, someone who's doing it as this month's craft. Very slow, very deliberate, every stitch an effort. Little old lady knitters, they're fast, they have a lifetime of practice behind them."

"She could have arthritis."

"Then she'd be holding her fingers different. Trust me. I spent years watching how my grandma and her friends handled their needles." He pushed off from the palm tree and ambled down the street. "Come on. We should have ourselves a word with this lady."

Lucy followed him to the concrete bench facing the exhibit, which consisted of over two hundred cast-iron street lamps. It was a lot less impressive during the day when the solar-powered batteries were charging up rather than letting off their light, but still a striking sight. The sleek design of the lamps, repeated in rows, was soothing to look at.

Ellis sat on one side of the little old lady. At a gesture from him, Lucy sat to the woman's other side.

"Howdy, ma'am," Ellis said. "Mighty fine day, ain't it?"

"It certainly is, young man," the woman said in a voice

that crackled like old wrapping paper. She stayed hunched over her knitting as she paused to smile at Ellis, then shot a sidelong glance at Lucy but didn't say anything more.

"Mind my asking what you're making there?" he said.

"Why, it's kind of you to take an interest, sonny." The old lady held up her knitting. "It's a scarf for my youngest. He's moving to Alaska, and I want to make sure he's nice and warm."

"That's mighty thoughtful of you. What's this here pattern?" Ellis pointed at the irregular mottled effect where mismatched stitches scattered unevenly across the otherwise smooth scarf.

"Oh, just some slip-ups, dear. My hands aren't as steady as they once were."

Except that those hands seemed perfectly steady now, holding out the knitting for Ellis to see.

"So they ain't, for example, a record of when you spotted undercover witches and wizards walking past, with each stitch on here representing a set amount of time?"

"Witches and wizards?" the lady said with a forced laugh. "Oh, young man, you do have quite the imagination." The stitches finished sliding from one needle to the other, and she pointed the empty needle at Ellis. "You know what they say: dormio."

"Renuo," Ellis snapped, his wand appearing in his hand in time to cancel the sleep spell coming from the needle. "You'll have to do better than that to catch me out."

"Lanio." Lucy pressed the tip of her wand against the woman's side.

For a brief moment, the air rippled, and the illusion shrouding the magical fell away. In place of a little old human woman, a young female gnome sat on the bench, wearing a gray beret and an old-fashioned dress. She glared at Lucy. Then the disruption passed and the illusion returned.

A passer-by blinked, rubbed his eyes, and stared at them for a moment, then shook his head and carried on, convincing himself that he hadn't seen anything odd and that he wasn't going mad.

"All right, you got me," the old lady who was really a gnome said. "What are you going to do, arrest me for knitting? Last time I checked, that wasn't any use of magic, never mind the illegal sort."

"You are wearing an illusion, though," Lucy pointed out.

"As I'm obliged to if I want to go out in public. Got to keep up the illusion of a non-magical world, or the Silver Griffins might arrest me, right?"

"You cast offensive magic against my colleague."

"Colleague, huh? So you are Silver Griffins. I'm sorry, I had no idea. I found myself surrounded by strange magicals, and when they got too close, I panicked. You two are awfully intimidating."

Lucy wasn't buying any of the gnome's excuses, but she could see how they might convince others. Should they take her in for questioning anyway?

She glanced at Ellis, who gave a small shake of his head.

"No need for more trouble." He pulled out his phone and pointed it at the gnome. There was a loud *ping* and a brief shimmer of magic. "I have you tagged now, so if you come within half a mile of the museum, I'll know. Same goes for your buddy taking photos up the street and the elf rideshare driver who keeps circling the block."

Behind the illusion of wrinkles and elderly weariness, the gnome's eyes went wide in alarm.

"How did you..."

"I'm a pro, and you're amateurs, or at least not experienced enough at this game. Fortunately for you, I have bigger fish to fry today. Get back to whatever petty grifts you usually spin, and we'll forget this ever happened. Remember..." He patted his phone. "Half a mile away or more."

The gnome might not have had Ellis's experience, but she managed a lot of calm under pressure. Maintaining her old lady act, she carefully rolled up her wool, put her knitting into her bag, and hobbled away.

"That was brilliant," Lucy said once the criminal was out of earshot. "That tracker, could we use it for other criminals around L.A.? That would make my work so much easier."

"What tracker?"

"The one you tagged her with."

"What, this?" Ellis turned his phone to show her the screen, which was full of colorful cartoon images of fruit. He swiped, three bananas lined up, and there was a loud *ping* as they disappeared.

"But the magic..."

Ellis waved his hand, and there was a small shimmer of power. "Cheap tricks and bluffing. If it convinced you, I don't see her seeing through it. That's one lot out of the picture."

Lucy laughed. "All right, I'm impressed. This is turning

into quite the learning experience. Now what?"

"Now we take a walk along the transport route, see who else is hanging around." Ellis stood and stretched. "First though, could you give me a minute? I have to give Sarah a call, see if she's free for dinner tonight. I hear that might make her happy."

CHAPTER SEVEN

Twylan cast a cleaning spell over the test tubes and beakers she had been working with, then carefully placed them back in their box. Around the room, other teenagers of the Underfoot Brigade were doing the same thing. The chemistry equipment was a new addition to their underground classroom, an expensive-looking addition. While they didn't know where their teacher had gotten it, they all instinctively understood that it wouldn't be easy to replace, so they took extra care with every piece.

"That's it for today," Heather Fields said from the front of the classroom. "I have to go meet with the other Tolderai, so I won't be around to answer questions after class. If you need anything, leave a note in my staffroom, and I'll deal with it in the morning. Have a good evening, all of you."

The teacher hurried out, taking her bag with her. Twylan watched in disappointment. She understood that Ms. Fields had other things occupying her time, especially with her role leading a tribe of witches and wizards, but it seemed like she had a lot less time spare for the Underfoots lately.

"I wish Ms. Fields were around a bit more," she said. "It feels like she's only here for the lessons these days."

Leontine snorted and gave a small wave of his wings, the one natural and the other a mechanical device over his stunted wing. "You get the irony, right? With you off running around with the Silver Griffins, we see almost as little of you as of her."

Twylan frowned, and magic crackled out around her eye. That comment felt unfair. Sure, she spent some time each week shadowing Jackie, learning how the Griffins worked, but she was still with the Underfoots most of the time, eating and sleeping and socializing with them in the tunnels, attending lessons with the rest. Then again, Leontine had been their leader, the most prominent of the Brigade, and now she was moving past him into the adult world. Did he feel like she was leaving him behind?

"Don't worry. I'm not leaving. Not until I have a proper job with the Griffins and can buy a house for us all to live in."

"Griffin money won't pay for a house that big," Leontine countered.

"Then we'll take it in turns to live there. Or I'll find a way to get us all jobs so we can live like normal magicals out in the world."

"It's not money that keeps us down here." Leontine tapped his crippled wing, then pointed at the magic flaring from Twylan's eyes. "Don't go getting dreams that'll never come true. It'll only break your heart."

He placed the box of chemistry equipment on a shelf, then strode out of the room.

Twylan followed more slowly, not keen to catch up with him and his bad mood. Out in the main tunnel, she looked across the homes of the Underfoot Brigade, the shacks and huts built from discarded building supplies. Although they had only recently moved to this tunnel, following an attack on their old one, she could still see the history of the community in those constructions. There were pieces of old buildings, recycled multiple times as the teens had learned to build better shelters, then rebuilt them here. There were plastic sheets that had been part of her home and were now someone else's. There was a new hut on the end where a deaf Willen had recently joined them.

"You all right there?" Kix appeared at Twylan's elbow. The gnome was wearing a new skirt she had sewn from offcuts of sparkling and sequined fabric, and it caught the light from the bare electric bulbs like a sea of stars shining all around.

"Just thinking about the past," Twylan said. "Remember that time we had a disco? Siltor created a magical light show, but it ran out halfway through, and we were all left listening to ABBA in the dark?"

"I had such a good outfit that night!" Kix clutched Twylan's arm. "This red top I found in a dumpster with patches sewn over the stains, and a pair of roller boots with nearly all the wheels. You remember?"

Twylan laughed. "I remember the boots."

"I should dig them out and go skating again. In fact, do you want to—"

A shout of alarm interrupted her as Siltor the elf came

running out of the far end of the tunnel, waving his hands in the air.

"Attack!" he shouted. "We're under attack!"

"What?" Twylan stared at him, bewildered. Who on earth would want to attack them?

Then she saw them, a dozen creatures racing down the tunnel after Siltor. They were like woodlice but five feet tall and twenty feet long, charging along on dozens of legs. Pincers clacked from arms protruding at the front of their shells, and mouths full of pointed teeth gaped.

Twylan strode into the middle of the tunnel and held her arms wide. She could deal with this.

"Everyone, shut your eyes!" she shouted. Then she lowered her voice and cast the spell. "Lumina caeca!"

Light flashed from her eyes, from her hands, from her whole body, so bright that if she hadn't been the one to cast it, it would have blinded her. Siltor, having closed his eyes a moment too late, cursed. However, when the afterglow faded, the monsters were still charging down the tunnel.

"They must not have eyes." Kix raised her hands. A dozen needles floated in the air in front of her. "We'll have to fight them off."

The monsters were almost on them. As Kix hurled her needles with all the force of her magic, Twylan summoned another spell.

"Refrigero!"

A bolt of icy magic flew from her hands and hit the leading monster. It left a glittering patch of frost across its carapace, but the creature kept coming.

"Refrigero! Refrigero! Refrigero!"

She flung bolt after bolt of icy magic at the beast, trying

to freeze it in place, but it kept coming. It was almost on her as she flung one last blast, throwing all her desperate strength into it.

"Refrigero!"

The magic hit the beast in the center of its face. At last, its teeth stopped moving, its claws stopped clacking, its legs stopped twitching back and forth. It had so much momentum that it kept coming, sliding across the dirty concrete floor straight at Twylan. She braced herself for the worst.

The frozen monster skidded to a stop inches from the young witch, who stood staring at it, trembling with tension and relief.

Above her head, Leontine soared through the air, his wingtips almost brushing the tunnel roof. He saw the other Underfoots scatter as the monsters crashed into their homes, demolishing improvised walls and plastic sheeting roofs. Rage swirled through him as he tucked in his wings and dropped, landing with a *thud* on the back of one of the beasts.

If the monster noticed his arrival, it didn't show it. It kept moving forward, slower now as it trampled the broken remains of their homes, claws lashing out to try to grab the nearest Underfoots.

The creature's shell was overlapping chitinous plates, each one the width of its whole body. Leontine slid his fingers under the edge of one of the plates, then heaved. Muscles straining, he pulled at the hard edge until it came free at last, revealing the monster's soft flesh underneath.

In his rush to get into the air, he had forgotten to pick up a weapon. Now it was too late. He had to take this opportunity using whatever he had. He pulled his fist up, then swung it down, punching straight into the soft spot. Gore spattered him, and the creature screeched. Leontine pulled his fist out, then hit it again, up to his elbow in giant insect guts. The beast slowed, but it was still moving, its claws still clacking. Leontine punched one more time, driving his arm into it up to his shoulder. At last, the monster stopped chasing his friends and fell still.

Around the tunnel, other Underfoots were using whatever skills and weapons they had. Kix had levitated needles between the plates of armor and through the mouth of one beast, then sliced it up from the inside. Others had summoned mounds of earth to block the monsters' paths, blasted them with electricity, tangled them in plants, or attacked them with planks and tools. Half of the monsters were dead or crippled, and the others were turning away, making a break for the darkness at the end of the tunnel.

"Twylan, don't let them get away!" Leontine shouted. "They might come for us again."

Twylan raised her hands, and a wall of ice rose to block the monsters' way. They crashed into it, hard shells smashing through the ice, and scurried on, disappearing into the depths of the earth.

"What are these?" Siltor asked as the Underfoots gathered around the first frozen monster.

"I don't know," Twylan said. "Does anyone?"

They all shook their heads. In years of tunnel living, they had never seen anything like this.

"What should we do with them?" Kix poked at one of the bodies.

"Definitely not eat them." Leontine sniffed at the

grotesque gore that coated his arm. "It stinks like something that crawled out of a sewer."

"Maybe it did," Twylan suggested. "Or maybe they tunneled up out of the ground. Either way, we should send someone to follow their tracks and see if we can work out where they came from.

"I'll lead on that," Leontine volunteered. "I'm ready to fight them again if we run into trouble."

"Try not to. I'd much rather you stayed safe." Twylan looked around at their trampled homes. "As for the rest of us, I guess we get rid of the bodies and start rebuilding."

"Everything's in ruins," Kix pointed. "How do we build back from this?"

"The same way we always do," Twylan said. "Better than the last time."

CHAPTER EIGHT

The traffic moved steadily along Wilshire Boulevard under the blazing heat of the midday sun. Klara Schulz had half-expected the Trakai Hoard to be brought in under cover of darkness to keep its arrival concealed, but it seemed that the locals were smarter than that. They had arranged for this to happen in daylight, when there would be more people around to notice anything odd, and when they could hide security people in the crowd.

That worked both ways. The Knights of the Hinterland were used to hiding in plain sight, to fighting unseen battles beneath the magic-blind eyes of the mundane world. Unlike many of the magical monsters they hunted, they could survive beneath the light of midday.

Schulz stood in front of an office building, dressed in a loose-fitting pantsuit with her phone in her hand, pretending to answer emails. It used to be that she would have faked reading a newspaper in a moment like this, but in the modern world, that would have been conspicuous ostentation. That was the advantage of smartphones. You could be doing anything, and it would look innocent. So much had changed in her thirty years of service to the Order, new tools creating new opportunities, but the fight remained the same. Hunt the monsters, baffle the unrighteous, do God's will.

Without thinking, she touched the scar on her cheek, then lowered her hand. Best not to dwell on the past, not when she needed to pay attention in the present.

"They're almost at your position." Oskar von Konigsberg's voice emerged from her wireless earbud. "Black van, license plate starts KV, driver and passenger up front."

"Got it." Schulz saw the van approaching down the street. "All teams, get ready to move."

As she was about to move, a boy bumped into her. He couldn't have been more than ten years old and was wearing a baseball cap with some sort of gadget attached to the brim.

"Sorry," he apologized and hurried down the road.

Schulz shook her head. Children these days. They did not pay attention.

She flexed her wrist, and her dagger wand slid from its hidden holster into her right hand. She kept it there, hidden from view, as she approached the curb. Holding her phone as if she was talking into it, she muttered the trigger word for a pre-prepared spell that would mean no one noticed her standing there. Then she reached through her wand, into the world, and sprang her trap.

There was a *bang* as the transport van's tire burst. It swerved across the road, thrown off not only by the burst tire but by the telekinetic push that had come with it. Brakes screeched as other cars swerved out of the way.

Pedestrians screamed and leapt clear as the van mounted the pavement and slammed into a palm tree. The only person who stayed calm was a small girl sitting on a nearby concrete wall. She was perhaps eight years old, with her dark hair tied neatly back. She barely even looked up from the tablet she was playing on. The girl was clearly damaged inside if she could sit through this without flinching, but this was no time to be concerned with that.

"Team Two, go," Schulz said.

Two Knights of the Hinterland, dressed as tourists from Europe, approached the front of the van. They opened the door and helped the stunned-looking driver clamber down. Schulz couldn't hear what they were saying, but she knew the script, and she knew the suggestive magic they would use to make the driver do as they said. Of course, he was concerned about his colleagues in the back of the van. Of course, he should release the doors so that someone could check on them. He reached back inside the vehicle and rummaged for a control next to the steering wheel.

"Team Three, go," Schulz said.

Five more Knights, three dressed as construction workers and the others as a couple out on a lunch date, rushed to the back of the van as the doors swung open. With their hands hidden from the crowd, they cast stun spells at the guards inside, then climbed in to carry the guards out.

"These guys are hurt," called the Knight with the most convincing American accent. "Is anybody a medic?"

While three of the Knights used the stunned guards to block the way into the van, the other two Knights would be inside, melting their way through the locks protecting the Grand Master's Crown. Two more minutes, and they would be out.

Still, something was wrong. An incident like this should have drawn more attention. There should have been a crowd by now, one that the Knights could melt away into. People were watching, but there hadn't been the rush that should have followed the crash. Someone was managing the crowd, and now a select group of people was moving in. Diversely dressed, perfectly ordinary people who would have blended in on the streets of any American city, just like the Knights had done.

"Maria, are you in yet?" Schulz still stood on the sidewalk, hidden from notice by her magic.

"No, Chancellor," one of the pair inside the van replied. "The locks are tougher than expected. Someone magically reinforced them. We'll need more time."

"Get out, now."

"Chancellor, please repeat?"

"I said get out. It's a trap." Schulz hesitated, caught for a moment on the tip of a blade made of uncertainty. This was their best chance. She shouldn't squander it, but she mustn't sacrifice her people either. "Oskar, Plan Omega, now."

"Affirmative, Chancellor."

Then everything fell apart. The people approaching the van—Silver Griffins, she was sure—surged forward. Some reached for stunned guards or the Knights pretending to care for them. Others raised their hands, wands concealed but very much at the ready.

There was a strange ballet to a covert magic fight, one

in which both sides were sworn not to reveal their powers to the world. Schulz had seen it dozens of times, and aside from her people, the Griffins were the masters of the art. Hands shifted, magic flowed, but there wasn't so much as a shimmer in the air to give away what was happening. To an innocent onlooker, it would seem that people were moving strangely around each other, hands rising and falling, some people stepping back while others advanced, until someone seemingly fainted or was led away unresisting by so-called friends. This was that sort of fight.

For half a minute, the strange battle swayed back and forth. Bodies shifted, spells were cast and countered, one of the Griffins even tried to grab Maria as she emerged from the van, but she shrugged him off. The Griffins had the Knights surrounded and pushed them back toward the van doors as the two sides talked loudly about helping the unconscious guards, trying to keep up an illusion for the crowd.

What the Griffins didn't know was that Schulz had more men on the way, ones who had prepared for a moment like this. There was a blast from a siren and a flash of blue light, then an ambulance screeched up the street, past the disrupted traffic, and stopped by the back of the van. Men and women in EMT uniforms sprang out. Men and women led by Oskar von Konigsberg.

"Let us through." Oskar rushed forward with a medical bag. He placed a hand on the shoulder of one of the Griffins, who fell to the ground. Another did the same as a second EMT reached her. "That van!" Oskar shouted and pointed at the crashed vehicle. "It's leaking something toxic. Get back!"

Now chaos truly broke out. The members of the watching crowd turned and ran while the Griffins whirled in alarm. They knew this was no gas leak, but they hadn't been ready for an attack from behind. Now they were trapped.

Watching from the curb, Schulz allowed herself a moment of triumph. This was perfect. Clear the Griffins, open the lock, get the crown, and get away.

Not everyone in the crowd was running. Some were closing in—more damn Griffins.

One strode past, mere feet from Schulz's place of magical concealment, a wizard in a charcoal suit with red sneakers. He was calling out orders.

Schulz raised her wand. "Stupefacio."

The suited wizard, caught by surprise and unable to defend himself, collapsed in the street as Schulz's hiding spell evaporated around her.

"Forget the crown, forget the ambulance," Schulz snapped into her phone. "Escape plan Beta, now."

The Griffins closest to the van fell like flies as the Knights unleashed a spray of stun spells using their hidden wands. Then they scattered, running off in pairs. Some of the remaining Griffins chased after them, but the Knights were trained warriors and athletes. They soon caught up with the fleeing crowds and disappeared into them.

Schulz joined Maria as she ran past, and the two of them dashed along the boulevard, then turned off down a pedestrian way, past a row of shops. Schulz looked back over her shoulder as they turned and saw a trim woman in a superhero t-shirt running after them. Then they were around the corner, out of sight and lost in the crowds of L.A.

By the time Lucy jogged back to the crashed van, Ellis was peeling himself up off the street.

"Dagnabbit," he said, with all the force that someone else might have cursed. "I thought we had them."

"Whoever they were, they were as prepared as us," Lucy said. "They would have been better prepared if not for a little help."

Ashley Heron walked up, tablet in hand, followed by a couple of slightly older kids. The boy was twitching on his feet, looking like he might burst with excitement, while Ashley and the other girl seemed calm although curious.

"So these are the fabled Mini Griffins, huh?" Ellis asked.

"Some of them," Lucy said. "Well done, Ashley. You guys did a great job of spotting the robbers in the crowd."

"It's mostly down to the pattern recognition algorithm." Ashley held up her tablet. "It's all about…" She hesitated. "This isn't the time to explain, is it?"

"Well deduced, sweetheart." Lucy kissed the top of her daughter's head. "You can tell me all about it later. Or better yet, tell your dad. He might understand."

"You never told us your mom was Scottish." The boy looked up at Lucy.

"I'm English."

"I've seen English people on TV. They don't talk like that."

"There are a lot of different accents in England, lad. This isn't the one from *Downton*."

"You know, this ain't the time for this either," Ellis said. "We need to start clearing up before the cops get here. Kids, we'll meet you in the museum. It's time for the big Griffins to get to work."

CHAPTER NINE

A crushed cola can flew through the air and *clanged* into the trash basket. Charlie looked up from his work and across the office to where Gail sat with her hands raised in the air and a triumphant grin on her face.

"Five in a row," she said. "Hand it over, loser."

A loud, soda-powered belch punctuated the last word.

"You're a monster." Steve handed her a ten-dollar bill. "I don't get how you can guzzle that so fast and sit still."

"Oh, I'll regret it when the sugar crash hits, but not as much as you'll regret this." She waved the ten around for a moment more, then slid it into her pocket.

"Are you guys actually doing any work today?" Charlie asked. The door to the IT office was firmly locked, so there was no chance of managers walking in and being appalled at their slacking, but he didn't want them to fall behind on their work. After all, people were relying on them.

"Waiting on a compile." Gail pointed at her monitor.

Steve tapped the phone headset he was wearing.

"Waiting for a manager's PA to switch his computer off and on again. Apparently, even that's too much for this idiot."

"You're on mute, right?"

For a moment, panic filled Steve's face. Then he looked at a flashing light on his work phone and nodded in relief. "Totally on mute. I'm not the idiot."

Charlie turned back to his screen. One of the reasons why he needed to be sure that the others focused on their work was that technically speaking, he wasn't. He was definitely productive, just not at the business his employers paid him for.

He switched windows on his machine, bringing up a browser connected to the magical web, that part of the Internet disconnected from mundane activities, where magicals could talk and share information about the hidden side of their lives, everything from troll sightings to the refinement of favorite spells. For someone with Charlie's tech skills, it was the best possible source of information for what was going on in the magical world, and that meant it was the best way he could help Lucy with her work.

He did a final check over the search criteria he'd created, relating to the attack on the van on Wilshire Boulevard and the upcoming exhibit at LACMA. He'd covered every relevant topic he could think of and a few more that Ashley had suggested. There was a risk of getting perfectionist over this stuff, checking and double-checking until the cows came home. That wouldn't help anyone, so he hit the button to set up the alerts and let the moment go. He could always add more later if needed.

"Charlie?"

He looked up to see Keiran, the youngest member of the team, looking at him across the top of the monitor. Even by Charlie's standards, Kieran spent too much time indoors in front of a screen, and his floppy hair framed a face that was becoming ghostly pale.

"What's up, Kieran?"

"You remember that problem with the client database last week?"

"No, I'm so old that I don't remember what happened seven days ago."

"Oh, well, you see, we had a problem with—"

"That was a joke, Kieran. I've not gone senile just because I'm in my thirties."

"Okay, cool." Kieran looked down at his feet. "So, um, do you want to know about…"

"I won't know until you tell me, so go ahead and do that."

"Okay, well, I've been trying to work out what was behind that database crash. It was really weird, you know, and since I got made responsible for the database, I want to make sure something like that doesn't happen again."

"Uh-huh," was about all Charlie could think of to say on the topic. The database problem had been the result of gremlins getting into their system, yet again. He'd now set up every trap he could think of that wouldn't draw his colleagues' attention, but there was only so much a wizard could do in a mundane office. Of course, he couldn't explain any of that to Keiran, whose knowledge of magic was limited to the spells in World of Warcraft. It was a shame to see the kid waste his time poking around for a software bug that wasn't there, but Charlie didn't see a better option.

"Well, I did find something in the code, but I'm not sure if it's what I was after."

"Oh." Charlie blinked. Maybe this wild goose chase would lead to something useful after all. "Why don't you show me?"

He followed Keiran back to his desk, where a long chunk of code was displayed across multiple screens.

"Well?" Keiran said. "What do you think?"

"Which bit am I looking at?"

"All of it."

"Huh."

Charlie started reading the code. After a few minutes, he sat in Keiran's seat and kept on reading.

The code was weird. That much was obvious. It wasn't that it wouldn't work, that was impossible to judge without knowing what it was supposed to do, but it was in an odd order, and there were some old-fashioned ways of doing things. Trying to work out what it was for proved impossible by simply reading. Charlie had seen jumbled code like this previously, in magical computer systems, where someone used it to embed spells, but as part of his company's client database, it didn't make any sense.

"Is it integrated with the rest of the program?" he asked.

"I don't think so. I don't think it's doing anything. It sort of sits there."

"Hm." Charlie didn't like the sound of that. Unknown code was like a bomb waiting to go off. This could be a long-buried virus for all he knew. "Gail, Steve, come have a look at this. Let me know if it's your doing."

They all gathered around Keiran's desk, staring at the code.

"Jeez, what a mess," Gail said. "This looks like Steve's dog wrote it."

"Hey, don't take Junior's name in vain! He's a smart boy."

"He's a dog. His smarts extend to fetching sticks for him and beer for you, and he doesn't even do the second one well."

"Just because he bites holes in some of the cans doesn't mean that—"

"Guys!" Charlie said. "The code, could you focus on the code?"

"Oh, yeah."

Silence fell as they read through it. It was an attentive and intrigued silence, one in which you could almost hear the *whirring* gears in people's heads.

"It's old," Gail said at last. "More than a decade. Probably been copied in from some other bit of software."

"Any idea why?"

She shook her head. "You're the old-timer here, remember? If you don't know, we have no chance."

"Could it be some sort of Easter egg?" Steve said. "Like those coins in Donkey Kong that you can't find if you play the normal way."

"An Easter egg has to mean something to the people who find it," Gail said. "Does this mean anything to you?"

"No, but neither do half the references in those Marvel movies. That doesn't mean they're not Easter eggs."

"Sure, but that's because they wrote those in for comics fans. If you put an Easter egg here, it would have to be for programmers at this company, and that's us, so if we don't get it, then it's a real stupid Easter egg, or you're stupid for suggesting it."

"Okay, okay, it was only an idea. No need to bite my head off."

"Sorry, I think the sugar's kicked in. I need a run right now, and I really need to go pee."

"That's fine." Charlie stepped back from the screen. "You go to the bathroom. I don't think we're gonna work this one out anyway."

"Thanks, old man." Gail rushed out of the room, letting the security door slam shut behind her.

"So what do you want me to do?" Keiran asked.

"Take it out," Charlie directed. "I don't want something we don't understand running on our system. Keep a copy somewhere, as a text file, in case we need to look over it again later."

"Thanks, Charlie."

Charlie went back to his desk. On his screen, the alerts he'd set were already popping off. Most of them would be false leads, of course, things about museums, vans, and crowns that happened to match his criteria, from Oriceran historical fan fiction to offers to sell magical vehicles. He should look through, just in case. He might not be saving the world, but he could help the woman who was.

Across the room, Steve answered a call.

"Hi, IT, how can I help you? Uh-huh. Uh-huh. Uh-huh. Have you tried switching it off and back on again?"

CHAPTER TEN

Kelly Petrie stood at the end of the test hall of the Silver Griffins' Special Equipment and Weapons division, staring at the target dummies lined up along the distant wall. Jell-O covered one of them, the one next to it in custard, and Bolognese sauce spattered the third. A wooden box sat on the floor in front of each dummy, the lids of the boxes tipped back.

"What on earth was the point of that?" she asked.

Toliver Jenkins, still holding the ends of the strings with which he had opened the boxes, ran a hand across his short red hair and looked at her in confusion.

"What do you mean?" he asked.

"I mean, why would you make something like this?" Kelly pointed down the range. "And why would you think I was interested in it?"

"All the agents like to have a first go with a new device from time to time. As head of the department, I try to make sure you all get your turn, so here you are."

Kelly sighed. She felt weary from talking to the walking

experiment in mad science that was Jenkins. His mind didn't seem to work like anyone else's, or perhaps to work at all.

"What are they for?"

"Well, whoever opens the box triggers the spell, and it covers them in food. That way we know who opened the box."

"Well done. You've reinvented the dye packets from banks, but at ten times the cost and a tenth of the practical ity. Congratulations, you're a genius."

"Thank you." Missing the sarcasm, Toliver beamed for a moment, then his expression faltered. "Wait, dye packets at banks? What's that?"

"Go look it up on the Internet. I have real work to do."

Kelly strode out of the room, through the blast doors at the department's entrance, and into the corridor. As she walked up the steps to the main agents' office, she took a compact from her handbag and checked her makeup. Still perfect, but of course it was.

Sam wasn't at the desk outside Applegate's office, so Kelly couldn't check if her boss was busy. Then again, she knew what his approach to work was, and he could do with more real work interrupting his day. She knocked on the door, and after he called a greeting, she pushed it open. It was only then that she realized he had company.

"Sorry, sir. I didn't mean to interrupt. I can come back later."

"That's quite all right, Agent Petrie," Applegate said. "No intrusion at all. Have you met Director Kowal before?"

The other man stood and extended his hand. He had neatly kept gray hair and wore an elegant three-piece suit, complete with pocket square and watch chain, every inch the dashing older gentleman.

"Harold Kowal. Pleased to meet you."

"Kelly Petrie, Agent 467." Kelly shook his hand. "It's an honor to meet you, sir. I've heard about your work."

"The honor's all mine, young lady. It's a pleasure to meet the up and coming stars of a new generation."

Kelly blushed and found herself very glad that she'd set her makeup to rights before coming in. "What brings you to town, sir?"

"Emergency inspection. They don't like you to know that we're coming." The former director winked at Applegate. "Just kidding, Roger. Everyone knows you run a tight ship here. No, Agent Kowal, I'm in town to catch up with friends and take in this new exhibit at the art museum. Of course, by old friends, I include my protégé here."

Kelly looked from one man to the other. She could see Kowal's influence in Applegate's dress sense, with the three-piece suits and the carefully chosen shirts. However, she had trouble matching the regional manager's work ethic to everything she'd heard about Kowal. Had the man who delegated away every task given to him really learned his trade from the hero who saved France from the mountain troll disaster?

"One of Petrie's first cases related to that French business of yours," Applegate said. "You remember, Kelly, that one with the forged grimoire catalog?"

"Forged grimoires, eh?" Kowal said. "Do tell."

Kelly smiled inside. This was amazing, a chance to show off her achievements in front of one of the most influential wizards in America. She only wished that the case had been as impressive as Applegate made it sound.

"It wasn't actually the grimoires that they forged," she said. "It was a late eighteenth-century catalog of grimoires, supposedly written by a witch named Madam Bompard."

"The one behind Napoleon's magical coterie?"

"Her mother, who ran a magical printing house at the same time. This catalog was supposed to be one of their products, except that I noticed something fishy about it. She supposedly published it in Paris in 1795, but it used the modern dating system. I don't know if that means anything to you?"

Kowal scratched his head. "I'm trying to remember my old lessons, but sadly my school days have also been lost to history. This isn't a Gregorian and Julian calendar thing, is it?"

"Good idea, sir, but no. What matters here is that the French revolutionaries created a new calendar in 1793. They only used it for eighteen years, but those years included the printing of this catalog."

"Meaning that the dates were wrong! Well spotted, Agent Kowal."

"Thank you, sir." Kelly beamed with pride. "This fake catalog was being used to establish the value of dodgy grimoires. Proving it was a fraud turned customers against the man behind it, and let us wrap up his illegal artifact sales for good."

"What does this have to do with my trolls?" Kowal winked at Applegate again. "All the best stories come back to me, eh?"

"The man behind the forgery was Javier Sadoul," Applegate said. "The same Sadoul who…"

"…released all those trolls!" Kowal laughed and slapped his thigh. "So you got to lock Sadoul up, eh, Agent Petrie? Well done. It felt dirty letting him get away with the troll business, but what choice did we have, eh? I'm glad someone got him in the end."

"Thank you, sir." Kelly beamed with pride.

"I presume you got Robail as well?"

"Robail, sir?"

"Olivier Robail. He and Sadoul were thick as thieves, always working together on their schemes. I swear Robail was half the reason Sadoul kept getting away from us back in the day. No way Sadoul was running a scam like that without Robail's help."

Kelly looked nervously at Applegate, who gave a little shrug. This was clearly news to him too.

"Nobody named Robail turned up in our investigation," Kelly said. "When we arrested Sadoul, he confessed to his crimes, and we sent him off to Trevilsom. That was the end of that."

"Oh, well then, perhaps I'm wrong." Kowal shrugged. "I daresay Sadoul and Robail had some sort of falling out or started running separate schemes. Plenty of reasons you might catch one without the other, eh?"

"Yes, sir," Kelly said uncertainly.

There was an awkward silence.

"Enough of that," Applegate said. "Was there something in particular you wanted to talk about, Agent Petrie?"

Kelly blinked. She had wanted to ask about a current case, but now her head was too full of worries about an old one. What if she'd missed something? Had this Robail been involved, and he'd slipped through her fingers? She'd been younger then, but that was no excuse for gullibility, for simply accepting a suspect's word when he said no one else had helped him.

If her younger self had been there with her, she would have given her a sound kick and a lecture on bucking up her ideas.

"Actually, sir, I think I need to check something out before I talk to you about my case. Can I come back later?"

"Of course, of course." Applegate smiled. "Off you go, Agent Petrie, go save the world while us old-timers try to remember where we left our keys."

"It was a pleasure to meet you, Agent Petrie," Kowal said.

"You too, sir." She hurried out.

When she got back to her desk, she logged onto her computer and opened the Griffins' database of past cases, where she searched for the name of Sadoul. This was why paperwork and administration were so important, so you could find the information when you needed it. Some people scorned writing up reports, but Kelly was a big believer in following the rules.

She opened the file, read her report, and started scanning through the witness statements. She wanted to believe that she was getting paranoid, that there was nothing to worry about. The case had seemed perfect at the time. Why should it seem any different now?

The answer, of course, was that one of the world's greatest agents had poked a big hole in it. If she couldn't close that hole, she needed to find out what lay on the other side.

Her desk phone rang, and she snatched it up.

"Petrie," she said sharply. "What do you want?"

"Humiliation!" Jenkins said from the other end of the line.

"Excuse me?"

"The point of those devices I showed you, it's humiliation. You let some magical criminal steal it thinking that it's full of treasure, he opens it in front of his men, and he gets covered in custard. Completely humiliating. Totally undermines his authority. How can anyone take him seriously after that?"

"That's the whole point of what you showed me?"

"Well, yes, now that I've thought about it. So, do you want the boxes?"

"Jenkins, don't take this the wrong way, but you really need your head examined."

Kelly slammed the phone down.

She stared at her screen. Humiliation. The word ran in circles around the inside of her head. That was what would happen to her if it turned out that one of her cases, the one with which she had made her name, had been so completely bungled that half the criminal team behind it got away. She had to fix this. She had to find out the truth, and if she had missed this Robail, then capture him before anyone else exposed her secret. It was the only way to keep her dignity intact.

She opened another witness statement and kept on reading.

CHAPTER ELEVEN

Ashley sat in the entrance room of the tunnel lair that she and her brothers had created under the Heron house. The walls were brightly colored, recently repainted at Eddie's request by her robot Octo, and finished off with rows of colorful handprints by Eddie himself. Bean bags lay scattered across the thickly carpeted floor, and in the middle of the room was a table with cookies, cups, and pitchers of lemonade and milk. Everything was ready, yet Ashley felt strangely nervous, in a way that she wouldn't have been when fighting criminals or sending her technology to hunt down rogue magical monsters.

It was a silly feeling, she told herself. After all, she had spent lots of time talking with the other Mini Griffins since recruiting them to help her with her work. They listened to her instructions, did as she asked, and generally accepted her place as leader, even though, at eight years old, she was younger than most of them. Yet, the idea of gathering them in person for the first time made her worry about how they would respond and how this meeting would go.

She pushed those feelings aside and got back to working with her construction marbles, the high-tech devices that she used to build designs and prototypes for her machines. The marbles clicked together, their electro-magnetic fields holding them in the shape of a new robot she was designing. When she hit a button on her laptop, the marbles moved, and the robot walked across the floor. The legs worked, but they needed more space in case it had to run. She walked the prototype back to her and started reassembling it, this time with a wider stride.

Footsteps from one of the adjoining tunnels told her that the first of her guests had arrived. She hastily set the robot down and sat smiling brightly for whoever it was.

Mia walked through the door, smiling and tucking back her dark curly hair. "Hi, Ashley."

"Hi, Mia." Ashley was pleased that Mia was the first to arrive. At twelve years old, Mia was one of the oldest Mini Griffins, and that could have made her one of the most intimidating to deal with. She was also one of the most cooperative, always standing up for Ashley when disagree-ments came up, bolstering her authority and encouraging her. It would be easier to deal with everyone else if Mia was there.

"This place is fantastic." Mia looked around the room. "Did you really make it yourself?"

"Me and my brothers," Ashley said. "With some help from Octo."

In the corner of the room, the robot waved a claw, then went back to standby mode.

"You want a drink and a cookie?" Ashley asked. "My mom baked them."

"Thanks." Mia poured herself a glass of lemonade and took a cookie, then settled onto one of the bean bags. "So, this is really cool, meeting up at last. What did you call us together for?"

"I wanted to—"

Ashley's explanation was interrupted by more footsteps and an excited shout. Ten-year-old Tommy, his baseball cap sitting wonky on his head, ran into the room and stared around, wide-eyed.

"This is so freaking cool!" he exclaimed. "It's like the Xavier school teamed up with the Batcave to make a place just for us." He grabbed a cookie and flung himself down on a bean bag across the room from Mia. "So. Freaking. Cool."

Other kids came in after Tommy, and while no one was quite as noisily enthusiastic, the room soon buzzed with lively chatter. Ashley wished that she'd made some sort of device to quiet people down. It was much easier to manage all these conversations over online chat channels, where she had a mute button. People were always messier to deal with in person.

It was Mia who brought things under control.

"All right!" she said loudly, clapping her hands together. "Ashley invited us all here for a reason, so we should hear what she has to say."

To Ashley's surprise, they all went quiet and turned expectantly to her. It was strangely exciting.

"We've done a bunch of missions now," she said. "Like tracking down those trash imps or helping stop the art robbery yesterday. I'm pleased with what we've done, and I want other people to know about it, now and in the future. I want to make sure it's recorded for future historians if they want to know about us.

"For that to happen, we need a record of our adventures. I'm going to start a log of all the things the Mini Griffins have done, and I wanted your help."

"What do you want us to do?" Mia asked.

"It would be cool if you could write about your missions after you do them. What you did, what you saw, things like that."

Tommy raised a hand. "Does this mean we have to do, like, homework?"

Some of the other Mini Griffins tried to shush him, but as many had the same concerned expression he did at the thought of writing things down.

"Nobody has to do anything," Ashley corrected. "It would just be nice."

Tommy made a face that told her how nice he thought it was to write things down.

"Wouldn't it be better to spend the time doing missions?" he asked.

Some of the others voiced their agreement.

Ashley sucked on the end of her finger as she tried to gather her thoughts. How could she explain this in a way that would make sense to other people, not only to her?

"There are times when we can't go on missions," she said. "At least, I can't. My parents won't let me go out after a certain time, and some days there's nothing we can do as Mini Griffins. You could write up your missions then."

"Or I could play Xbox," Tommy countered. It was an argument that Ashley could see she would struggle to beat.

"That's fine," Mia said. "If you don't want people to talk about what you did, then don't write it down."

That got Tommy's attention.

"Why wouldn't they talk about me?" he asked. "I found that lady who was in charge of the robbery. I helped catch the trash imps."

"Sure, we know that. Now think about what happens in the future when historians look back on all the great things the Mini Griffins achieved. You might not be around to tell your version of the story, to remind people how important you were. They'll have my version, but that'll be about the things I saw."

"You're leaving me out?"

"I wasn't there for your parts, so I can't write them properly, can I?"

"That's not fair!"

"What's not fair is expecting other people to do all the work while you get the glory. If only one side of history gets written down, that's the side people will remember."

Tommy's face went through a series of strange contortions as he battled with unseen thoughts and feelings. "How about if I make videos of what I saw and did instead of writing it down? Like, a vlog version of your reports?"

Mia looked at Ashley and raised an eyebrow.

"Sure, that's good," Ashley said. "I hadn't thought about it, but any way of recording it will do. Written or video or audio. You could do a picture if you want. Then I'll put all the pieces for a single adventure together so people can find them and get the whole story."

"Cool," Tommy said. "Because I'm, like, great at talking, but when it comes to writing, I get the letters all mixed up. They jumble together like a pile of spaghetti on a plate, and sometimes it doesn't matter how hard I try, they won't make sense." He frowned. "It's super frustrating."

Ashley blinked in surprise. She'd had no idea that Tommy had dyslexia. She hadn't thought at all about how difficult it would be for some of the Mini Griffins to make their voices felt in a record of the group's activities. Now she started to wonder what barriers other junior wizards and witches in the group might face.

"Really, any way of recording it is good," she said. "If any of you have trouble, you can come to me for help."

"Or me," Mia added. "I'm happy to help with things like grammar and spelling."

"I know how to edit audio," one of the other Mini Griffins offered, raising his hand. "I can help with that if anyone wants."

"I've been learning effects for videos," someone else said.

"I know how to draw imps."

"I have a great way to…"

Just like that, the room was full of excited chatter as the Mini Griffins talked about the best ways to chronicle their adventures. Ashley fetched out pens and paper, then pencils and crayons, before rushing off to grab microphones and video cameras from her stash. By the time she returned, Tommy was halfway through explaining one of his adventures to Mia, who was making notes for what to include in his first video.

Ashley grinned. There was no way people could forget their adventures now. Whether they became written articles, videos, or drawings, they'd remember the legends of the Mini Griffins forever.

CHAPTER TWELVE

"I'm proud of you, sweetheart," Lucy said.

"Thanks, Mom." Dylan looked around the carriage of the underground train hurtling toward the Silver Griffins' HQ. He didn't get to come to his mom's work often, and he was super excited for the chance to do it now. It was cool that she was saying nice things, but that wasn't where his attention was. He focused on the pair of witches bringing in a rogue elf they had arrested, the two gnomes debating magical theory in the corner of the carriage, and the strange tentacled creature that let out a musical note every time the train turned a corner.

"You used real maturity and good sense in a difficult situation," Lucy continued. "Who knows what would have happened if you hadn't been around to deal with that broken wand."

She patted the locked box in her lap. Its original design was a toolbox. Jenkins had stripped out all the inner dividers and fixings before strengthening the locks and hinges, then adding magical wards and radiation shielding.

It was the ultimate in secure, inconspicuous transportation for small magical artifacts, and right now it held the broken wand from the dig site.

The train rounded one last corner to the sound of a shrill solo from the tentacled magical, then stopped in the station below Griffith Observatory. Lucy led Dylan out and across the platform.

"Afternoon, Agent Heron." Normandy tipped his cap. "And Master Dylan, if I remember correctly?"

"Hi," Dylan said. "I love your uniform."

"Thank you." Normandy beamed with pride. "I polish the buttons every day."

Lucy led Dylan up the tunnel, around the winding staircase, and through the hidden door into the observatory. He had been to the building on a school trip, but that had involved a very different route than when he went with his mom. This way was much cooler.

In the entrance room of the Silver Griffins' offices, the receptionist was on duty as usual.

"I assume he doesn't have a security clearance?" The receptionist nodded at Dylan as Lucy pressed her wand against the ID box.

"No," she said. "He does have an appointment to meet with Agent Applegate."

"Ah, yes." The receptionist peered at something on his screen, then hit a button. The side of the ID box opened and a small plastic frog jumped out. It hopped into Dylan's hand, where it turned into a badge with his name and picture hanging from a lanyard.

"Please wear that at all times while in the building," the receptionist said. "And of course, have a nice day."

A pigeon buzzed past their heads as they walked through the door into the main office. The place was relatively quiet although a few agents were at their desks, and a cluster of gnomes stood around a hole in the floor, tugging out wires and arguing about how things should be connected.

To Dylan's surprise, a gray-haired man in a suit was sitting at the desk opposite his mom's, drinking from Jackie Kowal's favorite coffee mug. This was the sort of behavior that would get most people murdered when Jackie turned up, but the man seemed perfectly relaxed.

"Director Kowal!" Lucy exclaimed in surprise. "What are you doing here?"

The man got up and hugged Lucy.

"You know you can call me Harold," he said. "Is this Dylan?"

"The very same."

Harold held his hand out for Dylan to shake. "Young man, the last time I saw you, you were still in diapers."

It was the sort of comment that Dylan was used to, from whenever they met old friends of his mom or dad, and he'd never worked out how he was supposed to respond.

"I've grown out of those now," he said.

Harold laughed. "I like you, kid. You don't seem like the sort to put up with nonsense."

In Dylan's experience, he had to put up with a lot of nonsense, from Eddie's incoherent explanations of cartoons to his math teacher's thoughts on modern music through some of the inaccuracies he found in history books. Still, Harold had said it like it was a compliment, so Dylan nodded and smiled.

"Thank you, sir."

Sam had appeared by the desk, tablet in hand. "Lucy, Mr. Applegate's last appointment got canceled, so do you want to go in now?"

Yet again, Dylan followed his mom, this time through the glass door that led into the regional manager's office.

Dylan had seen Roger Applegate a few times, usually at the office although once at a barbecue his parents had thrown. He always seemed very jolly, but there was something about him that made Dylan uncertain. It was as if Applegate's personality expanded to fill whatever room he was in, and that didn't leave much space for anyone else.

"I hear you have an incident to report." Applegate gestured for the Herons to take a seat. "And that this splendid young man played an important part in it."

"Yes, sir."

Lucy set the locked box down on the floor, pulled out her wand, and unraveled the spells holding it shut. Then she flipped the lid back and carefully took out the broken wand.

"Dylan's been taking part in an archaeological dig, along with some other pupils from his school. He found this."

The wand *crackled* and emitted a scatter of magical sparks. Lucy placed it on Applegate's desk, and he poked it with a pen until more sparks came out.

"Well, that's unusual," he said. "What do you make of it?"

"I think it was more than a wand," Lucy said. "Someone was using it as a storage battery and a sort of converter to turn one form of magic into others. The raw power inside is nature magic, the sort you would expect to have effects on plants and animals, but it's doing all kinds of things when it's triggered."

Applegate gave the wand another prod. Magic burst from the tip, hit a pile of papers on the end of his desk and turned them into stones. One rolled off the heap and clattered to the floor.

"Well, that's unfortunate, though I suppose it's one way for me to avoid doing my accounts." Applegate picked up his phone. "Sam, could you print off those receipts for me again?" He put the phone down and turned his attention back to his visitors. "Dylan, why don't you tell me how you found it?"

Dylan explained about the dig, finding the wand in the pile of dirt, and about the spells it had unleashed. He carefully avoided mentioning that Sofia and Lance had seen what had happened or that they'd helped him to cover it up. His mom understood that his friends knew about magic, but she had been very clear on the fact that it shouldn't have happened. If the Silver Griffins found out, they might want to wipe those parts of his friends' memories, and Dylan didn't like the sound of that. He felt bad taking all the credit for something they had achieved together, but he would have felt much worse if Sofia and Lance had gotten in trouble because of something he said.

"You managed to keep all this hidden from the people running the dig?" Applegate asked.

"Yes, sir. I undid the magic, hid the wand, and

convinced the professor that she had gotten sick. Then I called my mom to come and help."

"Quick thinking. I approve. I've said before that the whole Heron family is an asset to the Griffins." Applegate looked pointedly at the silver medal Dylan wore proudly pinned to his chest, a memento of a previous magical adventure. "Now, if your mother approves, I'd like to recruit your help for something more."

Eyes wide, Dylan looked at his mom, who smiled back at him.

"I trust you, sweetheart," she said. "Whatever this is, if you think that you're up to it, it's all right with me."

There was another *crackle* of magic from the broken wand. A cloud appeared above Applegate's head, rained for five seconds, and disappeared. He frowned through the water dripping past his eyes.

"This sort of thing is why I'm asking for your help. The owners of this wand left it behind hundreds of years ago, and we have no records from that time. Who knows what else is lurking around that site? I would like you, Dylan, to keep an eye out for more artifacts there. You'll be able to blend in with the dig far better than anyone we could send from this office, as you already have a place as a volunteer. Your mission, should you wish to accept it, will be to identify any other magic on the site, contain it if you're comfortable doing so, and if not, call in other Griffins for help." He took a card out of his desk drawer and handed it to Dylan. "This number will reach an emergency support team in case your mother isn't available. So, what do you say?"

"That sounds cool," Dylan said, nodding eagerly. "I

mean, um, I'll be proud to do my duty."

Applegate chuckled. "It's all right to enjoy doing your duty. Now, let's talk about—"

There was another *crackle* from the wand, and water started pouring across Applegate's desk. As it ran onto the floor, plants shot up: thick grasses, waving ferns, bright bunches of flowers, all of them expanding at an incredible rate.

"This is getting ridiculous," Applegate said.

He pulled out his wand and cast a counter-spell, but the magic kept coming. Trees were growing now, springing up in the corners of the room, their tops quickly slamming against the ceiling and smashing its polystyrene tiles. Dylan had seen magic like this before, and he was glad that this time it wasn't his fault.

Lucy whipped out her wand and tried another counter-spell. The water stopped, but the plants kept springing up, and now the office was half-full.

"Time to make a retreat," Applegate said.

They hurried out of the room and slammed the door shut behind them. Branches pressed against the glass and slender roots quested out from underneath, wriggling across the carpet like worms. Two of the office pigeons immediately started pecking at them.

"Sam, call in Jenkins, will you?" Applegate said. "This is going to take some experimental magic." He turned to Dylan. "Please, get back to that dig as soon as you can. We can't have things like this getting out into the world."

Behind him, the glass door shattered, unleashing a whole swathe of greenery. Dylan and Lucy hurried off to get the dig site under surveillance again.

CHAPTER THIRTEEN

The garage was full of activity. One mechanic was reassembling the engine of an old Ford Mustang. Another was replacing the tires on a small city car. A third was sorting through spare parts and tools, making the most of a quiet moment to get the team set up for future work. The sounds of machinery and the smell of engine oil filled the place, an atmosphere heady with reminders of what thinking, calculating creatures could achieve.

Gruffbar sat by his bike, a midnight black Harley Davidson Deluxe. He'd opened her up intending to do some fine-tuning, then got distracted by another thought. Now he sat with his back against the wall, sketching a mechanism on the back of an old receipt.

Heavy footsteps approached, and a long shadow swamped Gruffbar. He looked up to see Gunther, his face contorted by puzzlement, looking down at him.

"Thought you was working on your bike?" Gunther said.

"I was," Gruffbar replied. "I just..."

He just what? He had a flash of inspiration for a new type of mining drill, and now he was halfway through his third iteration of the design? That wasn't who he was or hadn't been for years. He was a lawyer, not an engineer, as he would point out to anyone who made racist assumptions because he was a dwarf.

Except that he had been that person once, someone fascinated by machines and the ways they worked. Someone driven to make bigger, better, more efficient devices, and since the defeat of Mr. No, he'd felt some of that passion return. It wasn't just a hobby anymore, and tinkering with his bike wasn't enough to satisfy the itch.

An itch. That was exactly what he felt. An irritant. Something distracting him from his real work. That Gruffbar was in the distant past, while the modern Gruffbar had lawyering to do. He crumpled up the paper and stuffed it into his pocket.

"How are the new contracts working out?" He picked up the housing for his bike engine and started to fasten it back in place.

"Good." Gunther scratched his head with one of the huge fingers that marked his part-ogre ancestry. "All the old guys is happy with the perks, and the new ones don't know better."

"That's good. You'll have more control over who you employ now. That clause four is great if you want to get rid of someone."

From Gruffbar's point of view, doing legal paperwork was a great way to pay rent on his office, at least until more work came his way. Payment in kind beat payment in dollars when real money was thin on the ground.

His phone *buzzed*. He pulled it out of his pocket. A client's name was flashing up on the screen: Anders "Redclaw" Dokken.

"What's up, Anders?" Gruffbar said.

"Get the fuck over here," Anders snarled, his voice half-ferocious, half-fearful, the tone of a cornered beast. "Right fucking now."

Gruffbar scowled. He didn't like people talking to him like that, but clients like Anders paid him a retainer to be available whenever a crisis came up. This sounded like crisis territory. Plus, the fees for an emergency call-out would go a long way to plugging the gap in his accounts.

"You at the shop?"

"Of course I'm at the shop. Get over here now." There was a strained silence, then the most unexpected word. "Please. They're gonna kill me."

Gruffbar pocketed his phone, put on his helmet, and climbed up onto the bike. "Gotta go, Gunther. Any visitors call, take a message for me."

He roared out of the garage, down the street, and into the L.A. traffic, heading west toward the Pacific. Anders didn't quite live on the coast, but he was close enough to put himself within easy reach of Topanga, so he had somewhere to run when the beast took hold of him. It was a smart move for a shifter, one of very few things about Anders that was truly smart, which was what made him such a valuable client. Smart people didn't keep getting into trouble with the law or the Silver Griffins, and it took a special, profitable sort of stupid to keep falling afoul of them without winding up in one jail or another.

Anders was *very* special.

As he got close, Gruffbar slowed a little to take a leisurely ride past Anders' vape shop. A pair of rental cars idled out front, with a couple of familiar-looking and athletic young humans leaning against their hoods, hands hanging loose and ready by their sides: people watching and waiting for trouble. Another rental car had parked around the corner, and a human stood by the shop's back door, the tip of a dagger-style wand peeking from his back pocket. No wonder Anders had sounded panicked. What kind of shit had he gotten himself into?

The guards had clearly made Gruffbar. They eyed him suspiciously as he parked two doors down from the shop and took off his helmet. As he approached the entrance, one of them moved to block his way.

"Can I help you?" she asked in a Spanish accent.

That was when he realized why they looked so familiar.

"Knights of the Hinterland, right?" he asked.

Her eyes narrowed, then she nodded. "You're the one who met us off the train. What are you doing here?"

"I'm Anders' lawyer."

"You serve monsters like him?"

"I'm a lawyer, not an activist. I'll serve any monster who pays me."

The woman snorted. "Disgusting."

"Maybe. However, if you folks let Anders call me, that means you were willing to let him have representation, and here it is. So, you gonna let me in?"

She stepped aside. "By all means, lawyer. Do your master's will."

Gruffbar had many employers, but he wouldn't have let any of them take the label "master." He also had many better things to do than argue in the street. He headed in without another word.

Vaping was, in Gruffbar's opinion, a monumentally stupid idea. If he was going to ruin his lungs, he was going to do it for the sake of a good cigar, not some tarry liquid concocted in a chemist's lab. He still admired the ingenuity behind it all, from those near-alchemical concoctions to the devices that turned them into gas and even the complex commercial construct that convinced people to buy it all. It wasn't the best application of humanity's inventive spirit, but any application had something to be admired. Sentience always came up with something better than nature, and one of the things it had made was Anders Dokken's vape shop.

Anders was sitting in a chair in the middle of the shop, his hands bound behind his back with silver cuffs, silver chains tying his legs in place. The smell of burned fur wafted from his torn clothes, and blood had crusted beneath his nose. When he looked up at Gruffbar, it was with a wolf's eyes.

"About time," he spat.

Beyond him stood Klara Schulz and Oskar von Konigsberg, both holding daggers that would also serve as wands.

"Well, this is an interesting surprise," Schulz said. "Does L.A. only have one lawyer for magicals?"

"There are a few of us," Gruffbar said. "All the best clients come to me."

"Really?" Schulz looked at Anders, then back at Gruffbar. "I wonder what the worst ones are like."

Gruffbar reached inside his leather jacket, pulled out a

cigar, and lit it with a chunky metal lighter, buying himself time while he considered his next words.

"We both know that you have no jurisdiction in this city. I assume you're not interested in legal technicalities, so why don't you tell me what I'm here for? Remember, Anders pays me by the hour so you can take your time."

"We are monster hunters." Schulz pointed at Anders with the gleaming tip of her wand. "The definition of monster may have changed in the modern world, but our duty has not. Wherever we go, we hunt the beasts that threaten ordinary humans."

"You think Anders is a threat?" Gruffbar blew out a long plume of smoke. "The only thing he's a threat to is the bank balance of dumb hippies who think it's worth paying thirty bucks for toffee-flavored nicotine or a tiny plastic tub of something that might once have borne some relation to weed."

"There was a murder in the state park," von Konigsberg said, his voice laced with the sort of rigid conviction that only the young or the irredeemably stupid could maintain. "A woman torn apart. The police are looking for animals, but we found the tracks of shifters leading away from the scene. The next night, when we watched the park, we saw this one come back to the scene of his crime."

"So? That's what shifters do, make the most of whatever wild ground is available near them. Would you rather he went for a run through the shopping mall, with his furry little tail in the air and his big old fangs on display?"

"I would rather he were caged or permanently dealt with," Schulz said. "However, I'm not unreasonable. I gave him a chance to explain himself, and he asked to bring in help because he can barely string two sentences together without tripping over his stupidity."

"Hey!" Anders snapped. "Who you calling dumb?"

"Not the time, Anders," Gruffbar said. "Let the nice lady talk, and maybe we both get out of here alive."

"Oh, no," Schulz said. "I'm done talking. Now it's your turn, lawyer. Play the advocate. Convince me that this abomination does not deserve to die."

Gruffbar walked around so that he was directly facing Anders and looked his client in the eye. He didn't care who the guy had killed, didn't care whether he told the truth or not, but knowing whether he was honest would help Gruffbar make a coherent case, and looking him in the eye would help with judging that.

"Did you kill her?" he asked.

"No!" Anders' clear, open panic told Gruffbar that he was telling the truth.

"Then why'd you go to the crime scene?"

"I didn't." His eyes darted back and forth. That one was a lie and a stupid one to tell right now.

"Don't be an idiot, Anders. They saw you. Why'd you go there?"

Anders, his eyes wide, looked at Schulz and von Konigsberg, who flicked his knife around in a pointed fashion, then back at Gruffbar. The shopkeeping shifter was within inches of pissing himself.

"Is it as bad as murdering a girl?" Gruffbar asked.

Anders shook his head.

"Then tell us."

"I went for the blood."

"What?"

"The blood. It had soaked into the soil." Anders jerked his head toward a shelf of vaping fluids behind the counter. "Top left. Check 'em out."

Gruffbar wasn't going to put himself through the indignity of reaching for high places. He raised an eyebrow at the humans, Schulz nodded slightly, and von Konigsberg went to collect the plastic pots. He passed one to his boss, another to Gruffbar, and held a third up to the light.

"What is this?" he asked, his German accent adding "V"s and "W"s where they didn't normally belong.

Gruffbar peered at the label. It didn't have any words on it, only a round red dot.

"Seriously, a vaping fluid with extract of human blood?" He shook his head. "Who do you sell this crap to?"

"People in the program. Ones who still get cravings."

"The program?" Schulz asked. Her expression had darkened at the mention of human blood, and Gruffbar could see Anders' options shrinking fast.

"Some monsters that would feed on humans try to quit," Gruffbar explained. "The program helps them through. It's like AA, but for tearing people's throats open instead of getting drunk. Anders is selling a way for creatures addicted to the taste of human blood to get it without killing. That seems like a good thing to me."

"That depends where he gets his blood." Schulz set the vial down and approached Anders. She held her dagger wand an inch from his eye. "Well, beast?"

"I don't kill anyone, I swear!" Anders said. "I don't even need fresh blood, just anything stained with it. I buy medical waste from hospitals, old bits of carpet from crime scene cleaners, whatever I can get hold of."

"Then why, if you have these other sources, did you go to that crime scene?"

"Because I could get the bloody soil for free!"

Schulz looked at Gruffbar. "Is he really this stupid? That he would risk implication in a murder for a few hundred dollars?"

"Oh, yes. Trust me. I'm his lawyer. He's done dumber things."

"We should kill him anyway," von Konigsberg said. "He is feeding the hunger of dangerous beasts. That puts innocent people in peril."

"Actually, it keeps them safe." Gruffbar waved his cigar in the air. "You know how desperate an addict will become if they can't get their fix? Some of them will get desperate enough to kill, however much they want to follow the program. He's keeping them from stepping back over that line."

"You're trying to tell me that this pathetic worm is a hero?"

"By my beard, no! But in his awful way, he's making the world better, and if you kill him, you'll make it worse."

Von Konigsberg turned to see what Schulz said. Gruffbar could sense the balance of his client's life resting there on the tip of her blade, and he didn't know which way the scales would fall.

After a long moment, she stepped back and slid the blade into a sheath hidden up the sleeve of her shirt.

"Well argued, lawyer."

She said something to von Konigsberg in German, and the younger man strode out of the store. Then she reached into her pocket, fished out a small key, and handed it to Gruffbar.

"Once I'm gone, you can release him. Keep the cuffs. I have plenty more. Tell your other clients that there are worse things in this city now than the Silver Griffins. If any monster harms the innocents of Los Angeles, we will find them."

CHAPTER FOURTEEN

Lucy and Eddie ambled along the street with Buddy waddling ahead of them, yapping at cats, butterflies, and trees. The dachshund was in a good mood today, excited to explore the world, which made Lucy glad that he only had little legs. If he'd still been a bloodhound, keeping up with him or holding him back would have taken a lot more effort.

"I like cookies," Eddie announced.

To a less experienced observer of Eddie's thinking, this might have seemed to come out of nowhere, but Lucy knew how her son's mind worked. A moment ago, as they'd rounded the corner and came back onto their street, they'd passed Esther Romano's house. On a previous visit there a few months before, Eddie had been given cookies, and the connection between these two things had written itself firmly across his brain. His eyes had lit up as he'd passed the house, and there had been a conspicuous silence in the moments since, the silence of a three-year-old trying to work out the best way to get what he wanted.

"Lots of people like cookies." Lucy restrained a smile.

Eddie nodded thoughtfully. That line of conversation hadn't provoked the response he was after, so it was time to try a different approach.

"I like baking with you." He squeezed her hand. "Can we bake when we get home?"

"Definitely, yes. You can help me make dinner."

The face Eddie made almost made Lucy laugh out loud. He'd thought that he was so cunning, but it turned out that there were limits to what a little boy's mind could achieve. Who would have thought it?

As they approached their front door, he finally gave up and went direct.

"Can I have a cookie?"

"No, sweetheart, not now."

"But I want a cookie!"

"I want to live in a private palace with hot and cold running tea and Tom Hiddleston as my butler, but we don't all get what we want."

She opened the door and ushered both dog and boy inside. Buddy was flagging after his energetic walk, so he went straight to his basket and lay down, tail wagging slowly toward sleep. Eddie, on the other hand, still had sugar on his mind. He walked into the kitchen and stared up at the shelf where the cookie jar sat as if he could will it down through sheer force of desire.

Lucy took a small apron from its hook on the back of the door and put it on him. As she tied the strings behind his back, Eddie looked down in confusion.

"You wanted to bake, remember?" Lucy said as she put on her apron. "Because you like baking with me."

Eddie looked up at her. What she had said was true, but this wasn't what he had been trying to achieve. Would he accept a fun activity or try to open a new front in the battle of the cookies?

He smiled, took a stool from a corner of the kitchen, and pushed it over to the sink. "Wash hands." Apparently, today was going to be an easy day.

While Eddie splashed around, Lucy put the oven on to heat and fetched the ingredients they would need for a chicken pot pie. She had already made the pastry, and the chicken was leftovers from the previous night's roast. Flour, butter, vegetables, milk, and seasonings all went onto the counter, along with a bottle of sherry.

"Cook now." Eddie positioned himself at the little table that was his cooking zone, a private culinary arena where the Heron children had learned to cook for the past decade.

"Absolutely." Lucy sprinkled flour across the table, then presented Eddie with a ball of pastry and a rolling pin. "Can you roll that out for me?"

While Eddie tackled pastry, she did the work that needed a sharp knife, finely chopping onions, dicing potatoes, and cutting the chicken into small chunks. Eddie could do many things, but she wasn't ready to risk him with a proper knife yet. At least when he grew claws, he could feel where they were going and wasn't at risk of cutting himself.

Eddie grunted as he struggled to roll out the pastry. Then the air around him shimmered, and the little boy became a gorilla, still small but with bulging muscles beneath the fur of its arms. *Ooking* and rocking back and forth, the gorilla soon rolled the pastry flat, then looked up at Lucy with a pleased expression.

"Well done, sweetheart. Now I'm going to need you to stir something on the stove. What do you think would be the best animal for that?"

The air shimmered, and a slender monkey appeared, then climbed down off the stool and pushed it over to the stove. Lucy put the potatoes on to boil, then melted the butter in another pan and added the onions, which hissed as they gently fried.

"Can you keep stirring that for me?" She handed monkey Eddie a spoon. He *ooked* in the affirmative, then set to work.

Once the onions were soft, Lucy added the flour and seasonings, then helped Eddie stir to make sure the new ingredients mixed well with the butter. Eddie didn't like the intrusion. She'd put him in charge of stirring, and he wanted to retain responsibility for that role. His tail swished at Lucy's hand, trying to knock it away.

"Okay, okay, you can do it by yourself, but I need you to keep at it the whole time I'm adding milk, all right?"

Eddie nodded his monkey head.

Lucy poured milk slowly into the pan while Eddie stirred with focus, commitment, both hands, and a tail. At first, the flour mix thickened, then it started softening into a sauce as the liquid increased.

"Now, the magic touch." Lucy poured in a good glug of sherry, enjoying the sweet and heady fragrance.

Eddie looked thoughtfully at the bottle, then held out a hand.

"No, this isn't for you," Lucy said. "Not until the alcohol

has evaporated out of the sauce, or until you're a whole lot older. By then, I don't think sherry will be your first choice."

The sauce was bubbling nicely now, and the potatoes were tender. She drained them, then added them to the sauce, along with the chicken and some corn. She knew plenty of people who swore by carrots and peas in a chicken pot pie, but the memories of terrible school dinners with over-boiled vegetables put her off combining those things, and she made a face at the very thought of it.

Once the ingredients had a few minutes to mingle and warm through, she turned off the heat.

"Time to put it all together." She took out a large pie plate and draped one half of the pastry over the top. "Can you push that into shape?"

Eddie enthusiastically pressed the pastry down into the corners of the pie plate. He enjoying the squishing sensation so much that he pushed his fingers through the pastry in a few places, and Lucy had to fix the gaps with offcuts from around the rim. Then she steered Eddie away long enough for her to pour the pot of bubbling filling in, delicious chicken steam billowing around her. The two of them placed the remaining pastry over the top. Lucy ran a knife around the edge, trimming off the excess pastry, then handed Eddie a fork.

"You know what you need to do," she said solemnly.

Eddie's tongue stuck out the corner of his monkey mouth as, with incredible care and precision, he worked his way around the edge of the pie, pressing the pastry together and sealing it shut. Of course, the care and precision of a three-year-old weren't those of a grownup, and

Lucy knew that she'd have to fix a few spots before she put the pie in to bake, but it was worth it for Eddie's expression of immense satisfaction. At last, he got around the pie. Then the air shimmered, and the monkey turned back into a small boy.

"All done." He proudly held up the fork.

"Thank you very much." Lucy made a few holes in the top to let steam out, then donned her oven gloves and put the pie in to bake. "I think we're all done here. What would you like to do now?"

Eddie looked up at the cookie jar, then at Lucy, then back at the cookie jar. All hints having failed, he shrugged into surrender.

"Cartoons?" he asked.

"Sure, we can watch cartoons while dinner cooks." Lucy took off both their aprons and hung them up. Eddie was walking out of the room, his mind already full of animated robots and dinosaurs when Lucy reached up for the high shelf.

"That was some really good baking." She took the lid off the jar. "I think it deserves a reward. Would you like half a cookie so we don't ruin your appetite?"

"I like cookies," Eddie declared.

CHAPTER FIFTEEN

It was a bright morning as Lucy and Jenkins approached the Los Angeles County Museum of Art. The museum was only now opening, and the Silver Griffins who had been guarding it during the night shift were still around, doing their best to look like ordinary visitors, despite their yawning and blinking to stay awake.

"Don't worry." Lucy handed Jim a large cup of coffee. "The next shift are on their way, and we have some gadgets that might save us from having to watch this place twenty-four seven."

"Thank goodness." Jim let out an enormous yawn. "It's only been two nights, and I already feel like my body clock's ruined."

"Any problems during the night?"

"There was a security guard who started getting suspicious about us. We put a mild enchantment on him to put him off. I hope that's okay."

"We were bound to get attention sooner or later. Well done for dealing with it discreetly."

Lucy and Jenkins carried on into the museum, past a security guard with a slightly dazed smile. Jenkins was carrying a large backpack that rattled as he shifted its weight from one shoulder to the other.

"This would have been a lot easier if we'd set it up at night," he pointed out.

"Perhaps, but we would have had to disable the alarm system, distract all the guards, keep an eye out for the police, and we might still have drawn attention from passers-by wondering why the museum had lights on at three in the morning. This way, we can minimize disruption."

"If you say so."

They walked past a Griffin who was distracting a staff member for them and into the gallery where the Trakai Hoard was on display. Each piece rested on a pedestal, with a sign explaining the known details about its origins and craftsmanship. The ancient metal stood out starkly against the pale, minimalist modernism of the hall. In the center, gems gleamed red on the crown.

"We'll do this hall first," Lucy said, "then take a break and observe what happens before we set a wider perimeter, just in case."

"What do you mean, just in case?"

"I mean that your devices have sometimes had unexpected side effects, like that time you turned Nigel purple."

"It was only for a week."

"It was quite an awkward week for him, and that was only something affecting your lab assistant. If you turn a member of the public green, that could be a lot harder to deal with."

"I suppose you're right. We sometimes have mishaps in the progress of science. Let's get on with it."

Jenkins opened his bag and took out something the size and shape of half a soccer ball but made from aluminum and with sigils scored into its sides. It pulsed with magical power.

"Think of this as a sort of magical turret gun," Jenkins said. "It will detect any magical activity in the area and cast a spell to neutralize whoever cast it. We should put one in each corner of the room to make sure the space is covered."

They each took two of the devices, placed them in corners, and activated them using a button on the top. Once active, the devices became invisible, fading into the background of the area.

"These are full of banshee alarm ink." Jenkins held up what looked like marker pens. "Draw a line around each artifact you want to protect. If someone crosses the line with magic or with criminal intent, it'll alert us."

Between the two of them, they carefully drew a ring around each of the pedestals holding the Hoard pieces. The ink was invisible, but Lucy could sense its magic, and that let her find the beginning of each ring when she got back to it to complete the circle.

"One last touch." Jenkins pulled out a bag of powder and scattered it in the air. Like the previous two additions, it faded into invisibility.

"You're getting good at hiding these things," Lucy complimented.

"Thank you." Jenkins put away the empty bag and the pens. "I've had practice from hiding my lunch in the fridge at work."

With everything in place, the two Griffins retreated to a side of the gallery, where they stood as if examining one of the works of art. Lucy gave a quick nod to the Griffin outside, and she stepped away from the staff member, who walked into the gallery and took a seat.

A few minutes later, the first visitors arrived. A young couple headed straight to the center of the room and stood staring in fascination at the crown. They were soon followed by a school group, with a pair of teachers herding a class of chattering ten-year-olds.

"Who do you think the robbers were?" Jenkins asked. "The ones who attacked the van."

"They seemed to all be witches and wizards," she said. "So if they're a gang, they're not one of the big mixed magical ones. That could make them human supremacists or a group spun off from mundane organized crime, or it could just be a coincidence."

"Locals or from out of town?"

"There were some strange accents in the group, according to the Mini Griffins, so probably out of town. From the sound of them, more likely Russian mob than Mafia, though it's getting hard to keep track of all the Eastern European gangs. Assuming that's who they are, of course. There's always a chance that they're mercenaries hired by a powerful magical who wants hold of the Hoard."

"So what you're saying is that we don't know?"

"We have theories, and that's a start."

A change in the tone of the school group's voices made Lucy look around. One of the children stood stock still, a few feet from the pedestal with the crown on it. Her friends giggled as they tried to get her to move, and now a teacher looked at her in concern.

"Jenkins, how sensitive are those spell-casting orbs?" Lucy asked.

"Oh, very. They'll spot any magical coming too close to the treasure."

"So even a Silver Griffin would get caught?"

"No, don't be silly. I've set it to ignore people carrying our amulets."

"What about a witch's or wizard's child, in among a mundane group?"

"Oh yes, it could spot them. Nobody's going to sneak past us by hiring child criminals. I've read *Oliver Twist*."

The teacher looked worried now. She was waving her hand back and forth in front of the frozen girl's face.

"Ah, yes, I see the problem," Jenkins said. "Tell you what. I'll go over and cast a discreet counterspell. It'll all be fine."

Before he could move, Lucy grabbed his arm.

"What about that dust you put into the air?" she hissed. "What's it supposed to do?"

"It will adhere to anyone approaching the area with a hidden agenda. The particles will cling to them, gain color and substance, then create a sort of magical static that acts as a great weight, bearing the person to the ground. Makes it easy for us to identify and capture them."

On the other side of the room from the children, the young man who came in with his girlfriend was lying on the floor, his head and shoulders covered in bright blue-green dust. His girlfriend cried out in alarm.

"Ah," Jenkins said. "Yes, now I see why you ask."

"And the alarm wards? What do they do?"

"Start screaming like a banshee if someone magical... Oh."

They stared in horror as the teacher dragged her immobilized pupil across the room. The girl's feet crossed one of the wards, and a screeching noise filled the gallery. Children clapped their hands to their ears and cried out in alarm. The staff member looked around in panic. The girlfriend grabbed her boyfriend, trying to wrench him off the floor.

"Silencio!" Lucy shouted, whipping out her wand.

Silence fell across the room. People were still trying to shout and scream, but no noise emerged. Even footsteps did nothing.

Lucy cast another spell, and the doors slammed silently shut. She jabbed Jenkins with her finger and pointed at the alarm ward. He rushed through the swirling, panicked mass of visitors, pressed his wand to the ward, and gave Lucy a thumbs up.

She released her spell. People's voices returned, now without the screeching of the ward. They turned to look at her.

"Never was, never will be," Lucy chanted.

Magic rushed out from her, enveloping the people in the room. Aside from her and Jenkins, everybody went still and their eyes glazed over while the spell wiped away their last few minutes of memories.

"Quick," she snapped, "get that dust out of the air and clear away your sentry domes. I'll wipe out the wards."

She hurried around each of the pedestals, wiping away the magical ink. Then she cast a counterspell on the frozen schoolgirl, who went limp as the magic vanished. Lucy leaned her against one of the walls as if she had tripped and caught herself.

Then Lucy rushed over to the couple. She had to deal with this quickly before the "never was" ran out, and something like normality returned. She used a cleaning spell to remove the magical dust from the young man, then stood him upright as if he was having a conversation. As she was doing that, she felt a bulge in his pocket and looked in, curious. There was a small box, and inside a diamond engagement ring. At least now she knew what intention he'd been hiding and why they should never use the dust like this again.

She prodded at the girlfriend's face in the remaining few minutes, turning her expression of alarm into something happier. Hopefully, when consciousness returned, the couple would accept that they were in the middle of a lovely conversation. Lucy also repositioned some of the kids to look attentively at the displays or listen eagerly to their teachers. That was less likely to stick, but she could at least try to lend education a helping hand.

"Got everything," Jenkins called.

"Good." Lucy led him to the door, then released the magic holding it shut. As they headed out, sound and movement returned to the room.

"Is everything all right?" Jim asked as they hurried out of the museum and past his post.

"Let's just say that guard duties will have to continue for a while," Lucy said.

"I don't know," Jenkins said. "With a few alterations, some refinements to the magic, perhaps a different mix for the ink, we could—"

"Nope," Lucy interrupted. "Big bowl of nope. Huge helping of nope. We won't try anything like that again until I am one hundred percent certain it's going to work."

"Nothing in life is one hundred percent certain."

"Then we'll stick with the guards. Better to have a few Griffins miss out on sleep than to freeze half of L.A.'s art lovers."

CHAPTER SIXTEEN

"Ready?" Jackie asked.

Twylan looked nervously down the room, past heaps of packing crates, shadowy doorways, and half-open windows with only darkness behind them.

"Ready as I'll ever be," she said.

"Good enough."

The lights dimmed, and noises filled the room: the rumble of traffic and chatter of crowds, all the distracting ups and downs of noise that you'd hear on a busy street.

Twylan advanced slowly down the area, wand at the ready. In one of the doorways, a shadow shifted. She turned, caught a glimpse of an angry troll, and let fly with a freeze spell. Ice formed over the troll's cutout, and a green light lit up at the end of the room.

"One down." Jackie grinned as she watched from the start line of the assault course. "How many more to go?"

Twylan walked cautiously down the street, looking all around her for signs of movement. There was a *thud*, and she spun to see a dwarf in one of the windows, about to throw an ax at her. This time, she hit the dummy with a stun spell, and again a green light lit up.

"You're doing great," Jackie said. "Especially for someone who's never tried this before."

A movement grabbed Twylan's attention, and she whipped her wand around. She was about to let fly with a spell when she realized what she was looking at: an ordinary gnome with her hands in the air. There was a moment of quiet while the room registered her restraint in not shooting the gnome, and another light went green.

"Did Jenkins make this?" Twylan continued down the course.

"Of course. He had a phase where he'd watched too many cop shows, and suddenly everything was based on them. This was one of the bits we kept at the end of it, a sort of firing range assault course. No idea whether the police use them for real, but I like to come down here from time to time and play at being a commando."

Another pop-up opponent sprang from behind a pile of crates and Twylan blasted it. The next one she missed with her first spell but hit with the second, earning an amber light.

"Doesn't it get repetitive?" she asked. "Facing the same targets every time?"

"No risk of that. Jenkins and Nigel come down here from time to time to change things up. They don't tell us when, so it's always a surprise when you face something new, and you can't get comfortable with the old targets."

Twylan fired a series of sleep spells, catching three armed cardboard Arpak as they shot across the street hanging from a wire.

"That does lead to occasional accidents," Jackie admitted. "I once came in when they were making changes, but the darkness hid them. I ended up freezing Nigel when he popped up holding a plastic sword to attach to one of the dummies."

Twylan's enthusiasm grew as she got into the swing of the course. She picked up speed, and more wild magic spilled from her eyes. She dashed down the last twenty yards, twisting and darting as she flung spells to the left and right, her long brown coat spread wide behind her, then leaped over a pile of crates to reach the end. Her aim was messier in that mad final rush, and she missed a couple of targets, but she didn't mind. She was having fun.

"How'd I do?" She stood on the finish line with her hands on her hips, catching her breath. The target lights showed a string of green, with a few amber points and one in red.

"Eighty-five percent," Jackie said. "Good time as well, though you'll have to try a lot harder to beat Lucy or me." She grinned. "Kelly kept trying for a while, but she's given up now, claims it's not a realistic measure of how we perform in the field. I bet she'd think differently if she had the best score."

"It looked very impressive from up here," said a voice from above.

They looked up, and a light came on, illuminating a viewing gallery above the assault course. Harold Kowal stood smiling down at them. "I'd love to see you have a go at it sometime, little Jack-Jack."

Jackie's face contorted into something that was half smile, half scowl.

"What did I say about calling me that, Uncle Harold?"

"All sorts of things, but I stopped listening after a while. That's the advantage of getting older. People will assume you've gone a little deaf when really, you're rude."

Harold opened a door at the end of the viewing gallery and walked down a salvaged iron fire escape to the pretend street below. "Are you Jack-Jack's trainee?" He held his hand out to shake with Twylan.

"No, sir," she said. "I'm not old enough yet. Agent Kowal is showing me what sorts of things to learn and practice, to be ready for when I want to apply."

"'Course she is." Harold gave an exaggerated wink. "Definitely no trying to work around the rules here."

"I don't think that's—"

"Oh, don't worry about it. I used to be a big deal around here, and even I twisted my way around a regulation or two. It's the only way to get anything done. As a wise man once said, rules are there so that you think before you break them."

"Which wise man was that?" Jackie raised an eyebrow. "Calvin, Hobbes, or more likely Calvin and Hobbes?"

"To be honest, I think it was Pratchett, but great insight doesn't always come from books by big men with fancy titles." Harold walked over to the frozen troll image and prodded it with his finger. "Some people will tell you that you should listen to your elders, that things were better in the old days. You know what I say to that? Nonsense. We didn't have any of this in the old days. We barely had computers. Even the wand I started with was a grubby, erratic thing compared to the ones they make now. It's good for the new to replace the old from time to time."

"Yet here you are, telling stories to persuade us we should listen to you."

"Touché, Jack-Jack. I'm glad you haven't lost your touch. Now let's see whether I've lost mine."

Harold took off his suit jacket and draped it carefully over one of the crates. He pocketed his cuff links, rolled his sleeves up to the elbows, and drew a wand from inside his vest. The oak shaft was worn smooth, the silver bands polished by years of use.

Jackie pressed a button to reset the course. Dummies receded into their hiding spots, and the lights went dim. Harold stood at the start line, wand at the ready.

"Off you go," Jackie said.

Harold made his way slowly down the hall. When the first target popped up, he blasted it with a spray of mud, which hardened in seconds to a thick layer of clay, holding the target in place.

"That one reminds me of a troll I knew once," he said. "Fellow named Gringrin, led a small tribe of them in the Swiss Alps." He caught another target with a set of tangling vines. "We had some splendid nights drinking in a chalet up above the ski slopes, but in the end, I had to hunt him down and send him off to Trevilsom. Tragic, in its way."

The first of the Arpaks whistled down its wire. Harold spun it around with a wind spell and sent it hurtling back into the other two. They collided, tangled up, and stuck together with a huge blob of magical glue.

"So your friend turned out to be a bad guy?" Twylan asked. "That must have been so sad."

"Oh, I always knew what he was." Harold walked slowly into the final stretch, spinning his wand between his fingers. "It's not always a matter of good guys and bad guys, even in this game, even back in the days of the Cold War. Your ally one week can be an enemy the next, and that doesn't mean that they've changed or you misjudged them. It means that the world won't split neatly in two." As he talked, he casually flung spells around, catching each target as it emerged. "Even the best of intentions can lead people down dark paths. There was this group out in Europe, the Knights of the Hinterland. They were mostly active in the east, but they recruited from all over the continent. Big gang of monster hunters with a tradition stretching back to the twelfth century. We worked together several times, but they cared more about catching monsters than maintaining the peace, while the Griffins were the other way around. Inevitably, we clashed in the end, a messy damn business that nearly blew the magical world open in front of the Lithuanian press. Fortunately, it was easier to cover things up in those days, especially in the east."

He reached the end of the course. On the scoreboard, every light glowed green. Jackie and Twylan applauded enthusiastically.

"That'll do." Harold smiled. "Although I won't break the course speed record any time soon." He walked back to the start line, rolling his sleeves down as he went.

"Did you arrest them all?" Twylan asked. "Those Knights, I mean?"

"Goodness, no. Had to give up on the fight out of fear of exposure. We reached a sort of detente afterward, and a few of us had to promise to stay off their turf. One of these days they'll probably cross the line again, force us to put them down for good. For now, they're still out there, hunting monsters in the name of God and glory."

"I'd rather hunt monsters for the sake of people," Twylan said. "To keep them safe, I mean."

"I'll take any motive if it gets people on our side." Jackie started powering down the assault course systems. "So, what now, Uncle Harold? Are we taking this to the street so you can prove that you're better at detective work too?"

"I'm old, remember? I need to sit and have a coffee before I strain myself again, and as the revered elder of this establishment, I want you two to keep me company." He smiled at Twylan as he pulled on his jacket. "I want to find out what the future of the Griffins is like."

"Revered elder?" Jackie said. "I thought you said new things were better."

"I said sometimes they are. Other times, you can't beat a classic." He brushed an invisible speck of dust from his lapel, then nodded toward the door and the whole magical world beyond. "Shall we?"

CHAPTER SEVENTEEN

Ellis and Sarah sat across the table from each other, lingering over their cups of green tea. The pot was empty, as were the plates that had once held beautifully presented pieces of Japanese food. Around them, a gentle buzz of conversation filled the restaurant, but they were too caught up in each other to notice it.

"You've lived here your whole life?" Ellis asked.

"Is that so strange?"

"To me, yes. I'm not saying I don't like Texas, but I spent my whole youth planning how I'd get out of there and see the world. I can't imagine what I'd be like if I'd stayed."

"It's not like I've curled up and hidden from the rest of the world. I've traveled, I've seen the sights, I've had my picture taken pointing up at the Eiffel Tower. I simply never wanted to live anywhere else. Around here, I know where things are, I know lots of people, I'm comfortable with how I fit in. Why would I give up any of that?"

"It does have its advantages." Ellis sipped his tea. "You know all the best places to eat."

"Osen is pretty great, right? You can't beat good sushi. Still, we have been taking up their table for a long time, and my tea's getting cold. Maybe it's time to move?"

"Sure. Let me get this."

"No, we've had this conversation before. We're splitting the check."

"I'm staying away, so I get expenses."

"It's sweet of you to try to use that as an excuse, but I'm paying my half."

"This kind of thing is why chivalry's dead."

"Chivalry was a bunch of rules to justify men in chain-mail burning villages down. I can live without that."

They settled up and headed out into the street. The last of the summer sunshine was fading over Sunset Boulevard, and a thick, sticky heat was finally receding to something more bearable.

"If you don't believe in chivalry, does that mean I can't walk you home?" Ellis asked.

"I didn't say that." Sarah slid her arm through his. "Some traditions are worth preserving."

They turned off Sunset and ambled down Silverlake Boulevard, taking their time, enjoying each other's company. Their dates stretched out longer and longer each time they met, and now a possibility hung in the air between them, the implied promise that sometime soon they wouldn't part at the end of the evening.

"How's your hotel this time?" Sarah asked.

"No bed bugs, so that's something."

"They've cleaned the mattresses?"

"Oh, I ain't going back to that place ever again. I don't

care if it is on our preferred supplier list. I prefer to come out of the night with my skin intact."

The street was quiet apart from a jogger coming from the opposite direction, a distant figure growing larger as she approached through the twilight.

Sarah hesitated for a moment. She had known where she was leading the conversation when she mentioned the hotel bed, but now she felt unexpectedly nervous. She liked Ellis, was enjoying their evenings together. Any change risked disrupting that, but without change, things couldn't move forward, and she wanted them to.

"I did have a thought," she began, tentatively edging toward what she wanted to say. "I was wondering if—"

"Oh, no," Ellis said.

Sarah froze on the spot. She squeezed her eyes shut. That wasn't the response she had hoped for, and she hadn't even had a chance to get the question out yet. Still, if Ellis wasn't interested, she wasn't going to push this any further. She would take her losses and run.

"What's she doing here?" Ellis whispered.

Sarah opened her eyes and looked at him. His attention wasn't on her but the jogger fast approaching them, her dark, curly hair bouncing up and down in its ponytail. Ellis seemed frozen. The "oh, no" hadn't been for Sarah, but who was this woman who'd drawn such a reaction from him?

The woman's attention had been on the sidewalk in front of her, but now she looked up, only a dozen feet from them, and her eyes met Ellis's. She stumbled to a halt and stood staring at him, then slowly took out her headphones.

"Madre de Dios." The woman shook her head. "What are you doing here, Ellis?"

"I could ask you the same thing, Maria."

Ellis's usual carefree ease had fallen from his voice. Sarah felt the tension in him, his arm tightening beneath her hand.

"I'm here for work." Maria's Spanish accent lent her words a tuneful lilt.

"Photography work or the other kind?"

"That's not your business anymore."

"It is if it's the other kind."

"Then it's photography. Happy now?"

"Do I look happy?"

"Why are you here, Ellis?" Maria's gaze shifted pointedly from Ellis to Sarah, who clung tighter to his arm in response.

"I'm here for work too."

"You only have one kind."

"That's mighty observant of you."

A tense silence followed, the two of them staring at each other while the last light of day faded around them.

"Ellis, who is this?" Sarah asked.

"This is Maria Pérez," Ellis said. "My ex-wife."

"Your..." Without thinking, Sarah slid her hand from his arm and took a step back. Of all the people she might have run into during their date, this was one she hadn't known existed.

"And who are you?" Maria asked.

"My name is Sarah Smith. I'm his..."

Again she hesitated. They hadn't had a conversation about this yet, and that left her hanging in a void. Anything she said would either be presumptuous or dismissive of what was happening between them.

"Who she is to me ain't your concern, Maria," Ellis said through gritted teeth. "Neither of us has any claim over the other. You made that very, very clear."

"Maybe if you had been clear about some things from the start, we wouldn't have ended up the way we did."

"Maybe if I was the president, I'd hang out in the Oval Office wearing stars and stripes Underoos, but that ain't the case, so it doesn't matter."

"None of it does." Maria put her headphones back in. "Goodbye, Ellis."

She ran on past them and away.

Sarah stared after her until she was out of sight, then turned to Ellie.

"What was that?" she asked.

"Unwanted business, I suspect," Ellis said. "She and her people, they don't follow the same rules as us, and if they're in town, there's going to be trouble." He rubbed a hand over his eyes and groaned. "Maybe there already has been. They certainly have the skill to pull off something like that van heist if they had a mind to do it."

"That's not what I meant."

"Oh." Ellis's eyes darted back and forth. "You mean the whole, uh…"

"Yes, I mean that you never told me you'd been married."

"Okay, well…" Ellis gestured down the street. "Can we walk and talk?"

"Sure, but you'd better talk fast."

They set off down the boulevard again, toward Silver Lake Reservoir.

"I met Maria while the Griffins had me stationed out in Europe, part of the whole roving Griffin thing, you know?"

"They can send you that far away?"

"Depends on the job. At the moment, I'm only covering the US, but I've had other posts. While I was out there, we had some run-ins with another organization, a group of monster hunters. Sometimes we butted heads, and sometimes we worked together. They'd been through a lot of changes, were working more low profile, but somehow I kept bumping into them and the same faces. That's how I met Maria.

"You have to understand, I was young, and young folks, they mistake one day's infatuation for a lifetime's worth of love. There were a lot of feelings, working alongside Maria. Europe's magical underworld was in turmoil off the back of the big recession and the bloodbath it triggered in the Elven runic banks. Years of hidden warfare, and we were in the middle of it. The secret meetings, fighting on opposite sides one day and the same one the next, it built up into something that felt irresistible, and in the moments we weren't fighting for our lives, why would we resist?

"During one of the quiet patches, we got married. It felt like the right thing to do, and it made it easier for us to be in the same country. In some crazy way, we even figured it might bring some stability between the Griffins and the Knights. Shows just how young and dumb we were.

"The marriage didn't last two years. The same heat that fueled it burned it down. Turns out what I want from life is support and stability, while Maria, she thrives on chaos. There ain't no way to live together when you live like that."

By then, Ellis and Sarah had turned off Silver Lake Boulevard and uphill away from the reservoir. They were getting close to her house.

Sarah was reluctant to ask for more. It wasn't like she hadn't had relationships of her own. No one got into their thirties without a few emotional scars. Still, hearing Ellis talk about being married and about the intensity of the relationship leading up to it unsettled her. She didn't want to know, but at the same time, she needed to know.

"Why didn't you tell me about it?" she asked.

"I would have done, and soon, but it ain't exactly first date material. Hi, I'm Ellis. My ex-wife's a crazy Spanish monster hunter. You wanna go catch a movie? Trust me, it doesn't go down well."

"We've had more than one date, Ellis. You've had plenty of chance to tell me."

He looked down at the ground, and his voice went quiet.

"I know. I'm sorry. I probably should have gotten to it by now. It's just not something I like to think about, you know?"

"Hm." Sarah stopped outside her house and looked up at him. He was a nice guy, and he was so cute, even more so at moments like this when he was flustered. However, she felt pretty jumbled up now herself, and she needed time to process it all. She stretched up on tiptoes and kissed him on the cheek. "See you soon, Ellis. Enjoy your hotel."

CHAPTER EIGHTEEN

Lucy got out of the Rivian, drew a deep breath, and spread her arms wide.

"Here we are!" she exclaimed. "Angeles National Forest. All out for some fresh air and fun."

Eddie was the first out, climbing over his siblings to reach the door the moment it opened. He jumped down onto the ground and ran around, arms spread wide, singing the theme tune to a cartoon that Lucy couldn't remember the name of, despite being subjected to it nearly every day. Next came Dylan, unfolding himself from the back seat and stretching. He was starting to shoot up, and Lucy wondered how much longer she had before he was taller than her. With him came Buddy. The dachshund *yapped* and darted back and forth on the end of his lead.

Charlie walked around to join her. He had a backpack full of snacks and water, provisions for a day out hiking, and his phone in his hand, taking photos already.

"Smile, gang," he said, and the two boys posed with big grins on their faces. "Say, where's Ashley?"

Lucy poked her head into the rear of the Rivian. Ashley was still belted in, with a tablet resting on her knees. She'd set her construction marbles down on the book Eddie had been reading, a big illustrated guide to prehistoric animals, and she was rearranging the marbles into some sort of construction that Lucy didn't recognize.

"Time to get out, sweetheart," Lucy said. "We're here."

"I'm working on a design."

"I know, but the rest of us are waiting for you. We can't exactly leave you here on your own, can we?"

"Can't you?" Ashley looked up at her for the first time.

"No, we can't. So hop out now, and you can finish this later."

Reluctantly, Ashley put the marbles and tablet into her backpack and got out of the car. The bag came with her, of course, and Lucy wasn't going to object. If her daughter found a chance to work on her latest project while they were out and about, that was fair enough. She wasn't going to force her to spend all day focused on nature although she hoped it might provide a distraction.

They set off along one of the trails. Charlie had, with the sort of planning that came naturally to a software engineer, mapped out a route for them to take, with estimated times for each stage and stops along the way based on how long he thought the kids could last. He took the lead, holding hands with Eddie, keeping the little boy from running ahead in his eagerness to see the wilds. Ashley followed, taking photos and making notes on her tablet, apparently cataloging all the plants they saw. Lucy and Dylan brought up the rear, taking it in turns to hold Buddy's lead.

"How are things going on the dig?" she asked.

"Pretty cool. We've found a bunch of arrowheads and some pieces of pottery. There were some bones too, and Professor Angie says she's going to arrange for us to look at them under microscopes to see if we can work out whether someone cut the meat off with tools."

"No more magical artifacts?"

"Not yet, but I'm keeping my eyes open for them. Professor Angie says you never know what might turn up, and though she's not talking about that, I figure it's a good lesson to learn."

They passed a couple of hikers walking in the opposite direction and nodded hello to them. That was one of the things that Lucy liked about getting out into the country-side, the sense of all being in something together, of connecting through enjoying the natural world.

"It's a shame more people don't come out here," she said. "There are so many in the city, and most of them miss out on this."

"What if they want to be in cities? I mean, that's what some people prefer, right?"

"Sure, but I think they might be missing out."

"Me too."

Up ahead, Charlie had let go of Eddie, freeing up his hand to take a photo. Eddie wandered ahead a few paces, smiled, then sank to all fours.

"Look!" he announced. "I'm a dinosaur."

The air around him shimmered, and before Lucy could protest, a strange, four-legged creature with a round body, scales, and a curved beak protruding from its face replaced the small boy.

"What is that?" Lucy asked, staring at it in bewilderment.

"It's a kannemeyeria," Dylan said. "A prehistoric reptile."

Lucy glanced around. Fortunately, the hikers were out of sight. It would be hard to explain a living, breathing dinosaur wandering the wilds outside twenty-first-century Los Angeles.

"Eddie, change back right now," she said sharply.

If Eddie heard, he certainly didn't listen. He scuttled off into the bushes on his stubby legs.

"Hold this." Lucy handed Buddy's leash to Dylan. "Charlie, you stay here. I'm going dinosaur wrangling."

She hurried into the bushes after Eddie. She had to push the foliage aside, and branches scratched her arms, but she quickly emerged into a clear area where Eddie was scuttling around, prodding things with his beak.

"Eddie, you know better than this," Lucy scolded. "You can't just go changing in public. You have to ask one of us if it's okay first."

Eddie turned to look at her. His reptilian face crumpled.

"Change shape, please," Lucy instructed.

The air around Eddie shimmered, and the kannemeyeria vanished, but instead of being replaced by a small boy, it became a beaked reptile that flapped its wings and lifted into the air.

"That is not what I meant!"

It was too late. The pteranodon soared above the treetops and back toward the path.

"Charlie!" Lucy cried out as she ran after it. "Charlie, watch out for—"

She burst from the bushes and saw a group of half a dozen gray-haired walkers passing her family. One of them had stopped to pat Buddy on the head.

"Watch out for what, dear?" the woman asked. "This adorable little pupper?"

Buddy yapped and licked the lady's hand.

"I was going to say, watch out for big birds. I saw something exciting fly by overhead."

"I thought I saw something too," one of the other walkers said. "Great big thing flying over the path a minute ago. I must be going crazy, though, because I swear it looked like it didn't even have feathers.

"Oh, Zeke." The woman patted him on the arm. "I've told you before. You shouldn't be too proud to get varifocal lenses. It's not the old bifocals, where any fool could see how bad your eyesight had got."

"She's right," Lucy said. "The right pair of glasses can look really good on you, too."

"Well, if a charming young lady like you says so..."

"Zeke, don't be a creep." The lady rolled her eyes and offered Lucy a weary smile. "Come on. We should keep going."

As soon as they'd gone past, Lucy turned to Charlie. "The dinosaur, which way did he fly?"

Charlie pointed off the opposite side of the path.

"This is going to ruin our schedule," he said.

"Never mind, sweetheart. We can always come back another day for a long walk. Right now, I'm more worried about innocent walkers running into a T-rex."

She dashed off the path and through the trees, calling Eddie's name. Sure enough, a roar came from up ahead.

Lucy followed the sound until she found a two-legged lizard standing under a tree, its muscular tail swishing from side to side and its little arms raised, teeth bared in a long face. It would have looked a lot more intimidating if it hadn't been the size of Eddie.

"This looks like a lot of fun," Lucy said. "It's great that you're learning about history, and we're all impressed that you can turn into these animals just from seeing them in a book. However, do you think this is appropriate behavior when anybody could walk past and see you?"

The dinosaur waved a claw toward the surrounding trees.

"Yes, all right, no one can see you now. What's going to happen when you come back to the trail with the rest of us? Or are you going to stay out here on your own forever, without TV or cookies or macaroni cheese?"

At that, the dinosaur's mouth hung open. It looked at her with wide eyes and a trembling expression.

"I'll offer you a deal. You can be one more prehistoric animal while we walk back to the path, then you turn back into a boy for the rest of the day. How does that sound?"

The air around the dinosaur shimmered, and a woolly mammoth replaced it—not a full-size one, but an infant that stood waist-high to Lucy. It lumbered over and wrapped its trunk around her arm.

"Come on, then," she said. "The others will be waiting."

As they were approaching the path, Lucy heard voices. She stopped and peered out through the surrounding leaves. Someone looked back at her.

"Is this your wife?" said a smiling man with a beard in a lumberjack shirt.

"That's right," Charlie replied.

"Is that another dog with you?" the man asked. "I think I see fur."

"It sure is," Lucy said. "Right, Eddie?"

Behind her, the air shimmered for a moment, then a St. Bernard puppy bounded out, its shaggy coat flapping as it leapt about and barked. Buddy joined in, excitedly tugging Dylan around at the end of his lead. The man laughed.

"Aren't they both adorable?" He patted both dogs. "I should get going. You folks enjoy your walk. Nice meeting you."

"You too." Charlie waved goodbye.

When the man was gone, the Heron family carried on along the trail, following Charlie's directions. Lucy didn't bother asking Eddie to change back into a boy. He seemed very happy running around on four legs, and if this kept him from wanting to turn into a stegosaurus, that was a small mercy.

CHAPTER NINETEEN

When Twylan returned to the tunnels at the end of the day, she wore a backpack and carried two sturdy bags full of books and files. She brought them into the middle of the Underfoot Brigade's mass of shelters and set them down.

"Could somebody get me a table?" she called.

A moment later, Kix and Siltor appeared, carrying a table between them. Given the difference in heights between a gnome and a dwarf, one end of the table rested on her head while he held the other end close to waist height, but that didn't slow them down. They ran out into the middle of the tunnel and set the table down.

"What's this for?" they asked in unison.

"Research," Twylan said. "Get some seats as well, and I'll explain."

While they gathered chairs of various heights for various creatures, and while other curious Underfoots emerged from their homes, Twylan emptied the contents of her bags onto the table. There were books on history and biology, files full of old Silver Griffin reports, and several laptops with connections to Silver Griffin databases.

"What is all this?" Leontine peered at the heaps of papers. "Where did it come from?"

"Jackie found most of it for me," Twylan said. "Mr. Jenkins helped."

"Mister Jenkins?"

"He's a crazy man who makes weapons for the Silver Griffins. He also set up these computers so that we can access their records without seeing things we shouldn't."

"Why would we want to do that?"

"Research." Twylan looked at the gathered Underfoot Brigade. "We don't know what those monsters were that attacked us, where they came from, or why they did it. Until we know about those things, we can't be sure that they won't do it again, so we're going to use some of the analytical skills Ms. Fields has been teaching us, and we're going to work out what they are."

"You think they'll be in here somewhere?" Leontine looked dubious.

"I think it's our best option to get started," Twylan replied. "Unless you have a better idea?"

Leontine clearly wanted to have a better idea. Equally clearly, he didn't have one. He grabbed one of the books, sat, and opened the front cover.

"So how do we go about this?"

"I'm not totally sure." Twylan passed out laptops, books, and folders to the others. "If you're on a computer, try searching the archives for words that might describe what we saw. Think about how the monsters looked to you."

"Like a giant woodlouse," Kix said.

"Like an insect version of a tank," said Siltor.

"Their claws were like crabs," Leontine said.

"Great, so try looking for any of those things. If you have a book, try the index first, and if that doesn't work, start skim-reading from the front. If you have a paper file, then sorry, but you have a lot of reading to do."

Some of the Underfoots groaned, but no one made more fuss than that. Soon, they were all intent on their work, plowing through the heap of resources. After an hour, Siltor made enough lemonade and coffee to keep everyone refreshed. An hour after that, Kix and Leontine fetched snacks.

It was the most focused that Twylan had ever seen her community outside of Heather Fields' classroom. The destruction done to their homes, the ramshackle and incomplete repairs on display around them, that was enough to keep them motivated. There were occasional moments of conversation, as people showed what they'd found to each other or asked for advice on what to look up next, but for the most part, there was only the rustle of pages and the tapping of fingers on keyboards.

Not long after the snacks, Leontine spoke up. "I think I've found something."

He had a large book on the table in front of him, a dusty old hardback tome with a faded cover. When Twylan looked over his shoulder, she saw old-fashioned print on brittle, yellowing pages, with full-page illustrations in black and white.

"Look there." Leontine pointed at the background of a picture. Sure enough, there something like a giant woodlouse. The claws at the front didn't match what had attacked the Underfoot Brigade in their home tunnel but were what you might have got after describing the creatures to an artist who hadn't seen them.

"What's the picture of?" Twylan asked.

"Something called the Down Below Wars, from hundreds of years ago. Apparently, that's Deep Elves fighting against the Shadow Men and the Shadow Mage."

"That's an elf riding on the monster's back?"

"Sure. Look at the ears."

"Okay, everyone. Try looking up the Down Below Wars and the Deep Elves. We're looking for anything about monsters they used, things they rode, or how they fought."

Another period of intense reading followed. There was a sense of renewed excitement in the air, completely at odds with the calm and quiet of a band of teenagers absorbed in books. The fact that they had found a clue, that they were making progress, gave it all a strange sort of thrill. This was how the Silver Griffins operated, meticulous detective work digging into the truth, and now it was what the Underfoot Brigade did.

"Here." Kix held up a folder full of printouts from an old Griffin archive. "I wouldn't have thought to read it at first, but there's a description of the armies from that war. The Deep Elves used all sorts of creatures that lived in tunnels or under the ground. One of them was called the scythed borer, and it was big enough for a load of elves to ride on at once. That could be it, right?"

Twylan grinned. "Great work. Everyone, add scythed borers to your list of things to search for."

"Ooh, ooh, ooh!" Siltor waved. "I've got something."

With one finger in the index, he flicked through

another book, looking for a page number. The book was titled *Lost and Ancient Beasts*. The others gathered around, peering across the table or over his shoulder, wanting to see what he found.

"This is going to be awkward if you're wrong," Leontine commented.

"Thanks, that's just what I needed to hear." Siltor finally found the page and let the book fall open in front of him.

"That's it." Twylan stared at the image on the page. It looked like a giant woodlouse, with deadly claws on the front, rearing up out of a tunnel, threatening to tear in half an innocent dwarf who the artist had included for a sense of scale. The pages that followed held more information about the creature.

Taking it in turns to read paragraphs out loud, the Underfoots worked their way through the section of the book on scythed borers. They learned how most believed the creatures had evolved from isopods subjected to wild excesses of magic. They discovered how the Deep Elves tamed them in ancient times for use in warfare and that the beasts often turned on their masters, making them dangerous and unstable steeds. There were pages of illustrations showing the gear used to tame and ride them, much of which looked like cruel weapons. Twylan couldn't help wondering if that was part of why the Borers had turned on their riders—to escape the chains and pain.

At last, there was a section on the eradication of the scythed borers. Several groups had banded together to hunt down the wild herds that lived in deep underground tunnels and kept emerging to attack magical communities and even humans. They had wiped out most of the beasts and used magic to trap the remainder in caves, where they expected them to die out.

"Guess that didn't happen," Siltor said. "I wonder how they survived down there?"

"It was a stupid solution," Leontine said. "Trapping burrowing creatures underground and thinking that would kill them. That's where they live. It's where they hunt."

"Except that now they hunt in our tunnels," Twylan said. "I don't know why they're back, but they are, and they could come for us again.

"Keep reading. Find out everything you can about them: strengths, weaknesses, what sort of tracks they leave, where they like to make their dens. If we're going to be safe, we need to deal with these scythed borers. They destroyed our home. Once we know everything we can about them, we'll do the same back." She looked at Leontine. "You feel up to leading a hunt?"

He flexed his wings and grinned. "What do you think?"

CHAPTER TWENTY

"Where are we going tonight?" Lucy asked as she walked arm-in-arm down the street with Charlie.

"Guess," he said.

"Well, it's close enough for us to walk to, so it's probably on Sunset."

"Good start."

"Have we been there before?"

"Definitely."

"Did I like it?"

"I hope so, or this is going to be a very disappointing date night!"

Lucy laughed. "If we wanted that, we could have taken the kids to a family restaurant and saved ourselves the effort of finding a babysitter."

"Lovely as our kids are, even I didn't consider that. Making Eddie eat his vegetables is not anybody's idea of a date."

"So, it's somewhere we've been before, somewhere I liked, probably not somewhere we'd take the kids."

"I mean, we could, but it's not their thing."

"Hm. What sort of food?"

"That would give it away."

"That's the idea!"

"No, really?"

"Keep up the sarcasm, and I could go off you."

"That would make our living arrangements real awkward."

"Will you at least let me guess?"

"Can I stop you?"

"Good point. Is it Japanese?"

"No."

"Chinese?"

"No."

"Italian?"

"Still no."

"Ooh, are we going to Ostrich Farm?"

"Is that a sort of food?"

"No, but I don't know how to describe their food, beyond delicious."

Charlie laughed. "No, it's not Ostrich Farm."

Lucy slowed down as she tried to think of what other options there were. Then she sped up again as she remembered how hungry she was. Getting the kids fed and settled before they went out was always a time-consuming business and one that burned up energy.

"Giving up yet?"

"No, I'm just... Ooh, French! Is it French?"

"*Oui*, madam."

"Are we going to Taix?"

Charlie laughed again. "Given that we're now only

thirty yards away, that wasn't much of a guess, but yes, we're going to Taix."

"It's been ages."

"I know. That's kind of the point."

They walked into the restaurant, and a waiter whose hair was starting to turn to gray led them to the booth that Charlie had booked, where a chilled bottle of white wine was waiting, before leaving them alone to consider the menus.

"You remember the first time we came here?" Lucy beamed as she looked around and happy feelings flooded back. "It was one of the first places we ate out after I followed you here from London."

"The very first, I think," Charlie said. "Followed makes you sound like a lost pet that trailed me home."

"Or like Buddy when he sees someone with a sandwich, and he hopes they'll drop it."

That got them both laughing. It was easy to relax in a place that had such happy associations.

"Remember that apartment we lived in at the start?" Lucy shook her head. "There was barely space for one of us."

"It seemed like a good idea when I was planning for only me and my first graduate salary." Charlie reached across the table to take her hand. "I'm glad it turned out I'd planned wrong."

The waiter reappeared, notepad at the ready. "Are you ready to order?"

"I'll have the risotto, please," Lucy said.

"Pork chop for me, and can we have escargots to share for a starter?"

"Of course."

The waiter smiled, took their menus, and hurried away.

"Snails again." Lucy laughed. "Like that first time."

"If I'm honest, I'm not sure I liked them all that much, but I thought it would be fun to try again."

"I tried moving to another country. You tried eating snails. It was a big week for both of us."

"Here's to new adventures." Charlie raised his glass in a toast.

"To new adventures."

They *clinked* glasses, then drank. As she sipped, Lucy noticed a confused-looking woman standing nearby.

"Are you okay?" Lucy asked.

The woman blinked and looked around.

"I think so," she said. "I'm trying to remember what I…"

A man appeared at her elbow. He had amber eyes, a broad smile, and a distinct aura of magic about him.

"Hey, Alison," he said. "Our table's over here."

"Oh, yes, of course." The woman smiled at him. "How silly of me. I'll forget my head next."

The couple headed for their table, the man with a hand possessively on the woman's elbow.

"Odd couple," Charlie noted. "We probably seemed out of place here the first time, so young, you with the English accent, me desperately trying to impress."

"I think you were past the point of having to impress by then. After all, I'd crossed an ocean for you."

"True, but I didn't realize how well I'd done. All I knew was that this amazing woman was willing to spend more time with me and that I had a history of planting my foot firmly in my mouth."

"You must have done something right this time. If memory serves, we barely left that cramped little apartment the whole first weekend."

"I'm sure we went for a walk up by the observatory."

"No, that was the second weekend. You'd been working all week at your new place, and we'd spent the evenings in. I was determined to get us out for some fresh air."

"Oh yes, and I was still trying to show off, sprained my ankle failing to climb a tree."

"Good thing one of us had learned some healing magic."

"I've picked up a bit since then."

"Good thing too, given the scrapes and bruises the kids get."

While she was enjoying the reminiscing, something was niggling at the back of Lucy's mind. That couple, the woman with the faltering memory, it hadn't felt right. When she glanced over her shoulder at their table, the man's grin put her on edge.

"I'm going to the loo," she said. "Back in a tick."

She got out of her seat and headed toward the bathroom. Just past the couple's table, she stopped and crouched as if tying her shoelaces.

"Tell me about your eighteenth birthday." The man looked the woman in the eyes.

"Birthday…" The woman's voice sounded faint, confused. "I don't remember birthdays…"

"Come now. I haven't taken them all yet. Past loves, absolutely. Childhood anxieties, sure, those were delicious. I've been saving this morsel. It's always such a good one. Now, tell me about your eighteenth."

"I… Yes. There were candles. It was like the cakes when

I was little. I asked my mom for that." The woman smiled, but there was something sad about her expression as if she knew she was losing something. With every word, Lucy felt the magical aura around the man grow stronger.

A memory eater. She'd heard of them but never encountered one before. The man was like a leach that had fixed onto its victim, except that instead of draining blood, he drained memories, taking them away one by one until his victim would be little more than a zombie, a hollowed-out version of herself. Then, to cap off the horror, he would sell her as a pliant servant to some magical with no principles.

Lucy wasn't going to let that happen, but she couldn't make a big scene here, with so many people around. She had to do this subtly.

She slid her wand from her back pocket into her sleeve, with only the tip in the palm of her right hand and the rest hidden. Then she got up and approached the table.

"Brian, Alison!" she exclaimed. "Long time no see."

The woman looked up at her with a slack smile, the man with a sharp frown of frustration.

"I'm sorry, you've mistaken me for someone else," he said.

"No, I'm sure I haven't." Lucy held out her hand. "We met at that office thing last Christmas."

The memory eater's eyes darted back and forth. His ability to feed, his very survival, depended upon not drawing attention, and Lucy's loud voice, combined with her distinctive accent, had the opposite effect. He needed to placate her, maybe use a little of his magic to quiet her, and get out.

"Of course." He held out his hand. "You're from our Scottish division, right?"

"English, actually." Lucy took his hand. The point of her wand pressed against his palm, leaving no space between them for him to wield countermagic. "Stupefacio."

The memory eater's face went slack, and he slumped in his seat as the spell stunned him.

"Oh no, Brian." Lucy shook her head. She turned to the woman. "He never could take his drink, could he?"

Robbed of her memories, the woman was open to almost any suggestion. She nodded as if what Lucy had said was a long-established truth.

"We'd better get him out."

Lucy fished inside the memory eater's pocket, found a wallet, and emptied all his cash onto the table.

"That should more than cover the bill." She put the wallet away. "Now, let's get him out."

Getting the memory eater between them and sliding his arms over their shoulders, Lucy and the woman carried him outside, past concerned-looking waiters and customers.

"Sorry," Lucy said. "Our lad can't handle his beer."

Once they were outside, she pulled out her phone and dialed the Silver Griffins' duty desk.

"Agent Heron here. Badge number 485. I have a memory eater and his victim outside Taix restaurant near Echo Park. Can you send someone to pick them up? If he's processed soon, we might be able to restore the memories she's lost."

Within ten minutes, a van appeared. Jim and another agent leapt out, took the stunned memory eater, and lifted him into the back, where they secured him with magically reinforced manacles. Then they helped the woman climb in.

"Thank you," she said to Lucy, giving her a dazed but grateful smile. "I don't remember exactly why, but thank you."

Lucy headed back into the restaurant, where her meal was waiting for her, along with her grinning husband.

"Just going to the bathroom, huh?"

"Duty called."

"It often does. You remember my birthday, the year after you joined the Griffins?"

"I didn't miss dinner."

"No, but you missed coffee with my folks, drinks with my friends, and the only reason you made dinner was that Applegate realized what was going on and kicked you off the case."

Lucy laughed. "I'm going to be apologizing for that one my whole life, aren't I?"

"Never apologize for it. Your need to do good is part of why I love you." Charlie looked down at the plate between them. "Now remind me, how do we even eat snails?

CHAPTER TWENTY-ONE

Lucy didn't often go into the archives. While she loved the beauty of a well-made book, the Silver Griffins' old materials tended more toward plain, functional documents draped in decades of dust. It would have been exciting to Dylan, and maybe someday she would bring him down here so he could bask in it all, but for her it was a necessary evil. Despite all of that, she found herself down amid the stacks of cold, old shelves late in the evening, digging around for clues that might help her.

This was significantly harder than searching in a digital archive, like the Griffins' modern arrest reports. Instead of typing in a keyword and letting the computer pull up a list, she'd had to rifle through a box of file cards until she found some that seemed relevant to her goal. Now she was roaming the stacks with those cards in her hand, looking for reference numbers on the ends of the shelves, then for more specific numbers on the spines of books and ends of boxes. It was like walking through the mind of a vast and ancient beast, one made mostly of cardboard and cobwebs, its thoughts formed not from neurons but scribbles of ink on crumbling paper.

The inspiration to come down here had come partly from helping Jackie dig out books for Twylan, which had reminded Lucy of how much material there was down here. It had also come from something Ellis said. He'd asked her, with forced casualness, whether she'd heard anything recently about a group called the Knights of the Hinterland. When she'd said no, he'd looked relieved and said that it was probably nothing before hurrying off. Maybe he was telling the truth, and this wasn't anything she needed to worry about. Still, if Ellis was interested in it, then it could relate to security around the Trakai Hoard, and that made it Lucy's business.

She pulled a book off the shelf: *Military Orders of the Magical Past*. It was one of the books the file cards had specifically singled out for research into knights, and while the cramped text and dreary beginning were off-putting, she added it to her stack of books and headed on down the row.

To her surprise, she heard someone else moving a few rows down. It was late for anybody except the duty team to be in the Griffins' HQ and definitely late for the sort of work that involved rummaging around in archives. She peered through a gap between books to see what was going on.

Kelly sat on one of the wheeled stools that readers could use to reach the higher shelves. She had a box open in her lap and was rummaging through the papers within, her frown deepening with every passing page. She snorted, then swore to herself under her breath.

Intrigued, Lucy crept closer, stepping out from between the shelves where she was and down toward Kelly's row.

Kelly's phone *bleeped*. She dropped the papers back into their box and hurriedly shoved it back into its space on the shelf. Then she stepped out and jumped in alarm as she saw Lucy.

"Hi." Lucy beamed. "Working late?"

"Yes," Kelly said sharply, "and I have to go." She rushed off, heels clattering against the concrete floor.

Lucy glanced around the corner of the shelf. A box was sticking out slightly from the others. It was labeled *French Magical Underground Networks, 1974-2013.*

Lucy hesitated for a moment. On the one hand, she had a job she was trying to do and a pile of books to read. On the other hand, Kelly was up to something secret, and it was impossible not to be intrigued by that. Given the choice between the two, books could wait. Lucy set her selection down in an open space, made a mental note of where it was to retrieve them later, and hurried off in pursuit of the retreating footsteps.

Sneakers and some practice at stealth made Lucy's footsteps quiet as she followed the *clacking* of Kelly's heels out of the archive, down a corridor, up a stairwell, and finally around a bend to the transport room. It was a cavernous space lined with nineteenth-century brickwork. Along one side were the cage doors of the cells where they kept convicts for transportation, security runes glowing on their arched entrances. Opposite them, boxes and crates were piled up, supplies coming from or going to other Griffin bases. Between them, on the far wall, was a blank space laced with magic, primed to hold larger, better, more stable magical portals than those summoned in the empty air.

Lucy crept in behind the crates and watched as Kelly approached the lone duty wizard who had the night shift.

"You said he's on his way?" Kelly asked.

"Any moment now," the wizard replied. "Why all the cloak and dagger stuff?"

"If I told you that, it wouldn't be much of a secret, would it?"

"Fair point."

The wall glowed, and a portal appeared, golden light framing a gap in reality. Three people walked through —a gray-haired man in a prison jumpsuit flanked by wand-wielding guards. The prisoner's ankles were bound together with a chain long enough to allow shuffling steps, and manacles kept his hands close together.

"Thank you," Kelly said to the guards. "You can leave us now."

"You're lucky they let him out of Trevilsom like this," one of the guards informed her. "We're certainly not letting him out of our sight. You can ask your questions here and now."

"I said that discretion was important."

"We can be discreet. Now get on with it. The less time this one spends out of a cell, the more comfortable we'll all be."

Kelly glared, but they hadn't left her much choice. She turned her attention to the prisoner.

"It's good to see you again, Sadoul."

"Is it?" The prisoner's English was clear but run through

with a thick French accent. "Or is it an inconvenience you must suffer for some higher cause?"

"Does it matter? I would have thought that you would appreciate a chance to get out of your cell."

"This is hardly getting out." He raised his manacled hands. "Perhaps if you could release me from these bonds for a few minutes…"

"Nice try, Javier, but it's not happening," one of the guards said.

Sadoul shrugged. "Very well. Then why am I here?"

"When I arrested you, when we presented evidence of your magical crimes that you couldn't deny, you gave me a confession. You said that you had created and sold the Bompard forgery on your own, along with the grimoires listed in it. Once we dug deeper into your life, you confessed to further crimes. In every case, you said you acted alone. You were lying, weren't you?"

"Why would I do that? Confessing to other people's crimes is the act of an imbecile."

"Covering up for your friend and collaborator could keep him out of prison. You deliberately covered up for Olivier Robail, didn't you? He was part of those schemes, and you kept him hidden from us."

"No."

"What?"

"I said no. What did you expect me to say? You have my confession. I have my cell. None of that is going to change. So I say again to you, no, Robail was not involved."

"Don't you want to get out of prison someday, to see the light of day again?"

Sadoul's laugh was bitter as poison.

"When you Griffins got hold of me, you were ready to condemn before you even had the facts. You had been persecuting me for decades. Given a chance, you were going to lock me up and throw away the key. Why would I believe that things are any different now?"

"If you tell me the truth, I can approach my superiors, see whether we can arrange for you to—"

"Ha! You don't even have anything to offer me, do you? There is no time to be earned off my sentence. I know that. You know that. Do not play me for an idiot with your insinuations of something that will never be. The only way I leave Trevilsom is in a coffin, and even then, they will only take me as far as the prison graveyard. Nothing you say can make a difference to me."

Kelly scowled and ground her foot against the floor. She wasn't used to dealing with opponents who had so little to lose. There was no space to maneuver. Everything had relied on Sadoul's willingness to collaborate when she faced him with the truth.

Watching from her hiding place, Lucy could see Kelly's frustration. It was tempting to leave her to stew in it, but it seemed like she was trying to catch a criminal here, and that mattered more than any rivalry.

"If you're stuck in Trevilsom for life, you'll want that life to be comfortable, right?"

Lucy stepped out from behind the crates as she spoke. Everyone in the room turned to look at her, and Kelly's face fell.

"What are you doing here?" Kelly hissed.

"Well?" Lucy asked, keeping her attention on Sadoul.

"You present more vague offers," he said. "Nothing that

could make me share information, even if I had any to share."

"I've done it before," Lucy said. "When a prisoner cooperated with us. You know Turbit the gnome?"

Sadoul nodded, and a smile crept up his face. "Turbit has fine sheets and many books. They even bring him newspapers."

"I arranged that. I can arrange it for you too, can't I?" She caught the eye of one of the guards.

"If you want," he said. "This one's not a security risk. We can treat him nice if it helps with a case."

"So." Lucy smiled at Sadoul. "You have an offer. Books, sheets, newspapers, all in return for... What was the other lad's name?"

"Olivier Robail," Kelly said.

Despite his manacles, Sadoul managed to clap his hands.

"Well done, Agent Petrie. You and your colleague here have persuaded me. Yes, Olivier Robail was part of the Bompard forgery scheme and all the other crimes you imprisoned me for. I am willing to provide a detailed new confession, including all the elements I forgot the first time around, in exchange for a written contract for my new and improved terms of confinement. Do we have a deal?"

Kelly looked at Lucy, at the guards, and finally at Sadoul. "We have an agreement. I'll arrange with the governor to get the paperwork done."

"Perhaps you could send a little light reading in the meantime as a sign of good faith? One of your American detective novels, perhaps. It seems fitting, *n'est ce pas?*"

"Fine." Kelly nodded to the guards. "You can take him away. I'll be in contact tomorrow."

The portal opened again, and the guards headed toward it. As he was about to be led through, Sadoul looked back over his shoulder.

"Learn from your colleague, Agent Petrie. There is much to be gained from collaboration." He smiled, and there was mischief in his voice. "And please, I say this with all my heart, enjoy the fruits of your investigation."

When the prison group was gone, and the portal shut down, and the duty wizard back at his desk, Kelly stalked over to Lucy.

"That was completely unprofessional," she hissed. "Sneaking around after me, interfering in my case. I should report you to Applegate."

"What's that I hear?" Lucy touched her ear. "Was it you saying thank you for getting the lead you wanted?"

Kelly glared at her, then at the wall where the portal had been.

"Thank you," she hissed, then stalked away.

CHAPTER TWENTY-TWO

Twylan crept along the tunnel, a ball of magical light floating beside her shoulder. It felt strange to use stealthy movements when visible in the darkness, but the books the Underfoot Brigade had consulted all agreed that scythed borers were blind. It didn't matter how much light the teens used, it was sound that would give them away.

Leontine was ahead, his wings tucked in tight to his back, staring at the ground. The rest of the hunting party stopped, weapons and wands at the ready, while Twylan crept over to him.

"More tracks?" she whispered as quietly as she could.

Leontine nodded and pointed at some marks in the dirt on the concrete floor. Twylan had no idea what they represented, but she was happy to trust Leontine's judgment. This was an area where he knew far more than her.

"Scythed borers again," he whispered. "They've been coming in and out of this tunnel a lot. Must have been the route they took to attack us."

"So we can follow them down here?"

Leontine nodded. "There's something else too. Foot-prints from humans or magicals, following the same route."

"More hunters like us?"

"More likely someone's breeding borers again or stir-ring them up from the depths. That would explain why they've reappeared after all this time."

"So what do we do?"

"Keep following them, of course."

Leontine led the group on, down long-forgotten concrete tunnels. When those ran out, more roughly dug passageways carved from dirt and rock sloped down into the depths. Twylan couldn't tell if they had been made by people or by monsters, but they were wide enough for the scythed borers to pass through, and right now that was all that mattered.

The tunnel twisted and turned, then forked several times as it headed deeper underground. Each time the way split, Leontine paused to look at the tracks, to work out how many beasts had gone which direction and which was the best for them to follow. Every time, the other prints went the same way he wanted to lead the Underfoot Brigade.

After a while, they heard sounds from up ahead, the hushed noise of whispering voices, and the soft patter of careful footfalls. Out in the open, those sounds would have gone unheard, but it was deathly quiet in the tunnels, and the noise was amplified and echoed by the close walls.

Leontine pressed a finger to his lips and signaled for everyone to have their wands and weapons ready. Twylan remembered the pictures of Deep Elves riding the scythed borers, using them to chop through anyone who stood in their way. That would be a terrifying thing to face, and she gripped the handle of her wand tight in anticipation.

The Underfoots crept down the tunnel. They had been living in spaces like this for years and were able to move through them more carefully and quietly than anyone else. As soon as a hint of light appeared up ahead, they extinguished their glowing magic, ready to face whatever they met.

They rounded a corner and saw movement ahead. A group of witches and wizards in sportswear were advancing down the tunnel, holding wands and weapons. Like the Underfoot Brigade, they used floating magical lights to illuminate their way.

One of the witches said something in a language Twylan didn't understand, and another responded. These weren't native Angeleños, and from the way they advanced stealthily into the dark, she couldn't escape the feeling that they were up to no good.

There was a soft noise in the darkness behind Twylan, a stone shifting underneath Siltor's foot. At the sound, one of the wizards turned. He raised a sword and pointed it straight at Leontine.

Twylan didn't even have to think. The moment she saw the blade shift, her lips formed the words of a spell. Magic flew from the tip of her wand and knocked the weapon flying out of the wizard's hand.

The wizard shouted and pulled out his wand. His companions turned, their weapons raised.

"Get them!" Leontine shouted and leapt from the ground, soaring down the tunnel on his wings.

The Underfoot Brigade charged. Magic flew, and

weapons crashed as the two groups collided. The tunnel became a mass of tumbling bodies and flying spells. Twylan dodged a blast of icy magic and flung a bolt of electricity back. Next to her, Siltor flung up illusions to confuse the enemy: fake combatants, impossible objects, spells that weren't there. While Leontine grappled hand-to-hand with one of the wizards, others surged past him to try to grab the Underfoot spellcasters.

Someone swung a fist at Twylan. She dodged and grabbed the arm as Jackie had taught her, then twisted. Her opponent was stronger and more experienced. She flowed with the movement, spun, and kicked Twylan in the stomach, knocking her back against the wall.

"Madre de Dios, they're only kids," the witch exclaimed. "Try not to kill any of them."

Twylan flung a spell at the witch, who dodged aside as she drew her wand. Now Twylan was more concerned with her attacker's words than her actions. That hadn't sounded like the sort of murderous person who would unleash monsters out of the darkness to prey on innocent people above.

"Who are you?" Twylan held out her wand but didn't cast.

"Who are you?" the woman replied in a Spanish accent, aiming back at her.

"We live in the tunnels. What are you doing down here?"

"Hunting monsters."

Twylan lowered her wand.

"Stop!" she shouted. "This is a mistake."

The woman joined in, shouting in several different

languages. The fighting subsided, and the combatants backed off, watching each other warily. Fortunately, no one seemed to be seriously hurt although there were some bruises, a few frozen limbs, and more than a little damaged pride.

"These monsters you're hunting," Twylan said. "Do you mean the scythed borers?"

"Yes."

"We're hunting them too. They trashed our home. How did you know they were down here?"

"When we come to a new city, the tunnels are one of the first places we look for hidden evil. It is fitting that Hell's beasts are often hidden beneath the earth, yes?"

"I guess." Twylan wasn't a great believer in Heaven or Hell, but she wasn't going to argue with the woman's logic. Whatever her reasons for looking underground, it made sense that this would have led her to the borers or their tracks.

"I'm Twylan." She held out her hand. "This is the Underfoot Brigade."

"Maria Pérez." The woman shook. "We are the Knights of the Holy Order of the Hinterland."

"And you came to L.A. hunting monsters?"

"We had other reasons to come here, but wherever we travel, our core mission remains the same."

"Drive back the darkness," the Knights chanted together. "Lift the light. Hunt down the monsters. For the glory of God and a better world."

"This is an awful lot of darkness to drive back." Siltor waved at the dim tunnel around them.

"Then we will stick with the spiritual darkness," Maria said. "Starting with these scythed borers."

"In that case, why don't we work together?" Twylan suggested. "We'll stand a better chance against the borers that way."

Maria looked around at her companions and one by one they nodded.

"Why not?" she said. "Local guides are always useful."

Together, the Knights and teens made their way down the tunnels. Leontine and one of the Knights led the way. As they walked, Twylan noticed that Maria wore armor under her hoodie, not the stiff, metal armor of a traditional knight, but modern body armor. The Knights' weapons were also noticeably better than those of the Underfoot Brigade, sharp swords and dagger-shaped wands instead of lengths of pipe and baseball bats.

"You're better equipped for this than us," she said.

Maria shrugged. "You are children. We are professionals, crusaders against the blackness that threatens to consume humanity."

"Have you been doing this long?"

"My whole life and the Order had been fighting for centuries. We will never give up, not while the least risk remains."

Up ahead, Leontine and his fellow tracker had stopped. When Twylan and Maria caught up, it became immediately apparent why. The tunnel had opened into a wide chamber, and at the far side, the light of their magic glinted off the edges of vast, layered shells.

Maria drew her sword.

"On my signal, give us lots of light, yes?" she whispered.

The Knights fanned out across the near side of the cave, spreading out through the gloom. The Underfoot Brigade joined them, casting hands at the ready.

"Now!" Maria shouted.

"Lumen!" Twylan bellowed, spreading her arms wide.

Bright light flooded the cave, revealing a dozen scythed borers. The creatures turned toward the shout, then jerked their heads around as footsteps rushed toward them.

The hunters charged the beasts, swords and improvised weapons swinging, spells flying. One beast was quickly frozen in place by half a dozen spells, but another rushed forward, magic glancing off its flanks. It raced toward Twylan, who raised her wand.

Maria leapt into the air, dodged a snap of the beast's claw, and landed on its back. She raised her sword, point down, both hands around its grip, and steadied herself on the moving shell.

The beast was almost on Twylan. She flung ice and stun spells at the creature. Some seemed to slow it, but its shell deflected others. Claws rose, and its mouth opened, full of pointed teeth.

Maria thrust the sword down, stabbing through shell and muscle into the creature's brain. Dark blood spurted out as she withdrew the blade and leapt clear. The beast's legs stopped moving, and it skidded to a halt a foot away from Twylan.

Another of the beasts rushed toward her, but Leontine swooped in with a Knight hanging from each arm. They landed on its back and hacked at it until the shell cracked open and the monster ground to a halt.

Around the chamber, the hunters stepped back to

admire their handiwork. The beasts were dead, and no one was seriously injured. Having seen how many there were, Twylan wasn't sure that the Underfoot Brigade would have gotten so lucky on their own.

"Gracias." Maria wiped her sword as she approached. "That would have been much messier without your help."

"Do you think we got them all?"

Maria shook her head. "This is a newly dug nest, so they must have come from somewhere else, probably deeper down. That is where you need to go if you want to make your home truly safe."

"Will you help us do that?"

"If we can, we will. However, we have other duties in this town. For the sake of my honor, I make no promises, only the hope that we will fight side by side again."

CHAPTER TWENTY-THREE

It was another bright and sunny day as Lucy and Ellis approached the art museum. Jim was waiting for them on a bench by the outdoor street light display. He wore a baggy t-shirt and shorts and was drinking from a large cardboard cup of coffee.

"You look very relaxed today, Agent Lamont," Lucy said.

"I hope to get out to the coast after my shift. Catch some waves."

"Does that mean you don't want these muffins weighing you down?" Lucy held out a paper bag, from which a delicious, fresh-baked aroma emerged.

"I'll need something to fuel me." Jim smiled as he took a muffin. "Thanks very much."

"My pleasure. Now, you said there was something we should see?"

Jim nodded.

"I think one of the gang from the van heist is in there." He gestured toward the gallery where the Trakai Hoard was on display. "I almost didn't recognize him since he's not disguised as an EMT now, but there was something familiar about him, and it soon clicked. He's been roaming the galleries for a while, pretending to be interested in the art while he scopes out the security. He knows we're here, and I'm pretty sure he made me."

"Can you lead us to him?"

"Better if I give you a description rather than show him that we're together. You can go in, and I'll follow."

"Sounds like a good plan. So, who are we looking for?"

"Tall guy, blond, clean-shaven, well-muscled, wearing a designer t-shirt and skinny jeans. Last I saw, he was in the same hall as the Hoard."

"Should we have some sort of signal to make sure we have the right guy?"

"Trust me, you'll know. He's the hottest guy in that place by a mile, and he carries himself as though he knows it."

Lucy laughed. "Are you sure you want us to arrest this guy and not get his number for you?"

"Thanks for the offer, but violent criminals aren't my type." Jim took a bite from one of the muffins. "Mm, this is good. Give me long enough to eat it, and I'll follow you guys in."

Lucy and Ellis headed into the museum, doing their best to look like an ordinary pair of tourists. The place was busy by the standards of an art museum, with plenty of people standing around in front of the works on display, quietly contemplating them or sharing hushed conversations. The biggest gathering was in the hall holding the Hoard, where couples, families, and other small groups

MARTHA CARR & MICHAEL ANDERLE

gathered around the medieval artifacts on their pale, modern pillars.

Jim was right. Even with so many people around, the guy they were after stood out. He was at the side of the room, arms folded across his chest, apparently looking up at a painting. A pair of aviator shades hid his eyes, but tiny twitches of his head gave away the fact that he was more interested in the people around him than he was in the exhibits.

Lucy opened her phone and brought up a photo, a grainy frame of CCTV footage that had captured the face of one of the fake EMTs from the attack on the van. She looked from the image to the guy by the painting and down again.

"What do you think?" she asked. "It's hard to judge when the picture's like this."

"It's him," Ellis said. "Check out the side of the backpack."

Trying not to stare, Lucy looked at the backpack the blond guy had slung over one shoulder. Sure enough, down one side was the distinct rod shape of a concealed wand.

"How do you want to handle this?" she asked. "Stun him and pretend he fainted?"

"Sounds good to me. In this heat, nobody's gonna question a story like that."

They separated, Lucy walking one way around the room, Ellis the other. As they approached their target, Jim appeared in the doorway, brushing crumbs off his t-shirt. Another Griffin walked in through a different door, part of the patrols that constantly surveyed the building.

The target turned, spotted Lucy, and smiled.

"Sorry." He took a step back and gestured at the painting. "I have been hogging the best view."

A German accent managed to sound cool and charming coming from him, helped by his winning smile. Still, he was a little too charming for Lucy, the kind of guy whose polished presentation would have made her worry about what was underneath, even if she didn't know about his criminal connections.

"Thanks." She took a step closer. "I don't think I've seen this artist's work before. What do you think of it?"

She slipped a hand around behind her, reaching for her wand.

"This piece?" The guy looked up. "Not my sort of thing." Another slight movement of his head, and he took a step back from Lucy. "I should be going, friends waiting. Excuse me."

He turned and almost walked straight into Ellis, who was approaching from the opposite direction. Ellis flicked his wrist and the wand shot from his quick draw holster. Keeping it pressed against his forearm, he started raising it, but the guy brought his arm up and knocked it aside so that the stun spell missed and the magic splashed unseen against the floor.

"Sorry," the guy said, loud enough to draw other people's attention, which froze Ellis in place. "Clumsy foreigner. Do excuse me."

The guy strode past Ellis, moving as fast as he could without it looking strange. While Ellis turned, Lucy followed, trying not to let the guy get away but also trying not to alert mundane bystanders that something was amiss.

As the man got to the doorway, he also reached into his bag. Jim walked up to him, wand hand hidden under a map of the museum.

"Excuse me," Jim said. "Do you know where I can find—"

"Sorry, I am in a hurry," the guy said, then muttered something else a second before Jim could start his spell. Jim stumbled back, slumped, and slid down the wall.

"Are you all right?" a woman crouched by Jim with a concerned look on her face. Lucy gestured to the other Griffin to deal with that situation while she and Ellis hurried out to pursue their target.

They followed him out of the museum area and into the adjacent park. He kept his bag in his hand, the wand in reach but not revealed. He didn't want to show his magic in public any more than they did. That was something, at least.

For the first time that day, Lucy wished that the weather was worse. Then there might have been fewer people sitting in the sunshine, and she might have been able to get away with casting a spell to stop him. Instead, she split off from Ellis and raced around the outside of the park. She caught a couple of curious glances as she tried to get ahead of her target.

She dashed around a building and back onto the pedestrian route, away from the crowded grass but not yet on the street. The target was approaching fast, picking up speed without quite running, and as he saw Lucy, he stopped in his tracks.

For a moment they stood frozen, like gunfighters at the end of a western, while they evaluated each other and their surroundings. There were people in sight, but none too close, and Ellis was closing in the opposite direction. The target didn't have time to delay. He started walking again, straight toward Lucy, using his body to block the view of his dagger-shaped wand from passers-by.

"Agnietta," he called with a forced smile. "I didn't know you were in town."

"Heinrich." Lucy did the same, drawing her wand hidden between them, keeping up a façade of friendship. "It's been too long."

They were within feet of each other when the target cast his first spell. Lucy countered it, fired one of her own, and saw it deflected to stun a nearby pigeon. Then they were so close that he flung an arm around her, a pretense of a friendly hug.

They clung to each other, both muttering spells under their breath, magic surging between them, invisible spells and invisible counters, things that non-magicals wouldn't see even if the pair broke free. The sheer force of magic made Lucy's skin tingle, but she kept going as her opponent tightened his grip, trying to wrap an arm around her neck and gain control by sheer strength.

With a twitch of her wand, she finally managed to knock his aside. She cast a stun spell, and his counter didn't quite catch it. One side of his body slumped, and he staggered to a nearby tree. The wand slipped from between his fingers as Ellis arrived.

"You okay there, buddy?" Ellis placed a supportive hand

on the target's shoulder and kicked the wand into some bushes right before a jogger went past.

"You got me," the target said. "I will tell you nothing. Not even my name."

"Sure you won't…" Lucy pulled a wallet out of his backpack and read the name on the bank card, "Oskar von Konigsberg."

"I have done nothing wrong. I am only a wizard in a strange town, and now you people have assaulted me."

"You were part of a team that tried to steal a set of priceless artifacts," Ellis countered. "And unless I'm mistaken, which I ain't, you're also a Knight of the Hinterland."

"I don't know what you mean."

"Dagger-shaped wand, European accent, and you in town at the same time as Maria Pérez? Sure you don't know. But just in case you think of something, we'll take you in for questioning."

Von Konigsberg's eyes drooped as the stun spell overcame the rest of his body.

"On my honor, you'll never…" he mumbled, drooling down his designer t-shirt. "You'll never…"

Then he slid to the ground, his whole body limp.

"Fainted in the heat," Lucy said as a woman walked by, looking at them with concern.

"Oh, of course." The woman smiled and nodded. "This weather, huh?"

CHAPTER TWENTY-FOUR

"How are you kids doing?" Professor Angie Werner stopped by the trench where Dylan and his friends were digging and peered in to see what they had found.

"Really well, thank you." Dylan wiped the sweat from his forehead, and in the process left a smear of dirt there. "We found some more of those basket remains you talked about."

"I found more bones," Lance added while holding up one of his finds. "Look, it even has more of those marks you said were weird."

Professor Angie took the bone carefully from Lance and stared at it, tipping it this way and that to get a better view.

"Do you know what they mean yet?" Sofia asked. "I wondered if maybe it could be some sort of art."

Angie shook her head. "If it is, it's not like anything I've ever seen. We're not sure how the marks were made, never mind why." She gave the bone back to Lance and treated them all to an encouraging smile. "Keep going, though.

You're doing great. If you want to come over to the main site hut in half an hour, we're going to talk about what we've found here so far."

She walked off, and the kids got back to work, carefully clearing away dirt with brushes and trowels, looking for signs of what lay underneath.

"I heard they found a bunch of graves on the other side of the site," Sofia said. "And some stone that no one knows how to explain."

"Graves?" Lance asked. "Like, full of skeletons?"

"For a vegetarian, you seem way too into bones this week."

"Just trying to get into this thing, for Dylan's sake."

"For my sake? You wouldn't still be here if you weren't enjoying it."

"All right, fine, I admit it, this has turned out to be pretty cool. Like, every time I dig something up I imagine who it might have belonged to and what they did with it. Now there are graves, so maybe we'll disturb some ancient spirits, and they'll rise out of the tomb to haunt us." He raised his hands and contorted his face into a hideous expression. "The walking dead are coming for you, Dylan Heron. We've heard about your nerdy ways, and we're going to feast on your big fat brain."

"You call that scary?" Sofia shook her head. "It's hardly *Galactus*."

Lance lowered his hands and frowned. "Actually, could that stuff be real?"

"What, *Galactus*? No, you dummy, it's comics and films."

"I mean ghosts coming back to haunt us because we dug them up. What do you think, Dylan?"

"Not that I know of." Dylan looked at the bone Lance had found. "The only thing that's going to haunt you today is a chicken."

"Pecked to death!" Sofia gasped in mock horror. "The senseless brutality of it."

They got back to digging for a little while until a shout from the main hut told them that it was time for the Professor's talk.

From across the site, kids gathered in the temporary building set up to run the dig. The place was surprisingly large, but it didn't have air conditioning, and the walls were metal, so it was uncomfortably warm. Dylan didn't mind. He was ready to accept a little sweat in return for learning some history.

A table in the middle of the room held a map that the archaeologists had updated throughout the dig. It showed the locations of the trenches and everything they'd found in them, plus other objects revealed by geophysics, electromagnetic waves penetrating the ground to show the layout of what was underneath.

"Thank you all for coming," Angie said. "Plus, for the help you've given us on the dig so far. Since you're here to learn about archeology, I thought it would be useful for you to see what we've put together in these first few weeks and what we've worked out from it." She paused and raised her eyebrows. "Or in this case, how much we haven't worked out."

She started talking them through what was on the site. Some of it was what they had expected from digging up a centuries-old settlement: huts, animal pens, mounds of waste materials like the bones that Lance was so proud of.

There were tools, some broken and some left in a usable state, and pieces of weapons that might have been for war or hunting.

"As you can see from the map, we've also found a ring of standing stones, running around the outside of the settlement," Angie said. "Would anybody like to suggest what they might be for?"

"Ooh, could they be part of a giant fence?" Lance asked. "Like, it's a defensive wall in case of attack, only the wooden parts have rotted away now. When their enemies came, they could have stayed behind the wall with their bows and shot at people." He dramatically displayed mimed archery, shooting imaginary arrows at almost everyone in the room. "Then when people shot back, they'd duck behind the fence for safety." He vanished under the table, out of sight of his roomful of imagined attackers.

"That's a great idea, Lance," Professor Angie said. "Maybe it would be true for other settlements, but in this case, the stones aren't big enough to hold up a fence, and they're probably too far apart. Has anybody else got any ideas?"

A girl from one of the other schools raised her voice. "Could they be signposts? Like, each one's giving a direction to somewhere different?"

"That's another great idea, and a bit more likely. There are markings on all the stones, and we don't know what they mean, so they may be place names and distances, like on modern road signs." Angie laid some photos out on the table, showing the symbols on the stones. "The reason it might not be signposts is that the stones are evenly spaced apart, and unless interesting places nearby were also evenly spaced out, which is unlikely, that would make the signposts misleading."

"Could the stones be for a religious ritual?" a boy asked.

Angie smiled. "That's the most common reason for stone circles, and a lot of people will say it about this site. They might even be right.

"I have to admit that this was a bit of a trick question. We never really know what circles like this are for, and the conclusion that it's for rituals is speculation. We can't see a practical use, so we assume it's display or religion. Sometimes you have to take your best guess."

Except that, now he'd seen the symbols on those stones, Dylan knew what the circle was for, and he knew he couldn't tell her. The marks were magical runes from Oriceran, used to imbue power into objects. He didn't know all of them, but the ones he did know were for things like strength, toughness, and protection. Lance had been close with his talk about a defensive fence. Those stones had held together a magical field to keep the community safe.

The presence of the damaged wand wasn't a coincidence. This had been a magical community, probably home to witches and wizards. The risk of the archaeologists finding something they shouldn't had risen a long way.

"Something else has been baffling us on this site," Angie said. This time, the photos she shared were close-ups of damaged pieces of bone. "We're trying to work out what the markings are on these bones. They look almost like roots or creepers have attacked the bone, but from the context, that seems very unlikely. The damage happened quickly and suddenly. Was it done using cords, perhaps, and if so, why? We'll be doing some experimental archeology to try to work that out, but we might not be the ones to find an answer. That might be future generations of archaeologists, people with evidence we're missing. Understanding the past is a long game."

Again, Dylan realized that he knew the answer. Sudden roots and creepers could be the product of magic, especially nature magic. The people who lived here had used the sort of spells that made plants grow. They were nature magicals.

"At least one thing is less mysterious," Angie continued. "We know that there was a graveyard on the edge of town. We've only dug up a couple of the graves so far, but it looks like the others contain interesting grave goods."

A geophysics image showed the layout of one of those graves. It included the silhouette of a skeleton and what Dylan thought looked a lot like a wand, as well as something that could have been a scrying bowl. There were the artifacts he'd been watching for, and they were still safely underground.

"We'll be starting to dig those graves next week," Angie said. "Hopefully, they'll help us to understand the meaning of this symbol, which we've found on all the graves so far."

The last image she shared was a symbol carved into a rounded rock. Angie clearly didn't know what it represented since she was holding it the wrong way up, but to Dylan, everything had now become crystal clear.

The symbol was a simplified mortar and pestle, the icon of the Tolderai tribe. This whole settlement had belonged to those ancient nature witches and wizards. Why they had left, he had no idea, but they must have thought that their ancestors' artifacts were left safely buried, where no one would find them ever again. They were about to be proved wrong.

It was up to Dylan to make sure their magic didn't end up in the wrong hands.

CHAPTER TWENTY-FIVE

Klara Schulz sat in a coffee shop, a coffee and a pastry sitting half-eaten in front of her. Across the table, Maria Pérez picked at her sandwich.

"We're sure they took von Konigsberg at the museum?" Schulz asked.

"Almost certain. We know he went there in the morning, gathering information on the Silver Griffins' security operation, and that he stopped checking in after the middle of the morning. He would have told us if he was moving on. It's part of our procedures for operating in hostile territory."

"You mean he would have tried to tell us."

"Have you ever known Oskar to fail at something so simple?"

"There is technology to make it less simple."

"Still."

Schulz sipped her coffee and gazed out the window. The heat lay thick across the city. Fewer people were out and about. Perhaps some had gone to the coast of the countryside. Maybe they were staying indoors to make the most of their air conditioning. Regardless, it would make life easier for her and the Knights, for a little while at least.

"I'm wondering how sure we can be that this was the Silver Griffins," Maria said.

"Who else would it be, your sewer-dwelling teenagers?"

"They're friends. They wouldn't hurt us."

Schulz snorted. "You are naïve if you believe that those statements follow each other. Still, teenagers clearly wouldn't be a threat to von Konigsberg."

"We have other enemies, Chancellor. Maybe they followed us here or hired locals to attack while we're exposed."

"*Nein*. It makes more sense to prepare for us in Europe, where they know our movements best. The Silver Griffins are the enemy here, and they are the ones we must worry about. They will have von Konigsberg."

"Do we rescue him?"

Schulz shook her head. "He knew the risks. Our mission comes first."

"Drive back the darkness."

"Exactly. God's glory and a better world. Speaking of which..." Schulz set down her empty mug and tapped the earpiece hidden beneath her blond hair with its subtle streaks of gray. "All units, report readiness."

"Ready, Chancellor," a voice replied.

"Ready," said another.

"Ready."

"Ready."

"Ready."

Schulz looked at Maria, who tapped her hidden

earpiece and nodded. "Ready, Chancellor."

"Then in we go. Remember, this is reconnaissance, gathering information for a future strike. We go in together for safety, not to pick a fight."

"Yes, Chancellor."

"Understood."

"Yes."

"*Oui.*"

"As you say."

Maria got up from her seat and walked out of the coffee shop. A minute later, Schulz followed. She walked down the street, on the opposite side from Maria, then crossed at a junction and walked into the art museum.

This wasn't the way that Schulz wanted to operate. Reconnaissance in force was for war zones, not a civilian center. Going in with so many at once risked triggering a panicked response from their opponents and getting innocent people caught in the conflict. However, war was about balancing risks, and theirs was an eternal war, a never-ending crusade to make the world a better place. In seizing Oskar von Konigsberg, the Silver Griffins had forced her hand. Now it was time to see how that played out.

The moment she was in the building, she pulled out her phone and started waving it around, like she was one more dumb tourist taking photos of everything they saw, a digital wanderer with poor impulse control. Instead of photos, Schulz took video, recording every place and person she passed.

Around her, the other Knights were doing the same. They remained widely spaced out, not acknowledging each other or even making eye contact, for all the world like entirely separate people who had come from different places and happened to be here now, together, in this gallery.

They moved from one gallery into the next. She had already spotted one Griffin on a roaming patrol, their wand hidden not quite well enough in the sleeve of a flowery blouse. There would be others. Those they didn't spot on this pass, they would identify by reviewing the video footage in detail later, comparing what everybody had shot, as well as observations from smaller, earlier visits. Some of it would be evidence that von Konigsberg had captured before he gave his freedom for the cause.

The first Griffin didn't seem to notice them. Nor did the next one that Schulz spotted. The man by the door to the Hoard's gallery though, the one with shorts whose pockets were baggy enough to hold a wand, his gaze lingered on her a little too long.

"Someone spotted me," she announced. "Head into the main room and get footage from there before we have to move on."

"Yes, Chancellor."

"Affirmative."

"Yes."

"*Oui.*"

"*Si.*"

"Understood."

Like a flock of birds in the air, the dispersed band of Knights wheeled and headed into the hall where the Trakai Hoard was on display. They spread out through the room, watching, listening, sensing for magic around them, and the whole time taking video of what they saw.

Maria was closest to the door. When a familiar-looking man in a charcoal suit with red sneakers and tie appeared, he made straight for her. Schulz watched from the corner of her eye even as she moved her hand around, ready to grab her wand.

"Maria." The man's voice came clear through Maria Pérez's audio feed. "We've identified your people. We know why you're here. We already have your colleague. Can you all please come quietly so that no one gets hurt?"

"I don't know what your mean, Ellis," Maria said.

Schulz bit back a curse. That was why she recognized the face beneath that blond beard. It was Maria's ex-husband. An idiotic relationship for Pérez to have ever gotten into, and now it was back to bite them. No denying who they were with him around.

"All Knights, Code Silent Alarm," Schulz said. "I repeat, on my mark, silent alarm. We know who guards the door behind Ellis Ellis, so take him down and exit that way. On my mark... Now."

Every Knight in the building turned and strode toward the door they'd come in through. At the same moment, Maria reached out as if to hug Ellis.

"Oh, no, you don't." He took a step back. Her stun spell missed him, but he didn't see the other one coming as another Knight came close. The magic hit and Ellis fell to the floor.

"Is he okay?" one of the mundane visitors asked.

The Knights didn't answer. This wasn't about a smooth cover anymore. They could leave some mystery and confusion as long as they got out intact.

Beyond the door, Jim reached into his pocket. An invisible protective barrier rose around him a moment before the first spell hit. Sleep and stun spells, things that were invisible and easily explained away, hurtled past oblivious tourists and evaporated against his shield.

Jim had his phone out and was dialing Lucy's number.

"They're here," he said while frantically channeling more power into his protective spell.

"Sorry," Maria loudly said as she bumped into him, knocking the phone from his hand and slamming a boot down on it. The phone shattered. "So clumsy of me."

As the Knights stepped out into the blazing summer heat, more Griffins appeared, wands concealed in wide pockets or up sleeves.

"I'd stop if I was you." Jackie Kowal approached Schulz with a fake smile.

"No, you wouldn't."

The Knights kept walking fast, barging past the Griffins who stood their ground, while other Griffins backed off to keep up a cordon. Magic flew all around, no less dangerous for being unseen. Stuns and sleeps, magical glue, and tangling roots flew from both sides as the witches and wizards muttered incantations under their breath. Raised shields and rapid counterspells stopped most of them, though one young Griffin collapsed into a bush, causing passers-by to start shouting for a doctor.

"I thought you considered yourselves the good guys?" Jackie hissed, backing away so that she could keep facing the advancing Schulz. "Look at the people you're putting in danger for what, a robbery? This isn't how good guys act."

"You know nothing of good or evil, Griffin. All you do is try to keep the world as it is. We strive to make it better."

One of Schulz's spells almost broke through Jackie's defenses, and she stumbled. Schulz pushed past, her people with her, out onto Sixth Street.

"Code Urban Thunder," Schulz said. "On my mark…"

"What?" A dazed Jackie stumbled after her.

"Now."

In an instant, the focus of the Knights' magic shifted away from the Griffins. One car backfired, another veered off the street into a lamppost, and a third billowed smoke as its engine caught fire. A bus honked its horn as it slammed into the back of a truck. Suddenly, the street was in turmoil. Drivers leaped out of their vehicles, pedestrians dashed to help, and people rushed out of buildings to see what all the fuss was about.

"Code Air Burst." Schulz cast one last spell, and a lamppost crashed down onto an empty car. "Now."

The Knights scattered, each one sprinting off in a different direction amid the chaos of the street. Griffins ran after them but got blocked by crowds and broken cars or taken down by magic flung back by their fleeing prey. Within moments, every Knight was out of sight, lost amid the throngs of L.A.

Ellis staggered out of the museum, leaning on Jim, and joined Jackie on the sidewalk. With so much going on, no one paid them any attention. Sirens were screeching as emergency services rushed to the scene.

"So much for your carefully laid ambush," Jackie said.

"Yeah, well…" Ellis tried to think of a witty retort, but he had nothing. "At least they didn't steal anything yet, right? I'm calling that a win."

CHAPTER TWENTY-SIX

Lucy walked into the house and dropped her backpack by the front door. It had been a long day already, and the afternoon wasn't over yet. She had to hope that the Knights of the Hinterland kept from causing any more trouble while she had a nap and a cuppa and found some energy.

Buddy rushed into the hallway to greet her, tail wagging and tongue hanging out. Between his enthusiastic yapping and the way he kept nudging at a ball with his nose, it was clear what he wanted.

"Oh, lad, I'd love to take you for walkies, but I'm completely beat." Lucy patted him on the head. "Can't someone else take you?"

"We already did." Charlie poked his head out of the kitchen. "Someone's pushing his luck."

Buddy looked up at Lucy with wide eyes and an innocent expression, as if to say that he knew what they were talking about, but that wasn't going to stop him.

"Maybe later," Lucy said to the dog.

She walked into the kitchen, where Charlie was chopping vegetables for dinner.

"You're an absolute legend." Lucy leaned against her husband's back and wrapped her arms around him. "Have I mentioned how good you look in that apron?"

"Well, it is my turn to cook. Besides, if I left it to you, we'd all be living off cookies."

"Biscuits are a nutritious and balanced meal, as long as you put oats and raisins in some of them."

"I'm pretty sure that's not how nutrition works."

"Ah, but I have this sophisticated, cultured English accent, so if I say things with enough authority, they must be true."

"You have an accent that makes you sound like an Arctic Monkeys record. That's not as sophisticated as you think."

"How rude!" Lucy went to the cookie jar and fished out a chocolate chip cookie. "I'm going to go and spend time with people who appreciate my sophisticated ways."

"If you mean the kids, I should warn you that they're currently appreciating an episode of *Teen Titans*, so unless you're dressed in spandex and beating up the Joker, you might not get their attention."

"Works for me. I could do with some brain off time."

Lucy walked into the living room. She could tell that the kids were engrossed because they didn't even notice her cookie or demand that they get one too. She sat at one end of the couch and finished eating while watching superheroes charge around the screen.

Eddie and Dylan were sitting at the other end of the couch. Eddie had curled up against his big brother with a plastic dinosaur clutched in his hand. Ashley was on the floor, her attention split between the screen and her modeling marbles, which were turning into the outline for some new device. Lucy wondered what it was but decided not to interrupt the creative process. She would hear about it at dinner anyway.

Lucy enjoyed a good superhero show as much as the kids. She was even wearing the Green Arrow t-shirt to prove it, but she had seen this episode several times before, and her mind quickly wandered. Fortunately, she'd left her laptop beside the sofa. She opened it, intending to go onto Facebook, but instead found herself drawn to a folder she had left open a previous evening, the one full of family photos.

The first image to spring up was Eddie charging at the camera, waving his arms around wildly in an impression of a chimpanzee he had seen at the zoo. It was followed, inevitably, by a picture of him as a chimpanzee, still swinging his arms around. She laughed and looked over at her youngest son, who looked back at her.

"What?" he asked.

"Just enjoying some photos of you."

Eddie pulled his thoughtful face as he considered the relative merits of watching cartoons compared with talking about himself, then shifted down the sofa and slid in under Lucy's arm.

"I'm a chimp!" he exclaimed, grinning at the photo.

"Yes, you are, sweetheart. Here's one of you as a duck, as a bear, as a possum... Wow, we have a lot of photos of you as animals. Ooh, and here you are as a baby. How cute!"

Now they had the others' attention too, and they gathered around to see the pictures.

"Do you have us as babies on there?" Ashley asked.

"Of course. Hang on…" Lucy browsed through the photos, looking for something older. "Here you are, Ashley, when you were Eddie's age. You were disassembling two of your toys to turn them into a bigger car, I think."

"She's so small!" Dylan said. "That was forever ago."

Lucy laughed. To her kids, five years felt like a lifetime, while she could still remember each of them being in diapers as if it was yesterday.

They browsed through more of the photos, enjoying the memories of family holidays, Christmases, trips to the beach, or the park. It was amazing to see the past decade condensed down like this, to be reminded of all the magical moments that they had experienced together, some of them magical in a more literal sense.

"Do you have pictures from when you were small?" Dylan asked.

"Yes!" Eddie exclaimed, clapping his hands together. "Baby Mommy!"

"Not in here." Lucy patted the laptop. "Back in those days, we took photos on film, and you had to take them to be turned into pieces of paper so you could see them."

"No." Eddie shook his head. "Not real."

"It's true," Ashley said. "Photographs were originally taken using glass plates with chemicals layered onto them. Photographic film followed, which—"

"Baby Mommy!" Eddie clapped his hands again. "Please!"

Lucy laughed. "All right, let's see what we've got."

She reached for a shelf behind the sofa and pulled out a pair of photo albums.

"Who do you want to see first, your dad or me?"

"Baby Daddy?" That idea had Eddie intrigued.

"Dad it is." Lucy opened the album. "All this is from before I met him, of course. We got copies of the photos from your grandparents."

She started at the back of the album, with pictures of Charlie after he'd graduated high school and was about to head off to England. That had been before she met him, by a couple of years. From there, they traveled back in time with each turn of the page. Charlie grew younger, his hair shifting up and down with the fads of his teenage years. There were pictures of him out walking in the country with his family, of him reading or working at computers, of family holidays and birthdays, with fewer and fewer candles on the cake.

"What's gotten into you lot?" Charlie asked, coming in to see what the kids were cheering and laughing at. "Oh, wow. We're taking a trip down memory lane, huh? I forgot I even had that shirt."

As they reached the front of the album, the pages were rammed full of tiny Charlie in his first couple of years. Lucy had seen all of this before, but it still made her grin to see him as an adorable little toddler, waving his toy trucks around or getting stuck on a swing.

"You were so cute then," she said. "An omen of the man you would become."

Charlie kissed the top of her head. "Enough of me, let's see your pictures."

"Not so fast. We have to see the baby photos first." Sure enough, here was Charlie as a tiny, pink, wrinkled thing, his face screwed up as he protested at his first encounters with the world.

"Silly Daddy," Eddie said, shaking his head.

"You didn't look so different at that age, kiddo," Charlie said.

"Silly Eddie," the three-year-old said with pride. "Now Mommy."

Going through the other album brought out all the strange ups and downs of nostalgia for Lucy. It was full of places from what felt like ancient history, from her high school to her grandmother's house to the street she had lived on when she was a toddler. She could almost feel the weight and texture of her childhood toys as she saw them appear in photos, and she remembered all too well the scrapes and bruises that came with learning to ride a bike, as shown in other shots. However, one thing was missing, and it was the thing that the kids were most desperate to see.

"Where are the baby photos?" Dylan asked when they reached the front of the album.

"I guess I wasn't as interested in those," Lucy said. "They don't bring back memories for me."

"This isn't about what you're interested in," Charlie said. "Right, kids?"

"He's right," Ashley said solemnly. "We've seen photos of all of us as babies. Now it's your turn."

"I wish I could help, but I don't have them." Lucy felt a

little relieved. Seeing other people as babies was cute. Seeing herself was weird.

"I know who we can get them from." Charlie grabbed his laptop and fired up Zoom. "What time is it in England right now?"

"The middle of the night, so don't go waking my parents."

"It's okay, your dad's up and online, see?"

Lucy glanced at the icon on Facebook. Sure enough, her dad was still awake in the middle of the night, probably watching crafting videos while he worked on his latest project.

"It would be good to chat with him."

That was all the encouragement the others needed. Within seconds, there was the sound of a call trying to connect.

"Maybe Grandpa's fallen asleep?" Dylan said as the sound went on and on.

"He's probably trying to find the button," Lucy said. "He didn't grow up with computers like you."

Eddie's eyes went wide at that idea. "Grandpa's real old."

Then the call connected and Lucy's dad appeared on the screen, squinting at them through his glasses.

"Hello? Can you hear me?"

"Yes, Eddie," Charlie said. "And we can see you too."

"Splendid!" Eddie senior waved. "It's been far too long. How are you all?"

"We're great. Another sunny day here in L.A. How's Yorkshire?"

"Probably raining." He chuckled. "So, what inspired this midnight rendezvous?"

"We wanted to see you," Lucy said. "I miss you, Dad."

"I miss you too, lass, but by the look on Eddie junior's face, I suspect something else is going on."

"Funny you should say that," Charlie chimed in, "but we wanted to ask you a favor. It's about photos…"

CHAPTER TWENTY-SEVEN

Klara Schulz ran through the midnight streets of L.A. The heat had been too much for her to run during the day with the rest of the Knights. She didn't like to admit it, but each year made it a little harder to cope with the extremes, whether it was the cold of winter or the heat of summer. Last August in Berlin, she had gone out for an evening run during a heatwave and nearly fainted. She had learned from that mistake.

Some Chancellors of the Order had given up by now, retired from action, and handed over the reins to a younger Knight. That wasn't Schulz's way. She couldn't even begin to imagine a life beyond this, one where she wasn't leading the Knights. She had made it her mission to command them, had worked her way up the ranks with fierce determination, had led them to success after success. Now they were within days of their greatest triumph yet, when they would crown a Grand Master for the first time in centuries. She had earned the right to take that title, and she was damned if she would let age snatch it away from her. She had to stay in shape, both physically and mentally, to prove that she was worthy of the post. She had to keep up with the recruits by one means or another. So she went out religiously, night after night, ten kilometers running through the darkness, only her and her thoughts.

She rounded a corner into a street that was narrower but still well-lit. Schulz had little fear of muggers or other creeps in the dark, even relishing the chance they offered for her to practice her combat skills against someone who deserved the beating. Quiet streets had other advantages. With no traffic and no one around to pay her attention, she was free to stretch herself.

She ran toward a wall, propelled herself up, grabbed a second-floor window ledge, and pushed off. She dove across the sidewalk, landed in a forward roll, and sprang back to her feet at a run. Oh yes, she still had it.

Distracted by her sense of triumph, she almost ran straight into the spell, but some sixth sense, trained by years of fighting against monsters and magicals, told her there was magic in the air. She lunged sideways, and the spell shot past.

Schulz sank to a crouch and pulled her wand from the sheath at her back, then pointed it ahead of her. Where was the enemy?

A movement in the darkness and shadows shifted at the edge of the light cast by a streetlamp.

"Stupefacio," Schulz muttered, and magic shot from her wand.

The target moved as they countered the spell, and in doing so they stepped into the light. Schulz saw a wrinkled, gray-haired man in a three-piece suit, his watch-chain glinting. He looked back at her, and at that moment, the years fell away. Recognition dawned.

"Kowal." Schulz rose to her full height, wand still outstretched, and paced toward him. "It's been a long time."

"Too long," Harold Kowal said. "You made Europe an uncomfortable place for me."

"Good." Schulz's finger touched the long scar running down her left cheek, a bitter reminder of the last time they had met, a time that haunted her nightmares.

They stared at each other, opponents from a long-ago war, reunited at last. Nostalgia, that comforting feeling of sinking into the lost but familiar, almost made her think fondly of him. But the ridge of that scar was enough to chase the feeling away.

"You've aged well," Kowal said.

"Better than you."

He shrugged. "I had a few more years to begin with. Trust me. They'll catch up with you soon."

Schulz clenched her wand tighter. Light flashed off its dagger tip.

"What is this?" she asked. "They sent you out in the hope that you'd throw me off guard while others move in?"

"There are no others. Only me."

"Ah, of course. You want to regain your lost pride, to bring in single-handedly the woman who beat you before. The 'mere girl,' wasn't that what you called me then?"

Kowal scowled. "I want this over with, and this seemed like the least messy way to do it. Chop the head off and watch the beast fall."

"Take the head home and mount it on your wall, more

like. A hunting trophy for a sad little man whose peak passed decades ago."

"We'll see."

"Yes, we will."

His wand twitched. The next words out of his mouth would be a spell, not an insult, but Schulz wasn't going to give him space for that. As the magic flashed out, she countered and rushed at him. Another spell, another counter, another spell, a deflection. A swift flurry of magic, dueling wands, and she was on him. The edge of her wand sliced through the suit, shirt, and the flesh of his forearm. His wand slipped from his fingers. Her shoulder slammed into his chest, and he fell, crashing into a heap of garbage bags lying by the curb.

For over twenty years, he had harbored resentment against her, and she had ended the feud in seconds. It was sad, really.

She kicked his wand out of reach and leaned over him. Grabbing a fistful of suit, she lifted him out of the garbage, the seams of his jacket popping with the strain. She pulled her wand back, not for a spell but ready to thrust it into him, to finish this with honor and make sure he didn't come back for his revenge.

Some instinct stopped her. The man wasn't a monster, much as she wanted to see him that way. Yes, she had killed misguided magicals who got in her way before. Sometimes it was her or them or a necessary step to further the cause. This was only a sad, aging man, his ambition far outstretching his strength. She had robbed him of his honor, and that was enough.

She dropped him back into the garbage.

"It's over, Kowal," she said. "Leave the biting and scratching to those of us who still have teeth."

She slid her wand away and ran off into the night, carrying on with her run.

Jackie woke with a start and fumbled for her phone to see the time. One-thirty in the morning. Who on earth was knocking on her door now?

"All right, I'm coming," she called as she pulled on a t-shirt and yoga pants, then made her way across the apartment. "No need to wake the whole building. If this is a booty call, you're going to be bitterly disappointed."

With her wand in hand just in case, she opened the door.

"Uncle Harold?" She stared in confusion at the disheveled, smelly figure in front of her. "What are you doing here?"

She backed off, letting him into the apartment, and closed the door. Harold stood in the middle of her living room, his left hand clutching his right forearm.

"I had a little incident, Jack-Jack." He looked down at the clutching hand. Jackie followed his gaze and realized that there was blood seeping out between his fingers, and more soaking through the sleeve of his jacket, creating a dark stain.

"Holy shit, Uncle Harold, what happened?" She shook her head. "No, never mind that. First, come into the bathroom and let me clean that up."

One of the advantages of being a Silver Griffin, with all

the dangers the job presented, was that Jackie had prepared for moments like this. She took out disinfectant, wound closure strips, and a bandage while Harold took off his ruined jacket and rolled up the sleeve of his shirt, wincing as he pulled the cloth edges out of the wound.

"I should call Sarah." Jackie looked at the long gash left by Schulz's wand.

"No need to get anyone else involved," Harold demurred. "Trust me. I've had plenty of field treatment in my time. You can handle this."

"There's can, and there's should. You'd be better off with a real doctor."

"Please, Jack-Jack, I'd much rather keep this between ourselves."

Jackie sighed and ran the faucet, filling the sink with steaming water.

"All right then, I'll do my best, but you're going to tell me exactly what happened."

Harold sat on the edge of the bath while Jackie cleaned and disinfected his wound. It was the sort of treatment that would have made most people cry out in pain, but he bore it with a grimace and an occasional gritting of his teeth.

"An old nemesis of mine is in town," he said. "Someone from my days in Europe. She beat me then, and I wanted to settle the score."

"So you went after her on your own?"

"Well, yes. I do have some field experience, you know."

"You also have a bad hip and a liver that keeps threatening to fail."

"I don't need my liver to win a fight."

"And your hip?"

"I have magic."

Jackie snorted as she dabbed his arm dry, then reached for the wound closure strips.

"I know this might be hard for you to understand, Jack-Jack, but as you get older, sometimes pride is all you have. I did great things back in the day, and I want people to remember me that way. I don't want to leave a failure hanging in the air."

"So pride matters more to you than your safety?"

"My risks are my choice."

"What about the risk for Aunt Adelle? How would she feel if she lost you now?"

"That's not fair, Jack-Jack."

"It's not intended to be fair. It's supposed to be the truth." She started wrapping the bandage around his arm, covering the closed-up wound. She wound it a little tighter than it needed to be. "You can't go throwing yourself into fights anymore."

"What, because I'm too old?" Harold glared at her.

"Yes, exactly!" Jackie snapped. "It might not be fair, it might hurt your pride, but it's the truth. You're not as young or as fit as you were. You're still in fine shape for your age, but that age is real."

"I won't be consigned to the waste bin of history."

"I know you won't, but how is your story going to be remembered if it ends with you acting like an idiot? You're a source of wisdom, guidance, and inspiration for the rest of us, but you can't go picking fights on your own anymore."

"I think you'll find—"

"Do you want me to call Aunt Adelle and tell her what

happened?" Jackie grabbed her phone. "You know I will."

For a moment, Harold looked as if he was going to argue, but then he closed his mouth and hung his head.

"You're right, Jackie," he said in a small, lost voice. "I'm sorry."

Jackie wanted to reach out and hug her uncle, but she wasn't sure that his pride could take it. Instead, she set to cleaning up the blood and putting her medical supplies away.

"This nemesis of yours, did you leave her with some scars?" she asked.

"Not this time," Kowal said, "but I'd say that we're about even, in the long run."

"Maybe I can help next time. Who is she?"

"Klara Schulz, the Chancellor of the Knights of the Hinterland."

Jackie paused in the process of washing out a cloth. Water stained pink with blood trickled between her fingers.

"The people who have been trying to rob the museum?"

"Yes, that's them."

"The ones that Lucy and Ellis have been watching out for all week?"

"If you say so."

"The biggest problem the Griffins in this city are facing right now?"

"That sounds like them."

"You've been hunting one of them all this time, and you didn't tell us?" Jackie glared at her uncle.

"When you put it like that—"

"First thing tomorrow, you're coming into the office

with me. You are going to tell Lucy every last thing you know about this woman, her movements, and where we can find her. You're going to do it without any of your showing off or a single word of complaint because if you don't, I'm getting straight onto the phone to tell Aunt Adelle what you've been up to. Understand?"

"Yes, Jack-Jack." A grin fought its way past his scowl. "You're good at this, you know. Maybe you'll make director one day."

"I'd rather eat out at the sewage plant. Now let me go make up the sofa bed. You're staying where I can watch you tonight."

CHAPTER TWENTY-EIGHT

By the time she got to the Semi-Tropic on Glendale the next evening, Jackie was more than ready for a drink. She'd spent the day alternating between being mad at her uncle and worrying about what else he might do. She was emotionally exhausted and physically tired from a day patrolling the galleries at LACMA, looking for any sign of a return visit by the Knights of the Hinterland. Fortunately, she had the prospect of a ladies' night out to take her mind off it all.

Lucy and Sarah were already at a table in the bar with cocktails in front of them when Jackie walked in. She flung herself down in an empty seat.

"Guess I should order a drink," she said.

"We already got you one." Lucy slid a glass of something dark across the table. "It's called Two Cups of Blood."

"Sounds about right for my mood." Jackie sipped. "Mm, mezcal, that's what I've been missing all day. Thanks." She looked at Lucy. "So, how was your interview with the old troublemaker?"

"He turned the charm back on the minute you walked out the door." Lucy laughed. "Started in on the stories about the old days and everything he got up to back then. Asked me about how the family were doing and talked about how impressive it was that I achieved so much."

Jackie shook her head. "I knew it. The man has no shame."

"I wouldn't say that. Once I'd let him talk himself out, I brought the conversation back around to last night. Whatever you said, it had an impact because he looked really embarrassed about the whole business."

"I should think so too."

"Well, that embarrassment turned into a good motive to talk. He told Ellis and me a lot more about the Knights, some stuff that Ellis knew already, some that I'd found in the files, and some that no one around here seemed to know. He's also told me how he found Schulz and what he knows about her movements. That should help us track them down."

"At least something good's come out of this." Jackie looked at Sarah. "Sorry, we're talking shop, not a great way to start the evening."

"Hm, what?" Sarah looked up from her drink. "Oh, don't worry about it. Everyone needs to vent sometimes, right?"

"Exactly, yes! If your favorite uncle almost getting himself killed isn't vent-worthy, I don't know what is." Jackie knocked back the rest of her cocktail. "You guys want another?"

"Um…" Lucy looked at her glass, which was still half-full.

Sarah downed the remains of hers. "Same again."

Jackie leapt out of her seat and headed for the bar, leaving Lucy looking at Sarah with concern.

"Are you all right?" she asked. "It's not like you to be a pisshead."

Sarah raised an eyebrow. "That's an English thing, right, not a comment on the state of my hair?"

Lucy laughed. "Your hair looks great, but you're not normally the one heading straight for drunk town."

Sarah sighed, leaned her elbows on the table, and rested her head in her hands.

"It's Ellis," she said. "I found out he's been married."

"What? When?"

"Years ago, when he was working in Europe. To a Spanish woman from another magical organization."

"Wait, this other organization, it's not the Knights of the Hinterland, is it?"

"Something like that. It sounds like it was all very wild, very exciting." Sarah sighed. "And here's me, never even lived away from L.A."

"That scrawny, scraggly-faced little git." Lucy glared at the table. "No wonder he knew so much about them. Maybe if he'd told me about this from the start, we could have grabbed them before they caused trouble."

"The worst part is, he never told me before. I mean, he only told me now because we bumped into her, and he had to explain."

Lucy pushed aside her annoyance at Ellis, who would be getting an earful from her the next time she saw him and turned her full attention to Sarah. "I'm sorry, lass.

That's rough. Do you think he was deliberately keeping it secret?"

Sarah shrugged. "Maybe. I mean, how do you not mention something like that?"

Jackie returned to the table, clutching a new round of drinks.

"Wow, you lot look like I feel," she said. "What's going on?"

Sarah explained it again, with a few more details thrown in.

"Damn, that is rough." Jackie looked at her glass. "Maybe I should order the next round now because we're going to need it soon."

"I mean, who doesn't tell you that they've been married?"

"Someone who's worried how you'll react?" Lucy asked.

"Exactly! Wait, is that a good thing or a bad thing?"

"Depends," Jackie said. "Had you talked much about past relationships?"

"Not really. Everything was still light and fun and early days, you know? Being married isn't being in a relationship though. It's a much bigger deal, right?"

"If you're applying to be the pope, sure. If you're Larry King, not so much." Jackie took the straw out of her drink and waved it in the air. "Look, we all know that Lucy and Charlie are going to last forever because they're as adorable as a Disney dream couple. However, these days, lots of marriages end in divorce, and plenty of people have relationships that are as deep and important without involving a lawyer or a priest. I'm not saying that marriage isn't important. I'm just saying, what does it mean to him?"

Sarah took a long drink while she thought that one through.

"I don't know," she admitted. "We haven't really talked about it since he told me, and I didn't know what to make of it at the time. I mean, it's marriage."

Jackie blew a raspberry. "Marriage is a fancy word for picking someone you'll get a mortgage with."

"Hey!" Lucy said indignantly. "It's a lot more than that. It's a big deal, a loving relationship, something that's supposed to last forever."

"Tell that to Elizabeth Taylor. Point is, there are different sorts of marriages, so what was this one like?"

"Passionate." Sarah looked mournfully at her empty glass. "They'd had all these...all these big adventures together, you know? They'd fought each other, and they'd fought together, and they'd been in danger, and there was all this buzz around it. Maria's this exciting, international woman of adventure. You should see her. She's all..."

Sarah waved her hands in the air, making out an hourglass form.

"I think I have seen her," Lucy admitted. "You're not wrong. And her hair, it's all thick and dark and..."

"Yes! The curls! Those stupid, perfect curls. I hate her." Sarah clapped a hand over her mouth. "Oh my God, I can't believe I said that. I don't know this woman. I can't hate her. That's not fair."

"'Course you can," Jackie said. "She's his ex. It's your job to hate her. There's, like, a law about it or something." She waved a hand at a passing barman. "'Scuse me, can I get one more of these, and one more of those, and..." she pointed at Sarah's glass, "...make it two more of those."

"What sort of name is Maria, anyway?" Sarah muttered. "Stupid Spanish name to go with her stupid, tuneful Spanish accent."

"Bloody Europeans," Lucy said.

"You're European," Jackie pointed out.

"Ah, but British is a special sort of European. Semi-detached Europeans. Like Canada is to America."

"No, Canada's the fresh-faced, youthful neighbor. Britain's more like the grumpy old man, moaning at the others because their food smells spicy and their music's playing too loud."

"Hey, we have spicy food!"

"Yeah, but... No, wait, we're getting distracted." Jackie swiveled back to Sarah. "What were you saying?"

"She's glamorous and exciting," Sarah said. "I'm the sensible one he's settling down with. What if that's not really what he wants? What if he wakes up one day and realizes that he wants excitement again? How can I compete when that's who he used to be with?"

"Oh, honey." Jackie wrapped an arm around Sarah, who was trembling on the verge of tears. "She's who he used to want to be with, not who he wants. That's why they're not married anymore. I know it's intimidating, finding out that he used to be in a relationship with some secret warrior chick, but remember, he left that behind."

"Sure, but it says something about him, doesn't it? It must make a difference to who he is now."

"Everyone has history, and it shapes everyone. That doesn't mean it defines us or limits us. Ellis has grown into someone better than that and with much better taste in women. I can tell because he picked you."

Sarah smiled and wiped her eyes with the back of her hand.

"As for exciting," Lucy said, "you should see how excited he gets when your name pops up on his phone. Trust me. He hasn't settled. He has something that drives him wild."

"Aw, thanks, Lucy." Sarah squeezed her friend's hand. "Thank you, little Jack-Jack."

Jackie glared at Lucy. "You told her about that, didn't you?"

"I couldn't resist." Lucy grinned. "It suits you so well."

"I swear, if the Knights of the Hinterland don't kill that old man, I'm going to."

A barman appeared with a tray of drinks. "Your order, ladies. Hope you're having a good evening?"

"Yes, thank you," Lucy said. "Really enjoying the drinks."

"The drinks and moaning about men," Jackie added, grabbing her next glass.

"Oh, okay." The barman took a nervous step back.

"Don't worry, not all men," Sarah said, then gave the barman a moment to relax before she added with a scowl, "Just most men."

The three of them laughed as the barman hurried away.

Jackie slid two full glasses of green liquid in front of Sarah. "Feeling better now?"

"Much." Sarah took a sip. "I should talk to him, shouldn't I?"

"Yes, of course, you beautiful dumbass. First, we need to finish talking about how terrible this Maria woman is."

CHAPTER TWENTY-NINE

Lucy sat in her car in the dark, watching for signs of movement along the street. She was a lot more sober than the previous night and a lot more alert to her surroundings. She would need to be. Cheering Sarah up had been serious business, but tonight's was potentially deadly.

Her phone buzzed, and Ellis's number appeared on the screen.

"Yes?" Lucy answered in a hushed voice.

"Any sign of movement where you are?" Ellis asked.

"No. You?"

"No. I checked in with the others, and they all said the same. You think this is a dead-end?"

Lucy considered the possibility. It had been a risk, and they'd known that when they hit the streets in the middle of the night. Schulz had been varying her running routes even before Director Kowal tried to catch her. There was every chance that she would have given them all up now that he'd found her. On the other hand, wherever her L.A.

base was, there would only be so many routes she could run from there. If she was determined to keep exercising, she might retain some of the paths where Kowal hadn't been, and maybe, just maybe, the Griffins could catch her.

It was a long shot but better than waiting around the museum for the Knights to attack.

"I'm not ready to write it off yet," Lucy said. "Keep everybody in position, and we'll wait to see where the night takes us."

She hung up and set the phone aside, then slipped lower in her seat, trying to keep herself invisible to passers-by. With so many possible routes to cover, she was all alone for now, but she felt confident in the fact that the other Griffins would close in as soon as she called. For now, it was all a waiting game.

From the far end of the street, a movement caught her eye. Someone was running along the sidewalk, a tall, slim woman in leggings and a t-shirt, with a baseball cap casting her face into shadow. She ran right past Lucy's car, and Lucy watched her in the side mirror as she carried on down the street. Six feet tall and with a blond ponytail sticking out the back of her cap. It could well be Schulz.

Lucy slid her phone into her pocket, checked that she had her wand, then quietly climbed out of the car. She cast a spell to silence her footsteps, then ran after the woman.

The jogger kept up a good, steady pace, but nothing Lucy couldn't match. She might not have Jackie's stride, but regular runs with the girls kept her from getting out of shape. She settled into the meditative state that running created while watching the woman ahead of her for any sign of who she might be.

The woman passed under a street light, and there it was: a straight shadow at an angle across the back of her t-shirt, the shape of a concealed wand.

Still running, Lucy pulled out her phone and hit a button. Nothing happened. She tried again, but the screen didn't light up. Her skin tingled where it touched the phone, a sensation like static off an old electronic device, but with a hint of magic. Someone was screwing with it.

She looked up. The woman had stopped and turned to face her, wand in hand. The street was dark, deserted, but another figure emerged from an alley to one side and a third from the street opposite. Lucy looked back and saw someone else approaching out of the darkness.

"Are they with you?" she asked.

"All of them." Schulz took off her cap. Stern features and a long scar were cast into sharp relief by the white light of the street lamp. "You might as well give up on your phone. It is completely disabled."

Lucy slid the device back into her pocket and slowly drew her wand.

"You think that is a good idea?" Schulz asked. "That you can fight your way out of this?"

"I've fought my way out of worse."

"No, you have not. You are outnumbered and surrounded, completely cut off from your friends. We are not savage beasts or some idiot gangster relying on your fear to undo you. We are professionals, as you are. We have planned for every possibility, and there is none where you win."

"Then I guess I'll go down fighting."

"Save yourself the pain and surrender. We will not hurt

you but ransom you as a prisoner of war, part of the long traditions of knighthood. Your comrades in arms will get you back, and we will get our crown. All will be well."

"That's all this is about, not the other artifacts, only the crown?"

"That crown is enough. It is ours."

"I hate to tell you this, but there's a museum in Lithuania who'd say otherwise."

"They are wrong. The crown was ours. It will be ours again."

"If that's all you're after, surely there are better ways to achieve it?"

Schulz laughed derisively. "If you do not know better than that, you will soon learn. Now, put your wand away and come with us."

Lucy looked at the people who were surrounding her in a loose circle. All of them were athletic-looking, wearing loose, practical clothes, with wands held at the ready. She recognized several from security footage and previous encounters, including Maria, Ellis's ex, but none of that helped. She didn't know these people. She didn't know any of their individual weaknesses.

Still, maybe she knew something about their collective weaknesses. She thought back to the books she had read and the things that Director Kowal had told her. The Knights were grounded in tradition, in an ancient sense of glory, faith, and chivalry. They might wear modern body armor, but their mental armor was much older, a set of customs stretching back to the Middle Ages. In their heads, they were crusading knights, and for people like that, honor mattered.

"I challenge you." She pointed her wand at Schulz. "Instead of risking all your people here, a duel between you and me, a fight for my freedom."

"Why would I agree to that when I have you at a disadvantage?"

"Because if you win, I won't only come quietly. I'll help you persuade the Griffins to hand over the crown."

Schulz snorted. "Having you as my captive will be persuasion enough."

"What's the matter, too afraid to fight me on your own?"

"Hardly." Schulz ran a finger along her scar. "I've been thrashing more fearsome threats than you for decades."

"Is that how you lost your sense of honor, had it beaten out of you in one too many fights?"

"My honor is intact and more than a match for yours."

"Prove it. Fight me."

By now, the eyes of most of the Knights were turned to Schulz, watching to see how she would react, judging her response using their value system.

"Very well." She tossed her cap aside. "The rest of you, stand back. If the agent wins, she can leave, but that won't be happening."

Schulz stepped out into the empty street, and Lucy did the same. They stood facing each other, wands at the ready.

"Maria," Schulz called, "give the word."

There was a long pause in which the two witches stood staring at each other.

"Begin," Maria said.

Schulz's wand snapped straight up, and she fired a sleep

spell at Lucy, who countered it before it hit her. She responded with a freeze, which evaporated in a blast of fire. Spells collided and were obliterated in the muggy night air while the two women circled each other, each step bringing them a little closer.

It wasn't like the swashbuckling duels between swordsmen that Lucy had seen in old movies. There was no banter back and forth, no quick quips. It took all her energy to match what Schulz was throwing at her, and Schulz's grim frown of concentration told her that the pressure went both ways. Schulz had an edge in experience, Lucy in raw power, and as a tangle of magical vines withered in their attempts to grab Schulz, the fight balanced on a knife-edge.

"Occillo," Schulz said, the aim of her wand shifting by an inch.

The spell shot past Lucy, who didn't bother trying to counter. The window of a car behind her shattered and glass hit her in the back. As lines of pain slashed across her skin, she stumbled forward, distracted. She sensed the next spell coming a moment too late, and a blast hit that flung her to the ground, driving fragments of glass deeper into her back.

Schulz stood over her, wand pointing straight at Lucy's face.

"Do you yield?" the older witch asked.

"Not planning to."

"I admire your pride." Schulz's wand glowed as she summoned power for one final knock-out spell.

At that moment, Lucy felt a tingle in her wand. For a fraction of a second, she stood in familiar darkness, the world of dreams, the place where she had defeated Mr. No. In front of her stood two Schulz's, one in her greatest dreams, being crowned Grand Master of the Knights of the Hinterland, the other in her worst nightmare, as a sliver of stained glass slashed through her cheek, only a hair's breadth from her eye.

Lucy rolled aside in time to dodge the spell flung at her.

"Subvolo," she called.

A piece of glass flew up from where she had been lying and hung in the air in front of Schulz's face, blood dripping from its deadly sharp tip. Schulz stood, frozen in terror, as more glass rose to face her, a nightmare that had haunted her for years. Her grip loosened around her wand.

"Exarmo," Lucy said, and her magic knocked the wand from Schulz's hand. It rolled away beneath another car.

Schulz tore her gaze away from the floating glass. "How did you know?" she whispered.

Lucy touched her cheek in the same spot where Schulz had her scar. "Educated guess."

"That bastard Kowal. He's beaten me again, through you."

"Do you yield?"

"I am proud, like you, but pride should never override intelligence. I yield."

Lucy let the glass fall to the ground. She pushed herself to her knees, then got to her feet, wincing at the wounds in her back. "I'll be going now. We're going to meet again, aren't we?"

"*Ja.*" Schulz nodded. "I look forward to it. You fought with honor."

"You too."

Lucy pulled out her phone as she walked away. Half a minute later, the screen came alive, and her signal returned. As she called Ellis's number, she looked back along the street. The Knights of the Hinterland were gone.

CHAPTER THIRTY

"This is so exciting!" Dylan whispered. "I never get to stay up this late."

"Don't get used to it, buddy," Charlie said. "Your mom and I agreed that you could do it now because it's so important. This isn't a free pass to stay up past midnight reading about pirates every night."

"I'm not reading about pirates anymore. I'm reading about pre-Columbian civilizations, like the one on this site. It's amazing."

"You can tell me about it later. Right now, I think the Tolderai are here."

Half a dozen witches and wizards approached the spot where Dylan and Charlie stood outside the wire fence surrounding the construction site and archaeological dig. Dylan recognized his mom's friend Heather and several others who had been to a barbecue at the Heron house.

"Chuck." Heather nodded at Charlie. "And Dylan, right? I hear you're the one who found the graves."

"Not exactly," Dylan said. "The grownup archaeologists

found the graves, but they didn't recognize the signs on them. I did."

"Well, thank you for letting us know. We had no idea that this site was here or what was left behind." Heather peered through the fence. "Are there any trees in there?"

"I don't think so."

"Then we'll take a different route."

She pointed her wand at the ground around their feet. Plants burst forth, strong vines with thick leaves a foot across protruding from their sides. Heather planted her feet on one of the leaves and signaled to Dylan and Charlie to do the same. A moment later, they were lifted into the air and over the fence, carried by the growing vines.

"That's so cool," Dylan said.

"Keep it quiet, guys," Charlie whispered. "We don't want to draw the security guards' attention."

They stepped off the leaves onto the open ground inside the fence. Dylan took out a map he'd drawn, copying the information Professor Angie had shared and led them to the graves.

"One's under here." He pointed at the ground in front of him. "Another over there and two more beyond it. There are others too, but those are the ones with wands and things in them."

The Tolderai spread out, one or two to each of the places Dylan had indicated. He felt very grown-up, seeing these adults listen to him and act on the information he had gathered.

"How come you didn't know about this place?" he asked. "I mean, if it's an old village of your tribe…"

"Once, the Tolderai were widely scattered," Heather

said. "Living in secret among human societies. Secrecy doesn't lead to good record keeping. While we've tried to keep the history of those people alive, telling their stories and singing their songs, we've lost a lot. Far more than I care for."

"So this dig could tell you things about yourselves that you didn't know?"

Heather nodded. "Yes. We will be paying close attention now that we know what it represents. First, we have to make sure the humans don't find anything they shouldn't."

She pressed her hands against the ground and muttered the words of a spell in a language that Dylan didn't recognize. Nearby patches of grass shifted, then became still again. For a long time, it seemed like nothing was happening, though the other Tolderai were in the same stance as Heather, hands pressed against the ground.

Dylan pressed his hand against the dirt. It was trembling, and magic was flowing through it, connecting Heather to the nearby grass and something moving deeper in the ground. The trembling grew, and Dylan stepped back, excitedly waiting to see what would happen next.

Close to him, the dirt parted. A rippling cluster of roots emerged into the night air. Then something else came, pushed out by their movement: a wand, simply but elegantly made, carved from an old piece of pine. Dirt clung to its sides as it rose like a finger pointing to the sky, then fell on its side. The roots rippled again, and a bowl followed the wand. Then the roots withdrew, drawing the dirt in over them, leaving the ground as it had been before.

Heather picked up the bowl and the wand. The other Tolderai had similar artifacts in their hands.

"What about the bones?" Dylan said. "Don't you want to take your people's bodies, to stop the archaeologists from doing things to them?"

"Bones are only bones," Heather informed him. "Our people's spirits returned to the earth when they died, and their flesh has fed the things that crawl and grow. Archaeologists are welcome to the hard, dried-out pieces that remain. They are not people anymore, only a marker of history."

They all walked back to the fence and stepped onto the large leaves that had carried them over. The creepers rose, lifted their passengers a tiny fraction closer to the stars for a moment, then deposited them on the ground outside the fence. The plants retreated into the earth, which closed behind them.

"Thank you." Heather rested one hand on the ground where the plants had been. She looked up at Dylan and Charlie. "Thank you, too. You have done a good thing today."

"Could I..." Dylan hesitated, unsure whether he should even ask what he wanted to, but knowing that he would regret it if he didn't. "Later, could I look at the things you took? The only ancient wand I've ever seen was the one we found last week, and it's broken. I want to study ancient magical artifacts, and this would be such a cool opportunity."

"Of course," Heather said. "We are a little more open about our existence now, at least with the magical world. If you want to record the findings for a select few people like the Silver Griffins, that would be allowed."

"Wow, thank you!"

"It seems that we need a historian before more of our past is lost. I can't think of anyone better than you, Dylan Heron."

As the Tolderai stalked off into the night, Dylan turned to Charlie with an enormous grin.

"Did you hear that, dad? I'm a historian now!"

———

The next afternoon, when a teacher dropped Dylan and his friends off at the dig site, the place was buzzing with activity. Every archaeologist there had gathered around a new trench they had dug on the spot where Dylan had been the previous night, one of the graves.

"What's happening?" Dylan asked a girl from one of the other schools who had got there before them.

"I don't know. Nobody's given us anything to do yet, and they all seem really wound up about something."

"Let's go find out what."

Together, the kids made their way over to the gathered archaeologists. Professor Angie stood by the side of the trench, the geophysics scan of the grave in her hand, while other archaeologists worked in the bottom of the channel, sweeping dust from the bones and the gravestone they had found there. By the other graves, the geophysics team was walking back and forth with their equipment, taking new scans.

"This doesn't make any sense," the Professor said. "Those things are right here on the image. They were there, in the dirt, just last week."

"Could they be imaging artifacts?" one of her colleagues

asked. "Not something really there, merely a coincidental shape from background radiation?"

"For images this clear and this specific?" Angie shook her head. "Don't be ridiculous, John."

"I'm only trying to help."

"Sorry, didn't mean to snap. It's just…" She shook her head. "Has someone else been onto the site? Have we had grave robbers?"

Another archaeologist poked their head up out of the trench. "Not in the past week. There were no holes before we started digging, no disturbance in the soil caused by anything but tree roots."

"Then how on earth…" Angie flung her hands in the air. "I give up. It's as if they've disappeared. At least we have the other graves."

One of the geophysics team approached, holding a tablet with cables dangling from it. He tapped on the screen and frowned.

"Um, actually, those look different too." He showed the screen to Angie, who shook her head in bewilderment.

"I don't understand. The artifacts were there, clear as day. Now it's only bones."

"Bones are good," said the man in the trench. "You know how much we learn from bones."

"Yes, of course." Angie sighed. "I feel like I'm losing my mind. Evidence doesn't disappear by magic."

At those words, Sofia and Lance both turned to look at Dylan. He backed away from the crowd, and his two friends followed him until they were out of earshot of the others.

"Was this you?" Sofia asked.

"Sort of."

"What do you mean, sort of?"

"I didn't take anything, but I showed this place to the people who did."

"You've turned into a grave robber?" Lance stared at him in shock. "Indiana Jones would not approve."

"Indiana Jones is constantly robbing graves." Sofia scowled. "I don't approve. Professor Angie's been great, and now you're driving her mad."

"I'm sorry," Dylan said, "but there were magical things in there. I couldn't let them fall into the wrong hands. Remember what happened with that wand."

"You think she's the wrong hands?"

"People aren't supposed to know about magic, remember?"

"That doesn't seem fair."

"I know." Dylan shrugged. "You know I'd make the rules different if I could."

"So now what?"

"Now we carry on digging. There's plenty more history to find."

"What about Professor Angie?"

"Think of it this way. She'll have a great mystery story to tell all her archaeologist friends."

CHAPTER THIRTY-ONE

"New question." Steve looked out from behind his monitor at the rest of the IT team. He was wearing what Charlie thought of as Steve's "I'm clever" grin. It had a fifty percent chance of being followed by something stupid. "If you could be the protagonist in any classic computer game, who would it be, and why?"

The rest of the team leaned back thoughtfully in their seats. It was the middle of the afternoon, which meant that they all felt the need for a break from fixing the company's IT problems. Even Gail, for whom Charlie had finally found something she considered "real coding work," was ready to rest her typing fingers for a few minutes.

"Define classic," she said.

"You know, a classic."

"Tautology doesn't help. What's your measure here: age, sales, popularity?"

"Jeez, I dunno. That wasn't the point."

"Well, now it is."

"Fine." Steve sighed. "I can't believe you've almost

knocked the fun out of this already, but if I have to define it, I'll call it a classic if it's over five years old and people still talk about it. Nothing recent, nothing obscure and forgotten."

"Hm." Gail drummed her fingers against her desk. Now that the pedantry was over, she had to consider the question.

Charlie turned his gaze back to his screen. Much as he would have loved to spend the afternoon talking about games, an alert was flashing on his control panel, and as the senior member of the team, he had to pay attention when the others didn't.

"I'd be my World of Warcraft character," Keiran said. "He's strong and smart and built the way I want him."

"You can't pick your character," Steve said. "It's supposed to be someone important, someone we'll all know."

"You said the protagonist. When I play WoW, my character is the protagonist. Same for anyone else playing."

"That's not what I meant."

"It's what you said."

"Fine, then you can't pick WoW. That's a modern game."

"*Bzzzt*, wrong answer," Gail said. "You defined a classic as any game five or more years old and that people are still talking about. WoW has been around since 2004, and the world is full of nerds like Keiran who still won't shut up about it."

"Hey!"

"No offense. We're all nerds here."

"I guess…"

Steve sighed. "Fine, you can pick your WoW character,

MARTHA CARR & MICHAEL ANDERLE

though when you can be anyone, that seems like a dumb choice."

On Charlie's monitor, another alert was flashing, and another. Across the company, systems were slowing down or behaving strangely, and the Kanban board showed a worrying number of support requests in the past ten minutes. He leaned closer to the screen, looking for a pattern.

"How about you, Gail?" Steve asked. "Who would you be?"

"Doomguy."

"You'd be the protagonist from Doom?"

"Damn right I would."

"You'd choose to be stuck in a nightmare scenario of fighting your way through monstrous horrors?"

"Of course! In real life, if I have a problem, like a dumb support request from someone who doesn't understand email, I have to be calm and reasonable about it. I have to be patient and considerate and careful and blah blah blah urgh. In Doom, any problem I face, I shoot it. It doesn't get more satisfying than that."

"You'd be in mortal danger."

Gail shrugged. "Same with almost any choice. How many games worth playing don't involve violence left, right, and center?"

"I can think of a few." Steve was wearing his smug, knowing grin again.

"Sorry to interrupt this critical conversation," Charlie said, "but I need you all to get back to work. Something's going wrong."

"Hang on." Gail held out her hand, palm forward. "Steve

has an answer he wants to share, and he's going to be insufferable if we don't let him. Let's get this out of the way."

"I'm never insufferable!"

"Do you want to tell us your answer or not?"

"Fine." Steve pouted for a moment, but he couldn't hold back his pleased grin. "Leisure Suit Larry. I'd spend my days trawling around casinos and yachts, looking for lovely ladies. Life in computer games doesn't get any better. It's safe, it's comfortable, and it's all about getting—"

"Gross." Gail stuck out her tongue. "Your ideal lifestyle is a creepy old man in an old-fashioned suit hitting on women who want to be left alone?" She turned to Charlie. "I'm sorry, I was wrong. We shouldn't have indulged him this time."

"Hey, that's not fair!"

"What's Leisure Suit Larry?" Keiran asked.

"I'll tell you when you've grown into your big boy pants," Gail replied. "Right now, we need to..." She looked at her screen. "Holy cow, Charlie's right, we really need to work!"

Charlie shook his head and stifled a laugh.

"I did try to tell you. Steve, you do triage, go through those tickets and work out what's most urgent. Keiran, you, and I will work anything he passes us in order, no complaints or cherry-picking. Gail, you try to work out what's going on. All clear?"

"Yes, Charlie," the others replied as they turned their attention to their screens.

For the next hour, there was no conversation, only the frantic tapping of keys, interspersed with phone calls from managers concerned that their teams' IT systems seemed to be collapsing around them. Charlie could have worked on solving the problem, but Gail was as good at diagnostics as he was, and it wouldn't help the team dynamic if he took the interesting task while leaving the grunt work to the others. Instead, he worked his way through the help requests with Keiran, finding ways to get around the immediate problems. It was like sticking a band-aid over an open wound while a knife-wielding killer was still on the loose, but it was also vital to keeping the rest of the company happy.

Gail came over to Charlie's desk, a notepad in her hand and a serious expression on her face. "Everything I've looked at points to a virus, but I can't track it down. Not even a hint of what or where it is. The symptoms are there, but there's no disease for us to tackle."

"Huh." Charlie peered at her notes, then at his screen. There was a familiar pattern here, but it wasn't one he could explain to the rest of his team. "Can you get on the service requests while I take a look? I have a few tricks you might not have tried."

"Sure thing."

Once Gail was back at her desk, and no one else could view his monitor, Charlie pulled up one of the custom programs he kept in a hidden folder, away from mundane eyes. Within two minutes, it had produced a map of the company's IT systems and decorated them with a growing number of purple lines and dots, where the program had found magic in the system. The bubbles kept growing, more and larger chunks of magic. No wonder the system was on the verge of collapse, and no wonder Gail couldn't find it: they had a magical virus.

Charlie frowned. He'd been carefully maintaining the company's magical defenses for years, a secret project that no one else needed to know about. Every time he spotted a way for magical viruses or electronic spells to get in, he shut it down so that they only ever faced a tiny, manageable trickle. How had so many suddenly gotten in?

The magical heat map, with its web of connections, pointed him toward a client database. It was an old piece of software, one they had repeatedly patched and upgraded over the years but never replaced because it was in constant, critical use. Up until now, it had seldom caused problems.

Except that Keiran had been tackling an issue with the database recently, hadn't he? There had been that section of redundant code that he took out. Charlie had assumed it was an artifact of the database's long evolution, as redundant as an appendix was in a human body, but maybe something else was going on.

"Keiran, that bit of code you removed from the database, you kept a text copy, right?"

Keiran stared, startled, across the room. "Did I do this?" he asked in a tight whisper. "Am I gonna get fired?"

"You're fine. Just send me a link to the code, could you?"

Keiran gave a jittery nod while Steve and Gail exchanged a look. If this were the answer, it wouldn't be the first time Charlie had fixed a problem in a surprising way, and they were increasingly curious about how he did it. There were times when their senior colleague seemed like a miracle worker.

Charlie clicked on the link from Keiran and scrolled through the file full of code. Now that he understood what he was looking for, it made sense in a way it previously hadn't. This wasn't part of the database. It was barely code at all. It was a spell in the system, one translated into some old-fashioned code that had hidden its meaning from him before, and the database was merely a convenient place to hide it. Another wizard or witch who had worked for the company must have written it, years before Charlie even started there, and who wanted to keep the place safe from magical viruses after they left. A gift from history to Charlie and his team, and they had gotten rid of it, making themselves vulnerable in a way they had never been before.

Charlie laughed at his stupidity for not noticing this before. At least he'd had Keiran save a copy so he could set it up again, in a different part of the system this time. He would also find a way to leave information about it for future witches and wizards, in case he ever left.

His laughter made the others look hopefully at him.

"You solved it, chief?" Steve asked.

"Not yet, but I know how to do it." Unfortunately, he couldn't do it with the others around to ask questions. Aside from anything else, he'd have to get his wand out to activate the code's magical side. Fortunately, it would be straightforward to do once he was alone. "It's a one-person job. Steve, send out an email to the whole company. Tell them we've identified the source of the current problems and should have things fixed by the morning. Most of them finish work in less than an hour. They can find something else to do until then. Once you've sent the email, you can all go home."

"Really?" Gail sounded incredulous. "Won't you need help clearing up?"

"That's tomorrow's problem. For now, I have a long evening of work ahead, and it'll be easier if no one's talking about Leisure Suit Larry. Get on home, and I'll see you all in the morning."

Steve hit "Send" on the email, and the other three headed out. Once they were gone, Charlie locked the door behind them, pulled out his wand, and copied the code into a new file. Then he got down to the real work.

CHAPTER THIRTY-TWO

Ashley sat in front of her bank of monitors, watching the video feeds from the Mini Griffins. It was nearly dinner time, so they were getting near the ends of their after-school patrols, footsteps carrying them back toward their homes. It had been a quiet afternoon, and there wasn't much chatter over their communications devices, no sign that any of the Mini Griffins had stumbled across something cool. Instead, there was the quiet conversation of tired kids heading home from an uninspiring event.

Then suddenly, Tommy let out an excited shout. "Check it out! I'd forgotten I was walking past the ghost house."

As his head swung around, Ashley saw a tall, dark house appear on her screen. It was over a hundred years old, its bricks weathered and the paint peeling away from its woodwork, some of which was warping. The garden was overgrown, adding to the air of neglect.

"This is, like, the oldest house for miles around," Tommy said. "They say the ghost of the woman who built it haunts it, and you can hear her crying on stormy nights."

"Probably wind blowing through the eaves," Ashley said. "Statistically speaking, most hauntings turn out not to be supernatural."

"Yeah, but this place is totally for real. On Halloween, the bigger kids dare each other to walk up and knock three times on the door. If you can stand there a whole minute while the ghost watches you, everyone you're with has to share their candy with you. I'm totally going to do it this year."

"How do you know the ghost is looking at you?" Mia asked, her voice coming in over the comms from Pasadena.

"Of course it's watching you. You're knocking on its door."

"You're assuming the ghost doesn't have anything better to do, but what if it's reading a book or watching TV?"

"On Halloween?"

"Halloween might not be special for ghosts. Every day is haunted for them."

"Huh, I guess." The view shifted as Tommy tilted his head to one side, pondering the issue.

On another monitor, Ashley had pulled up information about the house, some of it publicly available, other bits drawn from government and business databases by her computer systems. The house had protected status because of its age and historical value. It had been bought by a real estate developer three years back, but he hadn't been able to make the changes he wanted and had eventually put in an application to tear the place down and replace it. The officials rejected that request as well, and Ashley hoped it stayed that way. Ghost or no ghost, it would be a shame to lose a local Halloween game, as well as the rest of the house's history.

Movement in one of the dirt-streaked windows caught her eye.

"Is there someone in there?" she asked. "It doesn't look like anyone could live in a place like this."

"Maybe it's the ghost!" Tommy exclaimed. "This is so cool."

Ashley didn't know much about ghosts, but that had looked more like an ordinary human to her.

"Go closer, Tommy," she said. "I want to see what's going on."

"You want me to go closer to the ghost?"

"You don't know that it's the ghost."

"You don't know that it isn't." He sounded a lot less confident than he had a moment before.

"I thought you wanted to go up to the house and knock on the door. You can't do that if you're scared of going close."

"I'm not scared."

"So go closer."

"I... But..." Unable to find an excuse that wouldn't make him sound frightened, Tommy reluctantly made his way up the garden path, pushing aside the branches of untended bushes and trees.

"Try to keep some cover between you and the window," Ashley instructed.

"In case the ghost sees me?"

"In case that's a criminal. We might need to gather evidence before we stop them."

"Oh, yeah, right."

Tommy drew his wand and stepped off the path, then crept closer to the building through the long grass and hanging trailers of the garden. Close to the house was a gap in the plants and a gravel path running around the building. He cast a spell to mute the sound of walking on the stones, then eased up to one of the windows and peered in.

No one had cleaned the windows in years, and the grime made it hard to see through them properly, both in person and through the video camera in Tommy's cap. He wiped a sleeve across a corner of the glass. The view improved, but dust on the inside still reduced patches of the interior to a muddy blur. Between those patches, Tommy and Ashley saw a man moving around a large living room. He tore peeling strips of paper from the walls, then picked up a crowbar and used it to smash the surround of a fireplace. Everywhere he went, he scuffed his feet and kicked the threadbare carpet as if he was trying to make it even more dirty and worn.

The man wore loose, dark clothes. As he swung the crowbar, a hood fell back, revealing his face. Ashley grabbed a screenshot, ran it quickly through a program that sharpened the image, and started a web search.

"Who do you think he is?" Tommy's knuckles turned white as he clutched the windowsill.

"David Bustle," Ashley read from the webpage of a business her search had led her to. "He's the property developer who owns the house."

"Then why is he wrecking it? Shouldn't he be repairing things instead?"

"If it deteriorates far enough, he'll be allowed to tear the house down the way he wants."

"Even if he's the one who does the damage?"

"He must be doing it secretly. If he can blame vandals or the place breaking down over time, he'll be in the clear."

"That's not fair!"

"I agree. We should come up with a plan to stop him. Does anybody have any ideas?"

Before any of the other Mini Griffins could answer, Tommy banged his fist against the window.

"Hey, mister! I see you!"

Bustle had been trying to pry up a floorboard. He jerked upright and stared around in alarm but didn't seem to see Tommy through the dirty window.

"Tommy, this could be dangerous," Ashley warned. "Get out of there."

"No, I'm not letting him tear the house down. Not until I've had my chance to win all the Halloween candy."

Ashley was more interested in preserving the house for its historical value, but at least they shared a purpose, even if they weren't on quite the same wavelength.

"Just banging and shouting won't help."

"It stopped him, didn't it?"

"Yes, but look, now he's coming out!"

Bustle had stormed out of the living room, crowbar in hand, and heavy footsteps approached the front door.

"Oh!" Tommy looked around. "What should I do?"

"Hide in the bushes," Mia said. "Quick."

The view from Tommy's camera became a blur of leaves as he dove into the overgrown garden, bushes rustling around him.

"He's coming after me," Tommy hissed. "I can hear him."

"Use a spell then. Quick."

Tommy pushed his way into the heart of a thorny bush, wincing as the spikes scratched his skin, then cast an obscuring spell. It wasn't as good as full invisibility, but with so much of him hidden from view, it might be enough to put Bustle off.

A dark shape approached through the swaying plants and David Bustle appeared. Between his black clothes, his raised crowbar, and the scowl on his face, he made up a menacing figure. He looked around, and for one terrifying moment, Ashley thought that he had spotted Tommy. Then his gaze moved on, surveying the other bushes.

"I don't know who you are," Bustle growled, "but this is my property, and if you're trespassing, I have a right to defend it. I'll beat you black and blue. Then I'll call the cops and tell them you were breaking in."

Tommy quivered in the bushes and held his breath in case that gave him away.

For all his confident words, Bustle seemed agitated and disconcerted that someone had seen him illegally trashing his house. He strode back to the front doorway, picked up a heavy bag of tools, closed the door from the outside, and locked it. Muttering to himself, he strode away.

Tommy let out his held breath. "What now?" he whispered. "Go to the cops?"

"Then we'd have to explain why you were trespassing in someone's garden," Ashley said. "No, we can find a way to save this place ourselves. It's time for another Mini Griffins adventure.

"Now get out of that bush and head home. Your mom will have dinner ready, and I need time to think up a plan."

CHAPTER THIRTY-THREE

Kelly's satnav announced that she had reached her destination. She checked the numbers on the low houses with their expansive lawns, then pulled over to the side of the road in front of the house she was after.

It was a quiet neighborhood, which made sense. If an international con man and notorious master criminal wished to retire from the limelight, he would want somewhere quiet. Somewhere the police were unlikely to be called and where he wouldn't bump into the people he had worked with, never mind the ones he'd swindled. When that con man had worked within the magical world, he would also want to get somewhere as mundane as possible, where no one knew about grimoires, wands, or spells. Here, a mile from the coast at Long Beach, was one of the most mundane places he could have chosen while retaining the benefits of sea, sun, and plentiful tourist distractions to keep from getting bored.

Kelly hadn't known whether to be relieved or disappointed when she had learned that Olivier Robail could be caught so close to her turf. When Sadoul had signed the confession implicating his old partner, she had imagined herself crossing the world to close down this zombie case, a thing thought dead but revived through the magic of fresh evidence. There had been a sense of drama to that version of the story. She would fly across the ocean, track Robail down in Budapest, Barcelona, or Berlin, and finally take in one of Europe's most notorious and elusive criminals. Great magicals like Director Kowal had tried to bring Olivier Robail to justice but had never had the evidence they needed. If she could bring him in, then her failure to implicate him a decade before would be forgotten before anyone even knew about it. A moment like that deserved some drama and confrontation.

On the other hand, keeping things local made it all a lot easier. To arrange the trip abroad, she would have had to make time away from her regular schedule at work and home. She would have to liaise with local authorities who had no idea who she was or what she was capable of, plus book travel, make connections and generally jump through administrative hoops. All of that would have meant explaining the situation, not only her discovery but also the error leading up to it. Inevitably, there would have been other people present when she finally made her arrest. This way, she could deal with the issue quietly, by herself, without rehashing what had gone wrong. She would simply present the prisoner at the end, telling a tale of triumph over time. That was a far better look on her.

She opened the car door and stepped out into the summer heat. The ocean's coolness was close enough to give a freshness to the air but not close enough to relieve the heat. She closed the door, locked the car, slid her wand discreetly up against her forearm, and approached the house.

She had considered bringing backup with her. After all, this was a renowned criminal, someone with proven cunning, ruthlessness, and magical power. Sensibly, it would have been good to have support if anything went wrong. Again, that fell foul of wanting to keep things on the quiet. Sure, there were people whose help she could have called on without informing her manager, but then she would have had to put up with Lucy or Jackie being present while she fixed her mistake. They might even have taken some credit for it, credit she needed to balance the past error. This was something she needed to do by herself, to preserve her professional standing and her self-esteem.

As she walked up to the house, she noticed the "For Sale" sign sticking out of the lawn. It looked like she had got here just in time. Another few weeks and perhaps Robail would have sold and moved on. The trail could have gone cold. That made it even more important that she deal with this now, alone.

She walked up four steps onto the front porch and knocked on the door. A moment later the door opened, revealing a woman around Kelly's age, wearing a navy blue suit and with her hair neatly tied back, a clipboard in her hand.

"You're here to view the place?" the realtor asked brightly.

"Sure." Kelly returned the smile. "I mean yes, I'm keen to have a good look around."

Perfect. This way, she could get into the house without

fuss and see the lay of the land. If Robail were around, she would take her chance to arrest him here and now, then use "never was, never will be" to blank the incident from the realtor's mind. If not, she would come back later to get her man, better informed about his lifestyle and the space he occupied.

"Are you looking for a family home?" the realtor asked as she ushered Kelly inside. "The previous owner lived here alone, but there's plenty of space for kids, good schools in the area, and of course the coast is great for family time."

Kelly looked around at a barren, empty room. When she stepped across the polished boards of the floor, her footsteps echoed back to her from blank walls. Open doorways revealed that the rest of the building was equally deserted.

Nagging details of the realtor's words finally snagged in her thoughts. "Previous owner." "Lived." Not the words you would use to describe someone in residence.

"Isn't there anyone living here?" she asked.

"No, it's currently unoccupied, and the owner is super keen to sell. We could have you moved in within weeks. It's not often you get an opportunity like this."

The realtor's smile was so bright that it lengthened the dark shadow stretching across Kelly's heart. Robail was gone. He had escaped her again. She would have to explain her failures to the others and get their help.

No. It didn't have to be that way. She had followed the trail this far. She could follow it further. Just a few details from the realtor and she could keep moving. Robail wasn't going to evade her again.

"Has the previous occupier been gone long?" she asked

as casually as she could. She strolled around the house, pretending to take it all in, while inside her mind only one thing mattered: Robail.

"Only a couple of weeks." There was something off in the realtor's voice, an edge that Kelly couldn't pin down. Something the woman didn't want to say. Was she in on some con with Robail? Had she been sent to put Kelly off the scent?

"Where did they move to?"

"Sadly, he passed away. It's his niece who's selling the house."

Then Kelly realized what the realtor was trying not to say.

"He died here?"

"Yes, I'm afraid so. I know that makes some people uncomfortable, but we factored that into the pricing. If you want, we can—"

Kelly held out her hand, silencing the woman.

"The man who died here, was his name Olivier Robail?"

"That's right, Ollie Robail." The realtor clamped a hand to her mouth. "Oh my God, I'm so sorry. Did you know him?"

"In a way."

"Oh, I am so sorry. Do you need some time to process this?"

Kelly drew a deep breath. What she needed to process wasn't what the realtor thought, but still... "That would be good, please."

"Of course. I'll be outside."

The woman left the house, closing the front door behind her.

Kelly stood for a long moment, silent and motionless, in the middle of the late Robail's kitchen. She drew another deep breath, then leapt up and down, cursing to herself, for two whole minutes.

Sadoul had cheated her. That lying pig had held onto his secrets long enough for them to become obsolete, then finally let her know what she had missed out on. He had done this to her on purpose. She was sure of it. There was no way it was a coincidence that she had persuaded him to talk right after this happened. He had been waiting until his partner passed away. Now that the coast was clear, he wanted to let the Silver Griffins know how clever and discreet he had been. Her triumph, her chance to make up for her past mistake, had been snatched away.

At the end of two minutes, she stopped, cleared her throat, straightened her jacket, and tidied away the strands of hair that had come loose while she vented her frustration. She took out a compact and fixed her makeup, making sure that her lips were just right. Then she put both the cosmetics and her wand away in her purse and went to the front door.

The realtor was waiting outside, clutching her clipboard tight. A couple stood on the lawn, waiting for their chance to look inside. All three looked at Kelly with sympathy.

"I'm sorry for your loss," the realtor said. "I assume you won't be interested in the house?"

Kelly shook her head. "No, it's not for me, but thank you for your time."

She got into her car, drove three blocks, then pulled

over again. Her hands trembled on the wheel as she tried to decide what to do next.

If she went back to the office without saying anything, her mistake might stay a secret. No one needed to know what had happened here or on her past case.

Except that Lucy knew, and she might tell someone. Not to mention the transport wizard and the guards who had brought Sadoul across from Oriceran.

She could try to keep this secret, tell no one, and hope that the others wouldn't think to tell. It was her best chance of protecting her dignity although it had the distinct downside of leaving Lucy with a hold over her.

On the other hand, she could go back, write all of this up, and leave an accurate history of the Sadoul case for future Griffins. It was what she ought to do. It was what duty and the rules called for.

The question was, which outcome was harder to face?

CHAPTER THIRTY-FOUR

The Underfoot Brigade and a contingent of Knights of the Hinterland made their way down the passage into the depths of the earth below L.A. Leontine and Maria led them. Magical lights floated around them, cast by Twylan and some of the Knights, the glowing orbs drifting along with the party as they walked.

Twylan carefully observed the Knights. They were outsiders, and that shouldn't have made her wary of them. After all, the Underfoot Brigade were outsiders themselves, driven into the tunnels beneath L.A. to find somewhere hidden, safe, and sheltered where they could live. No one here really belonged in the city above. Even helping the Silver Griffins, Twylan was an outsider, an observer to the actions of others. Still, it was strange working with these people she had never heard of until a few days before, with their international accents and their cold, hard way of looking at the world.

Perhaps it wasn't the Knights that were putting her on edge, but the hunt they were undertaking together. Twylan had never been a hunter, had never enjoyed violence, no matter who she turned it against. It was needed sometimes to stop bad people or to protect the Brigade, but the idea that they were pursuing the scythed borers to their death made her uncomfortable. Sure, the borers were a menace, and they needed to deal with them, but it was a shame to see anything die or to be the one killing it.

Leontine's outlook seemed far closer to that of the Knights. Together with Maria, he led them into darkness, clearly enjoying the thrill of the hunt and the challenge of trailing the creatures in the gloom.

"It is like the great hunts in the early days of our Order," Maria shared. "Parties of noble adventurers hunting boar, deer, and wyverns through the forests of Poland and Livonia. Strength of arms against the strength of the beast. The hunter's skill against the cunning of the prey."

"You make it sound like you were there," Leontine said.

Maria shook her head. "I have only read the chronicles, but the picture they paint is a glorious one."

The leading lights spread out as the tunnel opened onto a ledge overlooking a wider cavern. Maria whipped out the compact digital camera that she kept in a pouch on her belt, the sort of tool that her medieval predecessors definitely wouldn't have wielded on their hunts. Twylan had seen some of Maria's pictures, and even with such simple equipment and limited lighting, they were lovely works that captured the spirit of people and places. That was a hunt she found more comfortable, one for a perfect image. It was also a way to continue those glorious chronicles in a more modern format.

"There," Leontine whispered as the lights drifted across

the cavern, illuminating the shells of the scythed borers. "We've found their nest."

Twylan stepped forward between Leontine and Maria so she could see everything ahead of them. He was right. This wasn't like the areas where they found the borers before—tunnels the creatures had hunted along or chambers where they had stopped to rest. This place had nooks dug into the sides for them to curl up and sleep. It had a wide-open center where the beasts could tumble over each other, learning to fight or competing for dominance, and at the near end, it had heaps of bones and chewed-up fur, the debris of creatures that the scythed borers had killed and eaten.

The nearest borers had clearly felt a disturbance already as they raised their blind heads to point toward the hunting party.

"No time to waste," Leontine said. "Everybody ready?"

They drew weapons and wands, the Knights' daggers counting as both.

"Ready," everyone replied.

"Then let's do it."

Leontine spread his wings and kicked off from the ledge. He soared out over the cavern, mere inches from the ceiling. As he flew over the borers, he dropped a dozen glowing balls. They were magical bombs, made using a mixture of spellcraft and the chemistry Heather Fields had been teaching the Underfoots. As they hit the animals, the bombs shattered, blanketing the monsters in magically infused fire.

By the light of those flames, the Knights and the Underfoots charged down from the ledge and into battle.

Twylan raised her hands as she ran. Her wand was in her right hand, but a moment like this, a time of danger and tension, brought out her wild magic. It blazed from her eyes and *crackled* along her fingertips. Although she could channel much of it, she sensed it trying to break free, to escape her grasp.

She directed the magic through her wand and into a spell. A gust of wind billowed in front of her, flinging three of the borers off their feet and into the cavern wall. As they struggled to right themselves, the Knights fell on them with swords and knives, stabbing and slashing, reducing them to giant slices of insect meat.

Another creature rushed at Twylan, the magical wind parting to either side of its unusually pointed head, deflecting uselessly away. She abandoned that spell and summoned a burst of electricity, which cascaded off the thing's flanks apparently without touching it. Even the chemical fire blazing along the back of its shell didn't seem to put it off as it bore down on her, pincer clacking and its mouth open wide, revealing rows of needle teeth.

Then Leontine landed on the creature's back, a sword in his hand. He wedged the blade between two plates of its shell, pried them open, and stabbed down through the gap. The creature reared up, trying to shake off Leontine and the sword. Then Maria dived in front and raised her wand. A cloud of blades appeared in the air and slammed into the creature's soft, exposed underbelly, ripping it open. As the beast collapsed dead, dark drool running between its pointed teeth, Maria also sagged, and the magical blades vanished.

"Are you all right?" Twylan laid a hand on Maria's shoulder.

The Knight nodded, straightened, and looked around. "That took a lot of power, but I am ready for more. You?"

Twylan raised her hands, and sparks flew from her fingertips. "Of course."

Together, they charged through the fight between monsters and monster hunters to the back of the cave. There, the largest of the scythed borers stood. Its claws were as long as Twylan was tall, the plates of its shell inches thick. Two Knights of the Hinterland lay crumpled and groaning at its feet, and as Twylan approached, a swing of its claw sent Siltor flying.

Maria ran at the beast. As she went, she cast a spell. Her wand dagger grew into a long, heavy sword, blunt at the tip but heavy enough to hack through bone as easily as butter. She dodged a blow from the creature, then brought the blade down, severing its claw. The beast groaned, its rumble shaking the ground beneath their feet.

Maria swung again, slamming the sword into the creature's shell with all her strength. The blade bounced off, leaving only a long, pale scratch. The other claw came around and knocked her flying.

The borer pushed itself forward, teeth twitching as it advanced on Twylan. She shook with fear but knew she couldn't let that control her. This thing was a threat to her home, her friends, everything that mattered. She had to deal with it. But how? The shell was practically impregnable, and she had no way to make it expose its unprotected underside.

The mouth opened wide and inspiration struck. She

drew a deep breath, then leaped over the lower row of teeth, into the creature's mouth, and down its throat.

For a horrifying moment, she was alone in the dark, with the damp of the creature's saliva and the stink of its garbage breath. Its throat muscles rippled, threatening to crush her.

Twylan summoned all the magic she could from the world. For the first time in months, instead of controlling and channeling it, she let it fly free. Power bloomed, colored lights flashed, and the creature burst open, torn apart by the strength of Twylan's magic.

She stood in the remains as bits of borer guts dripped from the ceiling above. The monster's fluids drenched her, leaving her covered in its stench and the awful warmth of its insides. It was the most disgusting state she had ever been in.

She felt glorious.

"I did it!" She stared at the shattered remains of the creature's shell. "I killed it."

"Well done." Maria, one arm hanging limp, used her other hand to raise the camera and capture Twylan's moment of triumph.

"What about the rest?" Twylan asked.

"All dealt with."

Around them, the Underfoots and Knights of the Hinterland stood over the bodies of the slain monsters, celebrating their victory. A few were injured, but Kix and one of the Knights were already seeing to their wounds.

"Here." Leontine held out the borrowed sword to Maria. "You should have this back."

She shook her head. "You earned it today."

"Won't you need it?"

"I have another."

Leontine proudly wiped the gore from the blade and slid it into its sheath.

Behind the vast creature Twylan had killed, the packed dirt of the cave wall was broken and run through with roots. A gap, too narrow for a borer to get through, ran up and away.

"This must be what disturbed them," Twylan said. "Why they started digging out again and came into our tunnels."

"What is it?" Leontine asked.

"I don't know, but we're going to find out."

Emboldened by her victory, Twylan climbed into the rough, root-lined tunnel, directing one of the light orbs to come with her. In places, she had to push aside the loose dirt to make a wide enough gap to get through, and it tumbled down onto the others as they followed. By the time she emerged into another chamber, mud and borer gore coated her from head to toe.

The cavern they emerged into was like nothing Twylan had seen underground before. It was large and smooth-sided, the walls made of dirt so neatly packed only magic could have achieved it. Beneath bright magical lights stood rows of trees and bushes with grass and flowers growing between them. It was like an underground forest, hundreds of feet below the lowest naturally growing roots.

"What is this place?" Maria raised her camera and started snapping away.

"I don't know," Twylan said. "Given how close it is to our tunnels, I should."

Someone approached through the trees, someone who

radiated an aura of magic. They had their hands raised, ready to cast. Twylan raised her hand in response, ready for a new battle.

Then she saw who it was.

"Ms. Fields?" she asked, bewildered.

Heather Fields looked at Twylan and the rest of her pupils, as well as their armed and armored companions. She appeared equally unsure about it all. "Twylan? What are you doing here?"

"We were hunting monsters. The roots from these trees disturbed them and sent them up into the tunnels. What are you doing here?"

"The Tolderai have been planting forests down here to make the world a cleaner, greener place. If no one knows about our forests, no one can object to their presence or try to cut them down."

"That's a fabulous idea!"

"Thank you." Heather smiled, but then her expression grew serious. "No one but the Tolderai knows about this place. Would you be able to keep it secret?"

"Of course. We're used to living in secret, right, Underfoots?"

The whole gang gave their hearty agreement. Heather was their teacher, perhaps the most trusted adult in their lives. Whatever she wanted, they were there for her.

"What about you?" Heather turned her attention to the Knights. "Whoever you are?"

"This is a noble thing," Maria said. "A piece of ancient forest recreated in the modern world. It is to be treasured." She frowned. "Still, it drove monsters toward the surface. How will you stop that happening again?"

"We'll work with the Underfoot Brigade to place the forests more carefully and watch out in case they wake anything else." Heather looked at Twylan. "I mean, if that's all right with you guys."

"We'll be happy to help."

"Very well." Maria reached under her body armor and pulled out a crucifix that hung on a slender chain around her neck. "I swear by my honor and by all the saints, none of us will breathe a word of what you have here." She pressed a button on her camera to delete the photos she had taken. "Not even by accident. We too live with secrets, and yours is safe with us."

CHAPTER THIRTY-FIVE

Sarah walked along the bank of Silver Lake Reservoir, her arm through Ellis's. They'd had another lovely meal out at a local burger joint this time, and in theory, she should have been enjoying a gentle stroll on a pleasant summer evening. Despite her best intentions, despite all her attempts to let go, she was still tense. She couldn't help thinking about Ellis and Maria, about the significant relationship he had been in before her, about his marriage to a glamorous, exciting Spanish photographer-slash-Knight, and about everything that represented.

"Penny for your thoughts?" Ellis held out a coin. "Technically, it ain't a penny, but I figure a quarter will do."

"They're not that exciting," Sarah said.

"Really? 'Cause you've been lost in them for ten minutes, and that ain't what I'm used to with you."

"Well, maybe you don't know me as well as you think." She said it more sharply than she meant to and immediately regretted the words as he tensed, his expression shifting from curious to hurt.

"I guess not. But I want to. Could you maybe let me know what's bothering you?"

"I don't know." She let go of his arm and looked out across the reservoir, trying to muster her thoughts. When she had been out drinking with the girls, the idea of talking to him had become simple and straightforward, the most natural thing in the world. Now, the words clogged her throat and threatened to choke her. "I'll try. Give me a minute, okay?"

"Sure thing. I'll stand here and look at... Well, at that lost creature crawling out of the water."

Sarah looked at the opposite bank. Sure enough, something was coming out of the water. It was a beast eight feet long, its front dripping and its rear shining as the light caught the edges of scales.

"What is that?" she asked.

"Lost is what it is." Ellis frowned. "I'm sorry, I do want to hear what you're thinking, but as a Silver Griffin, I should investigate."

"I'll come with you."

They pulled out their wands and hurried off around the reservoir.

Maria pushed aside the drain cover and hauled herself out into the fresh air of evening. She'd sent the rest of the Knights home hours ago while she stayed behind to talk with Heather Fields about her underground forest. Maria might have promised her silence, but that didn't mean that she would simply let the moment go and forget what she had seen. The underground forest was a beautiful thing, and she wanted to know more.

Now she pulled herself up out of the depths of the earth, miles from the safe house, covered in the blood of dead monsters and the dirt of a hidden world. At least giving her sword to Leontine meant that she wouldn't have to explain it to curious passers-by. Americans were weirdly relaxed about weapons, but she'd had enough encounters with the police back home to know how awkward such a weapon was to explain.

The sewer tunnel had brought her out next to a body of water, some sort of reservoir or lake. She pulled out her phone and was about to call for a ride when she saw something emerging from the water.

She knew as soon as she saw it that the creature didn't belong here. Its front half was a goat, and its rear was a fish. As it pulled itself out of the water, sparks flew from its hooves, even though they were beating on mud.

Creeping through the still air, Maria drew her wand. The last of the scythed borers had almost killed her. In the end, the glory of killing it had gone to Twylan, not to her. This was her chance to redeem herself, to get a kill all of her own. She would slay the beast, hide the body, and once again keep humanity safe from all that was magical.

"Drive back the darkness," she muttered the Hinterland oath to herself. "Lift the light. Hunt down the monsters. For the glory of God and a better world."

Ellis slowed down a little as he and Sarah got closer to the creature. Then he laughed.

"It's only a sea-goat," he said. "Sure, it shouldn't be here, but it ain't anything we need to worry about too much."

"Sea-goat?" Sarah asked. "A goat that goes swimming?"

At this distance, she could make out the creature's goat features at the front: its long nose, curling horns, and shaggy fur dripping with water from the reservoir. Along its body, its coat gradually gave way to scales, and instead of hind legs, its rear half tapered to an oversized fishtail.

"They're Oriceran critters," Ellis said. "Basically harmless. Problem is, they have some magic in them, and it lets them hop across the gap between worlds from time to time. Never lasts more than a few hours, which is why they've never been caught over here or settled down and started breeding. We only have to keep this thing out of sight until it jumps back home again."

As he said that, someone else appeared through the twilight and stalked toward the goat. It was hard to make out details, but they were holding a knife, its edge gleaming as if preparing to dive in and stab the beast.

"Looks like there's a 'never was' in my future." Ellis raised his wand. "Stupefacio."

Instead of slumping as the stun spell hit them, the other person raised their knife, and with a flick of the blade, countered the magic. At least that meant they were a magical. That would make covering this up much easier.

Sarah and Ellis rushed toward the sea-goat.

"Aw, no," Ellis muttered. "It's her."

"Her who?" Then Sarah also realized who she was looking at. "Maria?"

The Knight stood six feet from the sea-goat, her wand knife at the ready. She glared at them.

"This monster is mine," she said, the tunefulness of her Spanish accent at odds with the harshness of her expression. "I won't have you stealing my glory, Ellis. Not anymore."

"There's no need to kill it," he said. "It's only a dumb beast. Help us get it out of sight, and I'll forget we ever saw you here."

"I wouldn't do what you told me when we were married. What in the name of God makes you think that I will do it now?"

"I never tried to order you around then, and I ain't trying to do it now. I'm asking for your help."

"I'm telling you that this is my prey. I will have the kill."

The sea-goat tipped its head one way and the other, peering at them, then leaned over to chew on a tuft of grass protruding from the mud on the reservoir's banks. Its big eyes and innocent expression caught at Sarah's conscience.

"No," she declared. "We're not going to let you kill some innocent creature. Right, Ellis?"

"That's right."

Maria brushed a clump of muddy, blood-slicked hair from her forehead and snarled. She looked a lot less glamorous than the last time Sarah had seen her. "Fine, I'll fight you for it."

She snapped off a spell with a single word, and an arc of icy air shot toward Sarah and Ellis. Before it hit, Sarah raised a shield around them, and there was a *hiss* as snowflakes melted against the warmth of her magic.

"Stupefacio." Ellis shot his spell around the side of the

shield, but his aim was off, and Maria easily dodged it. She responded with stun spells, which the Americans countered.

"I can't believe I ever married you." Maria flung more spells their way, this time turning the mud to a swamp beneath their feet, into which they started to sink.

"I can't believe it either," Ellis agreed as Sarah levitated them out of the mud. "I sure am glad it didn't last. Some things are a dumb idea from the start, like trying to kill this poor thing. Agglutino!"

This time, his spell hit, gluing Maria's feet to the ground. While she strained to free herself, Ellis and Sarah hurried forward, leaving a trail of muddy footprints to put themselves between the sea-goat and the furious Knight.

Having freed her feet, Maria raised her wand again.

"I'll fight you both with my bare hands if I have to," she said. "The hunt is on, and honor demands that it is complete."

"In my experience, honor ends up being another word for stubbornness," Ellis said. "And stubbornness is no reason to kill anything."

A sound like a giant balloon bursting filled the air. Sarah looked around. The sea-goat was gone.

"Looks like he went home," she said. "Where does that leave your honor?"

Maria scowled and started to back off. "This is not over." She turned and ran away.

"I sure hope it is," Ellis said.

He put his wand away and turned to Sarah. "Sorry about the distraction. Seems my past life ain't done messing with us yet. I hate that it's that way, but I promise, it ain't gonna stop me being there for you whenever you need me. Now, what was on your mind before?"

Sarah looked at the trail of the sea-goat they had saved together. She watched Maria's figure disappearing into the distance, looking bedraggled and grumpy instead of exciting and glamorous. She studied Ellis, standing waiting to listen to her the moment the fight was over, a fight in which he had, without question, leapt in to side with her against his ex-wife. The past was the past, and Ellis was very much here in the present with her.

"You know what, it doesn't matter," Sarah said. "I'm over it now. Let's get back to my place, get out of these muddy clothes, and get cleaned up."

"I like that in principle, but I ain't got any clean clothes at your place, for once I'm out of these."

Sarah smiled. "Oh, I know."

CHAPTER THIRTY-SIX

Lucy and Ellis crouched on the sidewalk close to Silver Lake Reservoir, peering at the dried bloodstains around a maintenance hole cover. A few passers-by looked at them curiously, but most people were on their way to work and didn't have time to consider anyone else's eccentric behavior.

"If you saw Maria here last night, why didn't you follow her then?" Lucy asked as she tapped her wand on the dried blood.

"There were other distractions," Ellis said. "Dealing with the sea-goat, keeping Sarah safe, that kind of thing."

"Keeping her safe, huh?"

"Yes, ma'am." Ellis kept a straight face as he pulled out his phone and captured the spell that Lucy had cast. On the screen of his magic viewing app, a series of trails appeared in different colors while sigils scrolled down the side of the screen. "Looks like we were right. This here is the blood of a magical critter, probably something she was hunting in the sewers. Your spell says there might be traces of it…" He turned on the spot until the tangle of lines came together on the screen. "...that way."

They got into Lucy's SUV, and she drove them south onto the Glendale Freeway while Ellis did his best to provide directions. The spell in the app only gave a direction they should go in and a rough sense of whether they were moving closer or farther away from their target, so it was hard to plan the best route. If they had followed Ellis's pointing finger, they would have crashed through houses or taken a winding series of small streets. Instead, Lucy relied on her local knowledge to pick out roads to take them where they needed to go.

"Looks like it's heading southeast," Ellis said. "Take a left when you can."

Lucy took them off the freeway, down a short road onto Sunset Boulevard. There, they headed southeast toward Chinatown.

"Looks like we're getting closer. Better find somewhere to stop soon so we can approach on foot."

They crossed under the 110 and down a couple more streets before Lucy found a spot to park. Then they got out, checked that they had their wands accessible, and looked at the app together.

"Probably not more than a couple of blocks over." Ellis looked at Lucy. "What's the plan here?"

"Reconnaissance for now. We see if Maria's here and who she's with. If she's alone, we can try to take her in. If not..." Lucy hesitated. "Well, I guess it depends on what they're doing."

She grabbed a couple of baseball caps off the back seat to conceal their faces. It was too hot for coats or other heavy disguises, but a loose floral shirt covered her distinctive Green Lantern t-shirt, and Ellis took off his jacket and tie.

"This might be the first time I've seen you out of that uniform," Lucy said. "I've gotten so used to it that it's like looking at a different person."

"That's what I'm counting on." Ellis held up the phone. "Let's do this."

The app took them down the busy streets to a building with a restaurant on the ground floor and apartments above. They did their best to look like tourists, waving around a map Lucy had taken from her car's glove compartment while moving closer to the building. There was no sign of Maria yet, or of anyone they recognized from the Knights of the Hinterland.

"Let's try around back," Lucy suggested. "That's where you get a lot of the best evidence."

The alley behind the building was no different from those in hundreds of other working streets, except for one important detail: the sleeve of a torn and bloodstained hoodie hanging out of a dumpster.

"That's it." Ellis held his phone close to the hoodie and watched as the readings shot up. "She was here." He peered at the rest of the dumpster's contents. "Protein powders, packets from Maria's favorite coffee brand, half a croissant, packets from German smoked sausage... I think it's safe to say that the Knights are staying here."

Lucy looked up at the building. There enough space to house all the Knights they'd seen so far if they were staying in one place. If that was the case, this was far more than the two of them could handle.

"I'm going in to get a sense of the place," she said. "You stay out here and call Jackie, tell her we need all the backup we can get."

"You sure that's a good idea, going in alone?"

"It's not ideal, but I don't want the others going in blind. If there's a chance I can confirm what's happening in there, I'll take it." She pointed her wand at her feet. "Silentium."

The magic wiped away the sound of her footsteps as she walked up to the back door of the building. An unlocking spell let her in, and she headed up the stairs, wand at the ready, looking all around.

There were several floors of apartments, all facing onto the stairwell. On the second floor, the door of one of the apartments hung ajar. Lucy carefully nudged it open, barely enough for her to slip through the gap and silently walk in.

The apartment's entrance was a narrow corridor with a bathroom off to one side and a bedroom on the other. Another door, this one closed, was probably another bedroom. Ahead, the sound of classical music emerged from another room.

Lucy crept down the corridor and peered into the living room. To one side was a kitchen area and a table littered with maps and papers. Clean bowls and cutlery sat stacked by the sink with empty takeaway boxes piled neatly at the other end of the counter. Past the table, a couch and an armchair had been pushed back against the living room walls, making space in the middle of the floor. Two young men stood there on yoga mats, facing away from Lucy as they worked their way through a routine while listening to Wagner. Their swords leaned against the wall, next to a set of dumbbells. Lucy couldn't see their faces, but she was sure that she recognized them from her previous encounters with the Knights.

She raised her wand. Now, with their backs turned and their weapons out of reach, was as good a time as any to take these two down. That way, the others would have an easier fight when they arrived.

"Did you think it would be that easy?" a German voice said from behind Lucy.

Lucy turned to see Klara Schulz standing in the corridor, wand pointing straight at her.

"I'm disappointed," Schulz continued. "After the other night, I expected better of you. Now drop your wand, or I will drop you."

Lucy let her wand fall to the floor. One of the other Knights came up behind her, kicked it away beneath the table, and pulled Lucy's arms roughly behind her back. He must have had the cable ties waiting for her under his yoga mat because he slid them onto her wrists in seconds.

"Careful there, lad. If you hurt your hostage, you might lose your bargaining power."

"Who says you're a hostage?" the man said in an Irish accent.

Lucy looked at Schulz and raised an eyebrow.

"Let's not insult Agent Heron's intelligence," Schulz said. "She understands what is happening here. Unlike her American counterparts, she may even understand the history behind this, that to be a hostage has often been a place of honor, a battlefield captive valuable enough to keep for later bargaining."

"This isn't the Middle Ages anymore. If you think the

other Griffins will accept this, you have another think coming."

"I have many things coming to me, *Frau* Heron, including the Grand Master's Crown." Shulz turned her attention to the men behind Lucy. "Signal the others. The Griffins have found us. Five minutes to pack, then we evacuate the building."

Lucy tried to do the math in her head. How long would it take Jackie to pull together reinforcements and bring them here? That depended on a lot of things, like who was around, how they traveled, and the state of traffic. Five minutes might not be enough time. Maybe Lucy could buy more.

"Now you have a hostage, don't you need some demands?" she asked. "Why don't you tell me them, and I can call through to headquarters, see what they say. It'll be more convincing if they can hear my voice, proves you've caught me."

"Nice try, but I will not waste time here and now." Schulz stepped into one of the bedrooms and emerged a moment later with a bag in her hand and a long cloth container, big enough to carry a sword, slung over her back. "We can discuss your ransom once we are in a safer place."

Footsteps rushed down the stairwell, and Maria burst into the apartment, hair wet from the shower, wearing a large backpack over her sports clothes and carrying her wand.

"The Griffins are here already," she said. "Emanuel spotted them from his window."

Schulz frowned, then shoved Lucy back so that she fell onto the couch.

"We must travel fast and light," Schulz said. "Another close escape for you, agent, but we will meet again."

She waved her wand, snapped a few words in German, then ran out into the stairwell, her comrades in arms running after her.

Lucy rolled off the couch onto the floor. Through the window, she heard shouts of alarm, running footsteps, and the *crackle* of magic. She rolled under the table and managed to grab her wand with her bound hands.

"Liquesimus."

Her magic melted the cable ties. The molten plastic stung her wrists, but there was no time to worry about the pain. She pulled her hands apart, leapt to her feet, and ran out of the apartment.

By the time she reached the alley, the fight was already over. Ellis was busily ungluing himself from a wall. Jim stood guard at the alley mouth, ready to distract any mundane passers-by, while Jackie defrosted a pair of frozen Silver Griffins. There was no sign of the Knights of the Hinterland.

"They got away again." Jackie scowled.

"True, but maybe they left some clues."

Lucy headed back up to Schulz's apartment, where she started going through the papers on the kitchen table. A few minutes later, the others joined her.

"What have we got?" Jackie asked.

"Maps, tourist brochures, details of some other apartments, hire car papers…" Lucy smiled grimly. "And they somehow got hold of blueprints for LACMA's security system."

"Could mean they're planning on going in when the whole system's fired up."

"A nighttime raid?"

Jackie shrugged. "They've been there in the day. Why not at night?"

"Then I guess we'd better beef up our overnight security." Lucy smiled at Jim. "Sorry, lad, it looks like you're not going to get much sleep."

CHAPTER THIRTY-SEVEN

"Dinner time!" Lucy called from the dining room of the Heron family home. There was a thunder of feet as three hungry children rushed in, one of them followed by a half-finished robot she had been building. Charlie ambled in at a more leisurely pace and licked his lips as he settled down at the end of the table.

"This all smells delicious," he said. "What are we having?"

"I decided to cook some old favorites." Lucy took the lids off pots and pans. "We have that three-bean chili your mom used to make, hot dogs and steamed vegetables from the phase when that was all Dylan would eat, French fries with cheese and onions, like Ashley got into on that holiday in Cornwall, and some mac and cheese, the first food Eddie learned how to say."

"Wow, this is great!" Dylan grabbed the hot dogs.

"What about you?" Charlie asked. "That's something for everyone else, shouldn't there be a Lucy Heron favorite in here?"

"There is." She set one last dish on the table and a jug next to it. "Yorkshire puddings and gravy, like we used to have for Sunday lunch back home."

Ashley looked at the meal with a puzzled expression.

"This is an unusual combination," she said. "None of these things are normally served together."

"Is that a bad thing?" Lucy asked.

"I suppose not…"

"Think of it as an experiment, a chance to see what flavors might go together well."

"I like experiments." Ashley picked up a spoon and started carefully measuring out equal amounts of everything onto her plate. "But you have to be scientific."

By the time Lucy got any food, Eddie had already smeared himself with cheese sauce and was waving a hot dog in front of his nose.

"Look," he said. "I'm an elephant. This is my trunk."

"As long as you don't turn into an actual elephant, that's fine," Charlie said.

The air had been starting to sparkle around Eddie, but he let the magic fade. Better to behave himself when there was mac and cheese on the line.

"Remember that trip to the zoo last summer?" Lucy asked. "We saw real elephants then."

"And lions," Eddie said excitedly. Fragments of pasta sprayed from his mouth. "And giraffes, and hippos, and deers, and snakes, and bats."

This time, the excitement was too much. The air around him shimmered, and a lion cub replaced the small boy, then a gangling infant giraffe, a hissing snake, and finally a bat that fluttered over his chair, clutching the hot dog between its claws.

"You know the rules," Charlie said sternly.

The bat dropped its hot dog onto its plate, fluttered over to the jar on the sideboard, and turned back into a small boy. With a cheese-covered hand, Eddie grabbed a piece of paper and made his mark before adding the note to the magic jar.

"Whose turn is it to give us a quiz?" Charlie looked for a distraction from any further attempts at magic.

"Me," Dylan said.

"So it's going to be history?"

"Yes, but this time I came up with questions where you might know the answers."

"Well done on learning from past mistakes."

Dylan pulled a piece of paper from his pocket, unfolded it, and cleared his throat. "Which American president freed the slaves?"

"Abraham Lincoln," Ashley replied while carefully spreading a layer of chili over her mac and cheese.

"Which president also led Allied armies in the Second World War?"

Ashley shook her head. "I don't know this one."

"Eddie, do you know any presidents?" Charlie asked.

"Biting." Eddie bit into his hot dog, doubling down on the message.

"Do you mean Biden?"

Eddie shrugged.

"Well, I don't think it's him." Charlie tapped the side of his head. "Is it Eisenhower?"

"That's right," Dylan said. "One point to Dad."

"These are very American questions," Lucy pointed out.

"We live in America, Mom."

"Still, do you have any questions I might know the answers to?"

Dylan scanned down his list.

"Okay, this one's British. Which king had six wives and founded the Church of England?"

"Henry the Eighth."

"Bonus question, what happened to his second wife, Anne Boleyn?"

"Oh, there's a rhyme for this." Lucy gazed at the ceiling as she tried to remember. "Divorced, beheaded, died, divorced, beheaded, survived, or something like that. So I suppose she got her head lopped off, poor lass."

"That's right. Point to Mom."

"Are we keeping score now? Because if we are, I think that I should get bonus points for cooking this delicious meal."

They all laughed, and reminded of the food in front of them, set to eating again. For everybody at the table, the food brought back happy memories, whether it was Charlie remembering meals as a kid or Ashley thinking back on her holiday. Of course, Ashley was thinking about the future as well, as she experimented with food combinations, pushing forward the boundaries of culinary science. If Eddie's memories were mostly of the zoo, not the meals he'd eaten, that didn't stop him from being part of the moment.

Lucy looked around with a smile at the scene she had created. Everyone in the family seemed content. She treasured every moment with them, but these most of all: her family together, happy, harmonious.

"We used to do more things together," she said. "Walks up at the observatory, that trip to the zoo, going out to the coast on the weekend."

"We went for a walk last week," Ashley pointed out.

"Still, it would be nice to do more, don't you think?"

"Sounds good to me, honey," Charlie said. "What did you have in mind?"

Lucy hesitated. It was one thing to desire a vague sense of family contentment, quite another to come up with a specific plan.

"Well, what are the things we've most enjoyed doing together, as a family?"

This time, the quiet came from people thinking, not eating.

"I liked going to the sea," Dylan said. "Getting in the water, letting the waves wash over me."

"I thought you'd say something historic."

"I thought of that, and I love history museums, but that's something I love doing for me. For something to do as a family, a place we'll all enjoy is best."

"Oh, sweetheart, that's so thoughtful." Lucy's heart melted at her son's words.

"Sandcastles!" Eddie piled up the food on his plate like he was already at the beach and building.

"I guess that's someone else who'd like to go back to the seashore."

"Me too," Ashley said. "The hydrodynamics of waves is fascinating, and there's no better place to study it."

"Looks like we're going back to the shore then." Lucy smiled. "Has anybody got other suggestions?"

Now they were into the swing of it, and the family soon came up with all sorts of suggestions. There were places they had been walking, unusual exhibits and museums, even coffee shops and restaurants that had served memorably tasty food and drinks. Dylan turned over the sheet of paper on which he'd written his quiz and started recording all the ideas.

"It's like another part of our family history," he said. "Same as when we were looking at the photos. All these places we've been, they're part of our past and part of what makes us who we are."

"So if we go back to them, will it be like an archaeological dig?" Charlie asked. "Digging up the family bones on Long Beach or tracing our ancestors in a tub of ice cream?"

"If you descended from ice cream, you'd melt in this heat," Lucy pointed out.

"Ice cream." Eddie banged his fork against the table. "Ice cream?"

"I think we have some in the freezer, but not until you've finished your mac and cheese. Main course first, then dessert, that's the chronological order of this meal."

CHAPTER THIRTY-EIGHT

Clutching a thick file of documents in her arm, Kelly stood at the door of Applegate's office. It had been a long time since she had felt this nervous about a meeting with her boss. She was used to working with him, understood how he would react to events and how to get her way. Managing him was part of the fine art of working in the Griffins' L.A. office. Today was different. Today, her whole body was tense, and her jaw clenched so hard it ached. Because today, she had to admit that she had made a mistake years ago and that for more than a decade, a criminal had gone free.

She knocked tentatively at the door.

"Enter," Applegate shouted in response.

Kelly opened the door and walked in. Applegate was sitting behind his desk, a pile of papers in front of him. He looked up at her with a smile.

"Ah, Agent Petrie, you catch me indulging in nostalgia. I've been reading old files."

"Me too, sir." Kelly took a seat across from her boss and

forced herself to look him in the eye. "In fact, I've been digging deep into one of my first cases."

"That must have been eye-opening." Applegate chuckled. "I dread to think how my earliest case notes compare with anything I would do now. I suppose my handwriting was a little neater, as I wasn't so used to typing everything, but the sort of things I considered important, the leaps in logic and the foolish observations…" He shook his head.

"I'm afraid this goes beyond foolishness." Kelly set her file down in front of Applegate. "I made a serious mistake."

Step by step, she talked Applegate through the old Sadoul case, from the first shreds of evidence through to his arrest, but with something that had been missing when she wrote her original report: an awareness of the role of Olivier Robail. Through gritted teeth, she talked about the hints that could have led her to Robail, details that she had been blind to at the time but could now pick out with startling accuracy. From there, she went on to discuss more recent events, her fresh investigation, Sadoul's new confession, and arriving too late to question Robail. Any more information they might have learned about the case had gone with him to the grave. There would be no arrest, no imprisonment, no justice. He got away with it.

At the end, she sat back, looking not at Applegate but her hands.

"As you can see, sir, I made a serious error. I should have seen the signs, and I didn't. Without other people correcting me, the truth might never have come out. Almost no one else knows, but I thought that it was important to set the story straight. I'm ready to accept the consequences of my failure."

She fully expected to receive an angry reprimand, a demotion, a loss of responsibilities, perhaps even to be fired. That would have brought some resolution and some relief that the whole business was over and done with. Instead, there was a long silence, broken only by the rustling of papers as Applegate leafed through the file she had presented. At last, even that sound stopped. Kelly looked up to see him gazing at her with an expression that she struggled to understand.

"Are you quite done with your self-flagellation?" he asked.

Kelly blinked. "I…"

"Agent Petrie, I admire your dedication to a thorough self-critique, but you can take a good thing too far. You made a mistake. Everybody does, especially in the early part of their career. Yes, this was a serious mistake, but it was also an entirely understandable one. The signs may seem obvious in retrospect, but they were far from evident at the time. Anyone could have made this mistake. Almost anyone would have, myself included. While giving yourself this overwrought verbal beating may be emotionally satisfying, it's neither helpful nor proportionate to the situation.

"Or, to put it more succinctly, cut yourself some slack."

Kelly stared at him, still too dazed to fully process what he was saying. "But Robail, and the fraud, and…"

"Yes, yes, yes, a master criminal slipped through your fingers. That's why they're called master criminals, not apprentice criminals or third from the left in a criminal chorus. He was an expert in his craft, a man who had evaded the law for decades. You said it yourself, even

Director Kowal wasn't able to pin anything on him, and he tried.

"Was your performance perfect? That's a ridiculous question because no one is ever perfect. You brought down Sadoul and eventually extracted the truth from him. If you expect me to punish you for the fact that you didn't make a clean sweep, then you don't understand what my job is about."

Now Kelly was utterly confused. This felt like a telling-off, except that he was telling her what she *hadn't* done wrong.

"What happens now?" she asked.

"It's your case. What do you think should happen?"

Kelly considered the question. If someone else had made a mistake, she would have clamored for him to punish them. After all, that was how the world worked. Actions had to have consequences for anything to function correctly. Now, on the receiving end, that felt unnecessarily harsh. Like Applegate had said, anyone could have made this mistake. Similar errors happened in the past, and they would in the future. She had tried her hardest, she had fallen short, but that didn't mean he should punish her.

Still, something had to come out of all of this. Otherwise, the whole thing was a waste of time, and she would have spent the past week in a state of tremendous stress for no reason. You couldn't discover failure and do nothing about it, or the world would never improve.

"We should find a way to learn from this," she said. "Examine what I did and didn't do, where I could have done better, and where our procedures could have led to better results. Did I need more training, more support, access to different information? What things did I do wrong that we can teach other new Griffins not to do?"

"That's very brave of you."

"It is?"

The hint of a grin raised the corner of Applegate's mouth, a small twitch of amusement.

"You're suggesting that the Griffins as a whole, from the highest to the lowest, look at what you did wrong so we don't do it again."

"That's not what I meant." Except that it was, wasn't it? How else would everyone learn from her mistake if not by hearing about it? She slumped as she thought about the reality of that, everyone looking at her, judging her, knowing what she had done wrong. She would be a laughingstock, and she wasn't sure she liked that idea any more than she liked the idea of demotion.

"Might I make a small suggestion?" Applegate said.

"Of course, sir."

"Let's not make this all about you, eh? Instead, let's take this moment as inspiration to better learn from all our mistakes, both the ones we've made and the ones we will make. To talk about the different ways that things go wrong."

"That sounds good, sir."

"Splendid. Let's put together a group to get started." Applegate picked up his phone. "Sam? Could you send in agents Heron and Kowal? I want my finest minds gathered together."

A minute later, Lucy and Jackie walked in.

"How can we help, boss?" Jackie asked.

"Agent Petrie has discovered a mistake she made on one of her cases," Applegate said.

"I bet she has." Jackie grinned. "Do you need us to fix it?"

Kelly cringed and sank into her seat.

"Agent Petrie has already pursued that line as far as it will go. No, I want us to take this opportunity to become more open about our mistakes. As is so often said, he who does not learn from history is doomed to repeat it. I want you three to draft a process for assessing our mistakes, identifying their sources, and learning from them so that we don't do the same thing again."

"A continuous improvement program." Lucy recalled the phrase from her management training.

"Yes, why not." Applegate beamed. "Come up with a system to continuously improve, and start finding some mistakes for us to consider."

Lucy looked from him to Kelly and back. Kelly didn't know what Lucy's expression meant, but the simple presence of that scrutiny left her feeling judged. She had been found wanting, and now she had to talk about it again with her biggest rival.

"I have a mistake for us to consider already," Lucy said. "Yesterday, we tracked down the Knights of the Hinterland. I went into the building to find out more, and that gave away our presence before backup could get there. If I hadn't done that, we might have rounded them all up. Now they're on the run and still planning to make a move against the artifacts at LACMA."

For a moment, Kelly felt a wave of smug satisfaction. Lucy had made a mistake, and she would make her squirm.

Except that Lucy had only mentioned it at all because of Kelly's mistake. Her rival was throwing her a lifeline, taking off the pressure that had pressed down on her. They were in this together. Lucy was so considerate, it was infuriatingly difficult to stay annoyed at her, so Kelly shifted her attention.

"What about you, Jackie?" she asked. "Do you have something to share?"

Now that it involved hearing about other people's mistakes, Kelly started to look forward to this. Maybe hers wouldn't look so bad by comparison.

"Now's not the time to start cataloging errors," Applegate said. "The three of you should come up with a procedure for evaluating and learning from them, try it out on your examples, then report back to me. If it all looks good, we'll set up this continuous improvement program. Now, if you'll excuse me, I have other things I need to get on with."

He waved them toward the door. Kelly was the last to leave. She was reaching for the door when Applegate called after her.

"Agent Petrie, you forgot this." He held out the evidence folder on her case. As he handed it over, he looked her in the eye and lowered his voice. "Remember Kelly, this is about learning, not throwing blame. Learn from the past, don't repeat it."

CHAPTER THIRTY-NINE

"I could have come here by myself," Ashley said. "I know how to use public transport, and I'm far safer on my bike than you."

Dylan sighed and patted his sister on the head.

"You're only eight years old. That's why Mom said I had to come with you."

"It's not like you're an adult yet, and it's not like we haven't done far scarier and more difficult things before."

"Look at it this way. How many moms do you think trust their kids to go fight crime after school?"

Ashley sucked on the tip of her finger while she contemplated that question.

"I don't have the empirical data, but if forced to give an estimate, I'd say almost none."

"So maybe don't complain that I'm here to help?"

"All right."

The lights changed, and they crossed the road to the playground where they had arranged to meet with the rest of the Mini Griffins. Most of them were already there, and the ones who weren't were the ones who wouldn't make it. That was how things went when your crime-fighting team also had curfews, homework, and after-school soccer clubs to fit in.

Tommy excitedly waved as they approached.

"This is so cool!" he called. "All of us out on a mission together."

"Ssh!" Mia said. "We're supposed to be a secret team, remember? The secret won't last long if you shout about it in front of the whole world."

"It's not like I shouted 'hey, we're off to fake a haunted—'"

Mia slammed her hand across his mouth. "Seriously?"

Tommy peeled her fingers away and muttered in an embarrassed tone, "All right, I got it that time."

Ashley set down her backpack, opened it, and took out a specially adapted drone with a host of sensors protruding from its underside. Its rotors started spinning, and it lifted into the air, hovering above the playground. Ashley pulled out a tablet, tapped a control, and the drone lifted across the rooftops, flying away.

"This is so cool." Tommy peered over her shoulder at the screen. "That's the house, right?"

"Correct."

All the Mini Griffins gathered around to watch as the drone's view descended. It made a loop around the historic building, its cameras taking in the view through each window in turn, then lifted for an overview again.

"No one's around," Ashley said. "Let's go for it."

With Tommy leading the way as their local guide, they walked a few blocks to the house. Along the way, they talked about school, TV, and the other things that filled their lives, like favorite pizza toppings or which was the best ice cream.

When they reached the house, they trooped up to the front door, then looked around. Fortunately, the over-grown garden hid them from the view of any passers-by, and the others were too busy to be bothered with a bunch of kids and a rundown building.

Dylan pointed his wand at the lock. "Recludo." The bolt clicked back, the door swung open, and they walked in.

They had worked out their plan in detail before coming here, but it still took time to get set up. With a mixture of magic, brute force, and information gathered from the building's plans, they set up individual hiding spaces for all of them. Ashley installed a hidden projector in each room, while others set up speakers to her specifications. While all of that was going on, one Mini Griffin sat in the corner at all times, looking at the video feed on Ashley's tablet, keeping an eye out for any sign of their target.

"He's here!" the lookout called as Ashley finished setting up the last projector. "Coming up the street now."

Hurriedly, they flung tools and unused wires into back-packs and dove into their hiding spaces, pulling covers into place over them. Some disappeared into cupboards, others under floorboards and a few into gaps in the walls. As the last door closed, Dylan pointed the tip of his wand out of his hiding place and whispered, "Propagationem pulvis." Dust swirled for a moment around the room, then settled, hiding the footprints they had made.

The front door opened and David Bustle walked in, looking as shifty as he had the last time. He wore all black, his hood drawn up around his face, and his gaze darted from side to side as he closed the door behind him and looked around the house. Watching on the feed from a hidden camera, Ashley feared for a moment that something had gone wrong, that he had spotted some sign of their presence. Then he shrugged, set his bag down, and took out his crowbar.

"Time to get to work," Bustle said to the apparently empty house. "This place isn't going to trash itself."

He walked into the kitchen, where a faucet was dripping intermittently into the sink. Mold had sprouted around the edges, and something dark stained the wall above the cupboards. Bustle drew back the crowbar, ready to smash in the front of the oven.

Hidden in a cupboard at the back of the room, Mia waved her wand. The handle on the faucet turned, and rusty water spurted out, rebounding off the edges of the sink and spattering all around. Bustle jumped, looked around, and sagged in relief.

"Lousy cheap faucets," he muttered while turning off the water.

Another twitch of the wand. The other handle turned, and water sprayed out again, hitting Bustle this time.

"Aw, come on!" He turned that handle back too, then shook off the water. A brown stain marred the front of his black top.

Deciding that the kitchen was too much hassle for now, he walked out into the hallway and trudged up the stairs. Straight ahead was the master bedroom with a rusty bed frame still sitting in the center of the room. Ancient springs creaked as he set his bag down on the bed, and he hefted his crowbar, ready to tear chunks from the plaster of the walls.

Another creak made him look around. The bed had lifted three inches into the air and was levitating above the dusty floorboards.

"What the..." He got close to the floor and waved his crowbar through the space underneath one of the bed's legs. "This isn't possible." He looked around. "Who's doing this?"

Ashley hit a button on her tablet while Tommy waved his wand in the bedroom closet, and the daylight faded from the room.

In the darkness, a figure appeared, projected by Ashley's gadgets. The woman wore white rags. Her face was wrinkled and pale with dark, sunken eye sockets. Even Lucy Heron's closest friends might not have recognized that the video was of her, with so much face paint disguising the figure underneath.

"Wooooooh!" The apparition waved her arms. "I am the ghost of old Mrs. Dunsinane. I have haunted this house for eighty years, looking for someone to take my place. Will it be you?"

"This ain't funny." Bustle backed up against the wall. He held his crowbar out as if using it to hold the ghost back. His eyes were wide, his jaw trembling. "I don't know who's doing this, but you stop right now, you hear?"

"Wooooohooooohhh! This house contains me. It is my prison. If it is destroyed, I will be released, freed to haunt whoever destroys my home. My home. My home, wooooooh!"

From his hiding place on the landing, Dylan stifled a

laugh and watched the proceedings through the open bedroom doorway. His mom had gone to town when they were making the video the previous night. At the time, he'd worried that no one could ever take this seriously, but Bustle was quivering with fear, his voice cracking as he responded.

"You can't be real," the property developer said. "You're a trick, some clever bit of electronics. I don't know why you're doing this, but—"

As Dylan waved his wand, the crowbar lifted from Bustle's hand and floated across the room. It spun through the air, then slammed down, its pointed tip first, tearing through Bustle's bag of tools, the rusted bed frame, and into the floorboard below.

"Aaah!"

Bustle screamed and ran for the door. At the top of the stairs, he skidded to a halt. Another version of the ghostly image had appeared in front of him, floating above the steps.

"I see you, David Bustle. I see your plans for my home. I will haunt you, David, haunt you until your dying day. Wooooh. Woooohoooooo!"

Bustle screamed so loud that the sound rattled the windows and scared birds out of their nests in the half-collapsed roof.

Dylan waved his wand again. This time, he levitated Bustle himself, lifting the shrieking man out over the stairs, straight toward the outstretched arms of the ghost.

"Hold me, David! Let me haunt you forever."

"Noooo!"

"Then leave, sell this place to someone who will care for

it, and never come back. Because I know your touch now, David Bustle..." The insubstantial image of fingers caressed Bustle's cheek. "...and if you ever return, you will be mine."

Dylan brought Bustle down to the floor with a *thump*. The projectors switched off, the lights rose, and Bustle was left pale and shivering in the hallway. It took him all of two seconds to wrench the door open and run out, sprinting away down the street.

Dylan gave his wand one last flick, closing the door. Then the hidden Mini Griffins emerged, laughing and grinning.

"That was brilliant!" said Tommy. "Can we do it again at Halloween, convince people there is a ghost here?"

"And risk angering the real spirit?" Mia waved her hands in the air. "Woooohoooo!"

They all laughed again, except for Ashley. As often happened, she was the serious member of the group.

"We won't do this at Halloween," she said. "Too much risk of someone realizing what we did."

"We should at least write it up," Tommy said. "Part of the Mini Griffin chronicles."

"No need, I caught it all on video."

"Oh." He looked disappointed, now that the moment was over.

"The good thing about video is we can watch it," Dylan pointed out. "Why don't you all come back to Mini Griffins HQ? We'll have milk and Mom's homemade cookies and watch our victory one more time."

They all cheered, then went to gather Ashley's devices before heading home to celebrate.

CHAPTER FORTY

Lucy arrived home early and let herself into the house. She'd had a few long days recently and been given the afternoon off in return, freeing up some time for house-work while the kids were at school and nursery. Of course, the house wasn't empty, and Buddy waddled up as she walked through the door, wagging his tail and looking up at her with his tongue hanging out.

"Hi there, mate." She bent to pat his head. "How's your day going?"

Buddy barked and licked her hand. He always appreci-ated it when his pet humans came home.

Lucy walked into the living room and stopped, puzzled. The place had been tidy when she left this morning, but now it was scattered with bits of paper that, on closer inspection, turned out to be the edges of photos. In the dining room, a collection of family mementos sat on the table, including shells from beach holidays, a ticket from her first flight out to the States, and a medal Ashley had won in a science contest. What were they all doing there?

From the back yard came the distinct rasping sound of someone sawing wood. Lucy followed the noise out the back door.

Charlie stood on the patio, a saw in his hand and sawdust around his feet, a collapsible workbench set up in front of him. He'd clamped a length of wood to it and had a chunk from the end in his other hand. Their neighbor Al, gray-haired and with weatherbeaten skin from years of outdoor work and leisure, was steadying the bench. They both greeted Lucy with smiles.

"What are you doing home already?" Charlie asked.

"Afternoon off in lieu. And you?"

"Same thing. I was in late the other day dealing with a, um, special bug." Charlie glanced at Al, then back at Lucy, and waggled his eyebrows. If Al noticed the not-so-subtle signal, he didn't mention it.

"That's great, sweetheart. Now, why don't you tell me what on earth you're doing?"

Charlie set aside the saw and placed the piece of wood with others like it.

"You know how we've been talking recently about happy memories?"

"I suppose we have, yes."

"Well, that got me thinking. We have so many of them, but they're not out for people to see. The photos are on our computers. We stashed the mementos in boxes. All those wonderful moments are sitting in the dark. I thought it would be nice to have them out, a reminder of our life together, so I'm building a display piece to go in the dining room."

"That's lovely, sweetheart, but how do I put this…"

"I'm bad at carpentry."

"That's not what I was going to say."

"It's what you were thinking, and you wouldn't be wrong. That's why I got Al to help. He knows what he's doing."

Al rolled his eyes. "I saw him out here, ruining perfectly good wood, and I couldn't help myself."

Lucy laughed. "It's kind of you to help."

"Well, it was this or go fishing, and I went fishing yesterday. Besides, I enjoy a good bit of carpentry. Fitting a neat joint, slotting the pieces together, making something you can use, or that'll make your home more beautiful."

"Well, now that I'm here, can I help too?"

"Of course!"

Under Al's careful tutelage, they measured and cut strips of wood, sanded down rough edges, and carefully carved joints into the ends and along the length of their chosen planks. Given Charlie's history in this area, Lucy did the more detailed work with Al overseeing them both and correcting when things were in danger of going wrong.

"This is more fun than I expected," Lucy admitted as she chiseled away a small chunk of wood to make a join match more neatly. "I mean, the result will be lovely regardless, but I'm enjoying the process."

"I told you carpentry was fun." Al was neatening up some other pieces, creating a perfect fit for a crucial joint. He did everything four times as fast as the others and ten times as precisely, thanks to decades of experience. He never boasted about it, instead offering helpful advice to improve the others' work. "You hear about Esther Romano?"

"What about her?" Lucy asked.

"Rumor is, people have seen her around town with her hairdresser."

"Nice that she's made a new friend," Charlie commented.

Lucy and Al exchanged a look. Apparently, Charlie didn't understand the nuance of gossip.

"Is this Chantelle?" Lucy asked. "I didn't think Esther's boat floated that way."

"Not Chantelle, the boss. What's his name?"

"Karl?"

"That's the one. Closer to Esther's age and style."

"Well, she does spend a lot of time in the hair salon. If she was going to meet someone, that was the most likely place."

"Oh, you mean they're dating!" Charlie looked up from his work.

"Yes, dear, that's it." Lucy patted him on the head.

Talking like this made Lucy realize how long it was since she'd gossiped with Esther or even with Al. Life had been so busy lately with one magical crisis after another that it seemed she was missing all the important events in her immediate environment. Not important on a Silver Griffins scale, of course, but they were to the people around her. She'd been so swept up in the big events that she'd missed the personal ones. She needed to catch up before those details vanished into the past.

"How about you, Al? What have you been up to?"

"Oh, you know, same old same old. Though the other

day, I got a catch you wouldn't believe…"

They talked about DIY and fishing, who was dating who in the neighborhood, who had bought a new car or gotten a new job, while the afternoon drifted by and the pieces of wood piled up. The design for the display stand was Charlie's concept, but Al had turned it into something workable and shown him how the pieces could best fit. Together, they had dreamed up something that Lucy thought would look lovely in the end, with shelves of different shapes and sizes to take pictures and mementos.

Once the wood was all cut, they slotted it together with a little glue to hold everything firmly in position.

"These joints should lock by themselves," Al said, "but it's good to be more secure when you have kids rushing around the place." He was kind enough not to mention that joints cut by Lucy and Charlie might also be less secure than his. "Now, where's the varnish?"

"Varnish?" Charlie looked at him in surprise. "I didn't think of that."

"Well, how were you going to finish it?"

Charlie shrugged sheepishly. "With wood?"

"I like it how it is," Lucy said. "There's something nice and simple about bare wood. Let's set it up like this. We can always take it down and varnish it another day."

Al glanced at his watch. "I should probably get going. I'm supposed to do the shopping today and cook dinner."

"Go on then, scram." Lucy smiled. "Thanks so much for your help."

She and Charlie took the display stand inside and hung it up in the dining room. It took a few goes to get the nails in the right places on the wall so it sat straight, but they got there in the end. Then they took the photos and mementos and put them carefully into their places. Pictures of the kids smiled out from behind holiday souvenirs. There were friends and relatives, tickets from special places and events, and a postcard of the painting they had been looking at when they first met. In the middle was a space the perfect shape and size for a photo of the two of them on their wedding day.

They took a step back and looked at what they had made. Lucy wrapped an arm around her husband's waist, and he draped his across her shoulders. They smiled as they held each other close.

"It's brilliant," she said. "Another wonderful plan from you, my carpentry genius."

"If I'm a carpentry genius, does that mean I'm allowed to put shelves up again?"

"Let's not get carried away." She stretched up, kissed him on the cheek, and disentangled herself from his arm. "Just one more thing to make it perfect."

She went out into the yard and looked around on the ground by the workbench. She picked up a pale and curling piece of wood, shaved off the edge of a plank to make it fit, took it inside, and laid it on the shelf in front of their wedding photo.

"A reminder of today," she said. "Of how it's not only our past that holds us together, it's our present, the way we keep finding new things together." She kissed him on the lips, and for a long moment, the world faded away, leaving only the two of them. "Now we'd better get out there and put those tools away. I don't want Eddie trying to play with a saw."

CHAPTER FORTY-ONE

Jackie sat in her car, looking up the street toward the doors of the private clinic. In honor of the stakeout, she had brought coffee and donuts to get the full cop movie feel. That element of absurdity helped take the edge off a tense situation. Plus, this was Twylan's first stakeout, and she wanted to mark the occasion.

Next to her, Uncle Harold sat with his hands clenched around his coffee cup. The jiggling of his knee gave away the tension beneath his usual calm, confident demeanor. The cardboard cup crumpled slightly beneath the pressure of his fingers.

"Are you certain about this?" he asked for the third time.

"About what?" Jackie asked. "My lead, or bringing you along to pursue it? Because if I'm honest, I have doubts about both."

"I was talking about the lead," Uncle Harold said stiffly. "Do you think it's likely to pay off?"

"The evidence was there in the Knights' safe house."

Jackie set her coffee cup down to count things off on her fingers. "First, the drug packets hidden deep in the trash. Someone there is going through some serious treatment. Second, the business card down the back of Schulz's bed. She's been talking to a doctor here in L.A., which means that it couldn't wait until she gets home. Third, that note scrawled on a corner of a map. That part's a stretch, I'll admit, but the initials match one of the doctors at this clinic, and the date and time are now. I think she had to jot that down in a hurry while talking on the phone, and the corner of that map was the first piece of paper that came to hand. Without the other evidence, it would have been meaningless but put it all together, and here we are."

She pointed toward the clinic's doors, a discreet private practice specializing in managing long-term illness.

"You have doubts about me too?" Harold asked, his voice brittle.

Jackie sighed. It was hard to deal with him like this, tense and defensive. She felt like she'd lost the fun, bombastic uncle she loved, and she hoped that he came back soon. If she'd given him the answer he wanted to hear, that she had every confidence in him, that he could still take on the world, then maybe that man would have returned, but it wouldn't have been an honest approach.

"Schulz beat you before. She could beat you again. I'm not going to pretend otherwise, but I didn't want to leave you out of this either."

"If you have so little confidence in my ability to beat her, why didn't you bring more of the Griffins?"

"Because I want to avoid drawing attention and because I think she's going to be alone. Schulz is proud, like you, and I know you don't like to tell people about your health troubles."

"I don't have health troubles."

"Tell that to your liver. Anyway, I'm counting on Schulz wanting to keep this secret from her colleagues. That means coming here alone, and that means we have a chance to take her down without giving away our presence with a big mob of Griffins."

"A mob that would have excluded me as a retired former agent."

Jackie sipped her coffee. "I don't know what you mean."

Her uncle finally looked at her. "Thank you, Jack-Jack."

A rear door opened and Twylan climbed into the back seat.

"She's there," the younger witch said. "Just came out of the doctor's office into reception."

"Then it's time." Jackie set her coffee aside and checked that her wand was readily accessible in her pocket. "Everybody ready?"

"Maybe, but…"

"What is it, Twylan?"

"The Underfoots, we've met these Knights. We've been hunting monsters with them. They seem like good people. Do we need to arrest their leader?"

"Even the worst people can seem good when they need to. Remember, they're thieves who have been trying to steal treasure and using magic to do it. It's our job to stop that."

"I suppose."

They climbed out of the car. Twylan and Jackie

approached the clinic's door while Harold set off down a quiet side street.

The clinic door opened and Schulz walked out. She saw Jackie and reached around her back toward a wand hidden beneath her t-shirt. "I know you. You're with the Griffins."

"I'm not alone." Jackie nodded at Twylan, who was moving around to flank Schulz.

"How did you find me?"

"The cancer. For what it's worth, I'm sorry."

Schulz shrugged. "I chose a hunt that led me into the land around Chernobyl. I accept the consequences."

"As I said, I'm sorry, but that won't stop me from taking you down if I have to."

"You would fight me at a place of healing? Have you no honor?"

"There's not a lot of call for it in my job, but I'd still like to avoid a fight here, with civilians passing by." Jackie nodded toward the side street. "Let's take this somewhere quieter. Then you can resist arrest for as long as our honor demands."

Head held high, Schulz walked down the street Jackie had indicated. Jackie and Twylan followed her. It was a quiet area, little more than a back alley between shops and offices, the only witness a rat rummaging through some trash. Uncle Harold stood halfway down the street, wand in hand.

"Kowal." Schulz drew her wand. "I should have known you would be behind this."

"Not me," Harold said. "My niece, Agent 782, Jackie Kowal. I'm very proud of her. My skills might be fading, but she will carry on our family's proud tradition of bringing magicals to justice. Magicals like you."

"You call this justice, trapping me in an alleyway outside a cancer clinic?"

"You think it's honorable to rob public museums?"

"When they have what is ours, yes I do."

"Then you and I have a very different view of honor." Uncle Harold raised his wand. "Shall we?"

Schulz looked over her shoulder. "Three against one. That hardly seems fair."

Uncle Harold gave Jackie a pleading look, and she felt a sadness she couldn't resist. This was the climax of his story, the end of a long history between him and Schulz. It would be cruel to rob him of the moment, whatever common sense or the Silver Griffins' operating manual said. Maybe this would turn into one more error for the improvement project, but she had to risk it for his sake.

"Fine," she said. "Have your duel. Twylan and I will be here waiting, whoever wins."

Schulz shifted, one leg going forward, finding her point of balance. The tip of her dagger wand gleamed as she pointed it at Uncle Harold. He shifted too, his fighting stance reminding Jackie that he had once been young, vital, and ready to take on the world.

Then their wands flashed, and the duel began.

The first spells collided in the middle of the street, a flash of light and power as they canceled each other out. Schulz was quicker to fire a second, glue engulfing Harold's foot, sticking him in place. He didn't try to free himself although Schulz was advancing, moving to get around him while he was stuck. Instead, he counter-attacked, flinging a dumpster at her with a levitation spell. Schulz leapt, but not quite high enough, and the dumpster knocked her legs. She fell, rolled, and came back to her feet as Harold blasted away the glue with a water spell.

The leg of Harold's pants dripped as he turned to face Schulz once more. A banana peel, flung out of the dumpster as it hit the wall, hung from her shoulder. They didn't care about these tiny indignities. They were too focused on the fight.

Schulz chanted and shifted her wand. Three spells shot out in quick succession, and Harold countered every one so fast that Jackie didn't even see what the spells were. Schulz's flurry of magic had put Harold on the defensive, and he backed away, flinging up shields and counterspells to deal with everything she sent his way. Within seconds, he pressed against the wall, his movements restricted, while Schulz swung from side to side, flinging magic at him from left and right, forcing him to respond to her.

Jackie could see that her uncle was growing tired, his hand trembling, his spells growing weaker. She clenched her wand tight. She desperately wanted to help, but she had promised him his duel. How would he feel if she leapt in to protect him now?

Schulz could see his weakness as well. She grinned as she closed in, wand flashing from side to side, its deadly tip coming ever closer. Her sickness did nothing to slow her down. She was as ferocious and determined as she had ever been.

Suddenly, Harold dropped. Jackie hadn't seen a spell hit him, and for one terrifying moment she thought that he must have suffered a heart attack, his body giving up under the pressure of the fight.

But he didn't fall to the ground. Instead, he rolled in a moment of surprising athletic grace, a moment from his lost youth. As he moved under Schulz's arm, magic flashed from his wand.

"Stupefacio!"

Schulz staggered, stunned, across the street. Harold leapt to his feet, wincing as his bad knee almost gave way under him but kept his footing. He slapped the wand from her hand and pointed his at her head, waiting for her to recover her senses.

With a blink and a head shake, Schulz recovered. She stared at her empty hand, at the wand pointing her way, and at Harold Kowal, his face wrinkled, struggling to catch his breath. He might not be the man she remembered, but he was still a deadly opponent.

"Well fought." She raised her hands. "Now what?"

"Now we take you into custody," Jackie said. "And you tell us where we can find the rest of the Knights of the Hinterland."

"I will never betray my comrades in arms. My time may have passed, but their glory lies ahead of them."

"Maybe," Harold said. "Or maybe this new generation of Silver Griffins will manage to do what I didn't and finish off your Order. What do you think, Schulz, is history going to repeat itself or is there a change coming?"

She looked at Jackie and Twylan, then shrugged sadly.

"It is not my place to say. The story is someone else's now."

CHAPTER FORTY-TWO

"This is it." Leontine pointed at the utility cover above their heads. "The closest tunnel entrance to the museum."

Maria clasped his hand. "Thank you for this. I know it was not an easy decision."

Leontine looked around at the other Knights of the Hinterland, their faces illuminated by the soft glow of magic spells.

"I like Lucy and the Silver Griffins," he said. "I like you guys too. You helped us hunt the borers to make our home safe again. I owe you this one."

He hurried off into the darkness, leaving the Knights alone.

"Are you sure about this?" one of them asked. "We don't have Klara or Oskar anymore. Maybe we should go home, leave the crown, go back to hunting monsters in the forests."

"No!" Maria snapped. "Chancellor Schulz gave up her freedom to bring us to this point. Oskar did the same. Would you dishonor them by abandoning their quest?"

"No, but..."

"There is no 'but.' The Grand Master's Crown belongs to the Order. It will be ours again, and in reclaiming it, we will show our courage and strength. Remember your oath."

"Drive back the darkness," the Knights chanted in unison. "Lift the light. Hunt down the monsters. For the glory of God and a better world."

Several of them crossed themselves or touched the crucifixes they wore under their body armor. All wore looks of determination.

"A better world," Maria repeated. "Let us make it happen."

She pulled a small laptop from her bag, opened it, and hit a key.

"That's it," she said. "The bot attack on the security company's systems has been launched. They will be busy for hours, distracted and uncertain, unable to respond if they notice what we are doing here. You all know your tasks?" The Knights nodded. "Then let us get to it."

She set aside the computer and opened the cover, then climbed out into the street. The other Knights followed her, their dark gray clothes helping to hide them in the darkness. It was past two in the morning, the city as quiet as it would ever be. Unseen, they hurried across the street toward the entrance of the Los Angeles County Museum of Art.

A few of the Knights dashed ahead of the rest. They didn't stop when they reached the building but kept up their momentum, using a mixture of magic and parkour to scramble up the walls. They grabbed security cameras, pulled wires from the back, and dropped black cotton hoods over their lenses, ensuring that what followed would go unseen. Others stood with plans of the building's security systems in their hands, wands waving over the diagrams, sending magical blades to cut wires on alarms around the building, or at least to cut the places where the cables should be.

This was the biggest risk to Maria's plan: change. If the systems had changed too much from their original design, the blueprints the Knights worked from would be useless. Instead of cutting critical wires, they would cut empty air, leaving the wires intact. She had factored in backups such as distracting the security company for when something inevitably went wrong, but if history had taught her anything, it was that you could never prepare for everything.

Approaching the museum's doors, she waved her wand. "Recludo."

Despite everything, she half-expected an alarm to sound and lights to flash, but they didn't. The locks clicked back, and she pushed the door open.

"Hey!" A surprised-looking security guard hurried down a corridor toward her with a flashlight in one hand and a radio in the other. "What are you doing here?"

"Dormio." Maria waved her wand, and the guard fell to the floor. He started to snore almost immediately. "Get him out of the way."

Two Knights grabbed the fallen guard and carried him away to have a long nap in a toilet stall. He would wake up confused but unhurt, unable to explain how he had slept through the museum being robbed. Perhaps he would lose his job over it, but Maria didn't give that much thought. Something more important was at stake.

The Knights spread out through the museum, disabling security systems and securing entrances. They moved like a military unit, covering each other's backs, using hand signals to communicate their intentions silently. Though their Order might have its roots in medieval warfare, they had learned from modern ways of fighting too. Time had not stood still, and neither had the Knights of the Hinterland.

Maria brought two other Knights with her and headed for the gallery where the Trakai Hoard was on display. The route was familiar, as it was supposed to be. Days spent reading, viewing materials about the museum, and walking around in the guise of a tourist had prepared her for this moment. Half of any victory came from preparation, and she had worked hard to make sure they won.

The uniformed security guard wasn't the only person in the building. As Maria and her comrades crept up to the Hoard's hall, they saw two wizards standing in the doorway, holding a whispered conversation over a phone screen. One of them laughed as he pointed at something on it, and the other one shook his head. Then he looked up and saw Maria.

"Hey, what are you—"

"Stupefacio!" The spell shot from Maria's wand and one of the wizards fell.

The other one, dressed in shorts and a baggy t-shirt, whipped out his wand and countered the spells from the Knights. He backed into the hall, phone in hand, frantically tapping on the screen with his thumb.

"Come on, come on, come on," he muttered as his wand swung back and forth, stopping spells right before they hit him.

Maria charged, running in low to tackle the guy around the waist. Her shoulder slammed into his gut, and she flung him to the floor, knocking the breath out of him. His phone slid across the floor in one direction, his wand in another. He swung a punch at Maria, but it was a pitiful blow. She caught his fist, twisted his arm back, and delivered a blow of her own, knocking him out cold.

"The phone," she snapped.

One of the other Knights already had it. "He was trying to call the Silver Griffins' headquarters."

"Did he get through?"

"No. The phone signal in here is bad. He was still trying to connect."

Maria almost laughed. How many times had she moaned about a poor cellphone signal, and now it had come to her rescue. She rolled the Griffin over, bound his hands with cable ties, then dragged him to a corner of the room. It was a lousy way to treat a valiant opponent and a worse way to secure an important prisoner, but they weren't here to take captives. All that mattered was the crown.

There it stood, on a pedestal in the middle of the room. The museum's curators understood that it had beauty and value, but they clearly didn't understand its importance. They had treated it with no more reverence than the rest of the Hoard, standing it on the same sort of plinth as crucifixes, bowls, and candlesticks, as if simply being ancient made them equal. However, this was the Grand

Master's Crown, used to appoint a true Master of the Hinterland. Without it, the Knights had been diminished, but soon they would return to their true power, and Maria was leading them to that goal.

The light gleaming off the crown's gems drew her, and it was tempting to simply snatch it. Still, she knew better than that. Her opponents had shown that they were cunning and gifted magic users.

"Revelare." She waved her wand and particles of magic fell across the room like glowing dust. They clung wherever there were spells or wards, revealing the defenses the Silver Griffins had put in place.

While the others stood guard at the entrances, Maria made her way across the gallery, sidestepping magical traps and alarms. As she approached the pedestal, there were spells she couldn't move around. She carefully unpicked them with her wand, detaching one strand of magic at a time. Who knew what other spells the Griffins had tied to these? This was no time for brute force.

Piece by piece, the first alarm ward fell apart. Maria stepped through the gap and examined the next spell.

"Time?" she asked.

"Ten past three," one of the Knights replied.

This was taking too long. They needed to be out of here before the city stirred. Maria's heart raced, but she kept her hand steady as she started dismantling the magic. Sure enough, she quickly found a hidden strand, one that would have triggered a freeze trap if she had used a simple counterspell to blast through this. Here was another, connected to an electronic alarm, of all things. Whoever had built this was a master in combining magic and technology. Now wasn't the time to stop and admire the craftsmanship. She unraveled the spell, severed the wires on the alarm, and finally made it through to the pedestal.

She was inches from the crown, so close that the light refracting through its jewels scattered across her cheeks, red as drops of blood. She couldn't take it yet. One more spell bound it to the top of the pedestal. The inevitable trap, a classic that no one could resist: the *Raiders of the Lost Ark* weight trap.

Maria detached a pouch from her belt. There was no need to test and adjust its weight, as Indiana Jones had done. The Knights knew everything about the crown and had prepared this bag to match it ounce for ounce.

She put one hand on the crown and held the bag next to it. Then, in a single deft movement, she slid the crown off the pedestal and the bag into its place.

For a minute, the whole world seemed to hold its breath. However, there were no alarms, no balls of stone rolling out of the ceiling. She had her prize.

Still moving carefully to avoid the remaining magic, she stepped away from the Trakai Hoard. At the entrance to the gallery, she held up the crown. Its power was unmistakable, both the magic throbbing in her hands and the sense of authority this circle of metal represented. She could put it on now, take her place as Grand Master. After all, who else would it be, now that Schulz and von Konigsberg were gone? The crown whispered to her, urging her to embrace her moment.

No. It was not her place to decide who led. Perhaps the Order would choose her, but such a historic decision should not fall to one woman.

With trembling hands, she slid the crown into her backpack and zipped it shut.

"Time to go."

Before she could move, one of the other Knights rushed down the corridor, her wand in her hand.

"The Griffins," she exclaimed. "The Silver Griffins are here!"

CHAPTER FORTY-THREE

Lucy emerged from a portal in front of the museum and ran toward the doors. Jackie, Kelly, and Twylan were with her. Other Griffins would be coming out of portals at the museum's other exits and on the roof, to cut off the Knights' escape routes. She hoped they weren't too late.

It was fifteen minutes since Jim had been due to call in with his hourly update. Fifteen minutes for the duty Griffins to get through to her, for calls to go out to others on the team, for everybody to wake up, find their pants, grab their wands, and get out here. Was that fifteen minutes too long? Would the Knights already have escaped, taking the stolen crown with them?

As they dashed toward the museum's doors, she saw her answer: a wizard and a witch, both dressed in loose, dark clothes with dagger-shaped wands gleaming in their hands. This wasn't over yet.

"Refrigero!" the wizard called, and a blast of icy air shot at the Griffins.

"Contego!" Lucy flung up a magical shield around herself and her colleagues. The freeze spell burst harmlessly across the barrier, and they kept running.

Kelly and Jackie flung spells ahead of them. The Knights countered and held their ground, waiting inside the museum's entrance, turning that gap into a bottleneck. More of them were coming from inside, but so were more Griffins, as they were woken up and sprang into action.

As they reached the open doors, Lucy let her shield drop and flung herself at one of the Knights. The two of them tumbled in the corridor, grappling and shoving as they each tried to pin the other to the floor. Lucy tried to turn her wand to point it at her opponent's body, but he twisted, grabbed her arm, and pinned her face down to the floor.

"For the glory of—oof!"

Jackie slammed into him, and he skidded away across the polished surface. Even reeling from that blow, he brought his wand up and shot a glue spell, sticking Jackie in place.

"Leave these to us," Jackie said. "Go make sure the crown is secure."

Lucy scrambled to her feet and ran down the corridor. Ahead of her, at the entrance to the Hoard's gallery, stood three of the Knights: two wizards and the Spanish witch Maria.

"Form to contain in bonds of chain," Lucy chanted.

Chains shot from the end of her wand and struck one of the wizards, wrapping themselves around him. Before Lucy could tighten those bonds, the others flung spells at her, and she had to leap aside to dodge them. She brought up a shield, and there were flashes of light as more spells burst against it. Her protection was strong, but so was the well-practiced magic of the Knights, and she could see the shield starting to crumble already.

Someone else flung a spell past Lucy, and the second wizard slammed back against the wall.

"Twylan?" Maria exclaimed. "What are you doing here?"

"You said you were monster hunters," Twylan said, "not thieves."

"Is it theft to take back what was ours?" Maria said. "What was stolen from us?" She held up her backpack, and the points of the crown pressed against its synthetic cloth. "This does not belong in a museum."

She waved her wand and shouted a spell. Twylan countered one freezing bolt, but another struck her shoulder, spinning her around and freezing her wand arm.

Lucy charged, flinging spells ahead of her. Maria's wand danced through the air, as swift and purposeful as a fencer's blade, her counterspells skewering each attack as it came in. The air was thick with magical power.

Lucy slammed into Maria, aiming to knock her down, as she had the wizard at the entrance. Maria swiveled as Lucy hit, stuck out a leg to trip her, and shoved her to make sure she went down. Lucy fell past the Knight, but as she went, she grabbed the strap of the backpack and wrenched it from the Knight's hands. The bag skidded across the gallery floor and between the pedestals, triggering magical traps as it went. Freezes, stuns, and sleeps flew harmlessly through the air while lights flashed and an alarm wailed.

Maria ran after the bag. She tried to kick Lucy as she passed, but Lucy grabbed her foot, and Maria fell, sliding across the floor. Her momentum carried her through one of the wards. A spell missed her by an inch, freezing the surface where her hip had been a moment before. She slammed into one of the pedestals. A medieval candlestick wobbled, then fell, setting off more spells as it hit the floor with a resounding *clang*.

Lucy got to her feet again and ran after the bag. The cacophony of alarms grew, and spells flew at her as she ran through the wards, but she fended them off with a flurry of her magic and reached for the bag.

"Refrigero!" Maria was on one knee, wand raised. Lucy tried to counter the spell, but she was a moment too slow. Ice gripped hold, freezing her in place.

Maria stumbled over, one hand rubbing the back of her head, and grabbed the backpack, inches from Lucy's frozen fingers. All Lucy could do was watch as the other woman snatched it away.

"Well, ain't this the darnedest thing." Ellis's voice rolled across the room, his southern drawl a low note against the shrill sound of the alarms. "I swear, I see you more now than when we were married."

Maria stiffened and turned to face him. He stood in the doorway, wand at the ready. Hauled out of bed in the small hours, for once, he wasn't wearing a tie with his suit.

"You just have to keep proving you're better, don't you?" Maria said.

"Maybe that's because I am."

"And you wondered why our marriage didn't work."

She spat out a spell and a whirlwind formed in front of

313

her, then rolled across the room toward Ellis. Its outer edges caught his jacket, flapping it around him, and forced him back before the wind could snatch him off his feet. Maria followed the wind as it headed out the doors and down the corridor, snatching paintings off the wall as it made for the museum's exit.

By the Hoard, Lucy strained against the ice holding her. It was like trying to push through a brick wall, but she kept going, determined to break free. There was a *ping* as a crack spread down one finger, then a *tap* as a piece of ice fell to the floor. Another followed, and another, until she could wiggle her fingers around her wand.

"Calor," she whispered between frozen lips and chattering teeth.

Warmth spread through her hand and out. The ice started to melt, dripping from her fingers, her hand, her arm, and out across her body as the heat spread. She flexed her legs and chunks of ice fell away. Dripping wet but no longer frozen, she rushed out the doors and after Maria.

The whirlwind had pushed the other Silver Griffins back, out of the museum and into the street. It now hovered in the entrance, rattling the windows and tossing the contents of a trash can around. Behind it, Maria was fixing her backpack in place, ready to make a run for safety.

"Nice try," Lucy said, "but it's not over yet."

"Madre de Dios." Maria shook her head. "Don't you ever give up?"

"Do you?"

"Never."

"Looks like we're going to have to fight this one out, then."

"Looks that way."

Maria's wand twitched. Before she saw what was coming, Lucy launched a counterspell. Magic shot back and forth between them as each witch tried to get past the other's defenses and gain a moment's advantage. The magical wind roared, and their hair flew around their heads as the air filled with the scent of magic.

"You'll never get away with this." Lucy shouted to be heard over the rising wind and the alarms still ringing in the nearby gallery.

"You'll never stop me."

Another flash, more magic evaporating. Sweat beaded both their brows as they strained for any advantage.

Twylan stepped out of a corridor. Magic flew like lightning from her eyes.

"Stop," she called. "Please, both of you."

Neither could stop while the other was still standing. The magic kept flying, deflected spells freezing and burning the walls.

"I mean it!" Twylan raised her hands. Magic poured out with her words. Lucy felt a pull. Then her wand was wrenched from her hand. At the same moment, Maria's shot from between her fingers. They flew into Twylan's hands, and the girl sank to her knees, exhausted from the effort of breaking through the defenses of such powerful women.

"It doesn't have to be this way," Twylan said. "You both want to make a better world. Can't you do that together?"

"The crown is ours." Maria clutched her backpack tight. "We need to crown a Grand Master to regain the power we have lost."

Through the wind and the windows, Lucy saw Griffins and Knights fighting each other to a standstill. Twylan was right. There had to be a better way.

"What if you could borrow the crown?" she asked. "To create a new Grand Master?"

"Why should we borrow what is ours?"

"Forget about ownership. You want a coronation. Other people want to see this amazing work of art. What if we could have it both ways? What if you could have your coronation and leave the crown on display?"

"This is not a one-time thing. We will have other ceremonies, other leaders to crown."

"Then we'll arrange that too. You stop trying to steal it, and in return, you get access when you need it, arranged by the Silver Griffins. What do you say?"

"It is not stealing!"

"But is it the best fight you could have? Is it the most honorable one?"

Maria glanced out of the window, to where noble Knights fought against the forces of magical law and order, two groups who were both sworn to keep the world safe and who made it more dangerous by fighting each other like this. She thought of the monsters in the forests of Europe and in the tunnels under the city, of the human monsters who preyed on the innocent. She thought of all the other quests they had set aside to come to Los Angeles.

She reached into her bag, pulled out the crown, and held it up. The gems blazed like a forest fire, their power threatening to burn everything else away. The temptation of power was there once again, to put the crown on, tap into its magic, and fight her way out.

"For the glory of God," she said, "and for a better world." She set the crown on the ground. "Let's talk."

CHAPTER FORTY-FOUR

The clocks struck midnight, the most powerful time for magic. In the hastily repaired Los Angeles County Museum of Art, the city's most powerful magicals had gathered. Leaders of the city's different magical tribes, CEOs of businesses that thrived through more than technology, scholarly witches and wizards from local universities, and of course, a contingent of Silver Griffins, led by one of their venerable elder statesmen, Director Harold Kowal. The great and the good of southern California stood around the edges of the room, champagne flutes in hand, holding quiet conversations and enjoying the refreshments delivered by tuxedoed gnomes.

"I'm not the only one who feels out of place, right?" Jackie straightened the hem of her skirt for the tenth time.

"Definitely not," Lucy agreed. "This whole do is so swanky that I don't dare talk to anyone in case I make a pillock of myself."

"We deserve to be here," Kelly said firmly. "Or at least I

do, and I won't have you two casting that into doubt. Act like you own the place, and they'll all believe it."

She smiled at a passing congressman, who smiled and nodded back.

"Twylan ought to be here," Jackie said. "None of this would have happened without her."

"A grubby teenager out of the tunnels?" Kelly shook her head. "Hardly a suitable guest to mingle with the great and the good."

Jackie shot Kelly a look so toxic it could have killed.

"She didn't want to come," Lucy informed them. "Said she hadn't been spending enough time with the Underfoot Brigade, though I think nervousness might have played a part too."

A bell rang, its single note crystal clear, and the room fell silent. Footsteps approached down a corridor amid long shadows cast by floating orbs of light. In two slow, decorous columns, the Order of the Knights of the Hinterland filed into the room. Chainmail had replaced their body armor, antiques flown in on an express flight from eastern Germany by a patron of the Order. Each one had a sword at their left hip and a dagger-like wand at the right.

Maria Pérez led one column, Oskar von Konigsberg the other. They walked up to a pedestal in the center of the room, on which the Grand Master's Crown sat, then stopped. The columns of armed magicals formed two lines, flanking an avenue from the pedestal to the door. In front of the pedestal stood Director Kowal, his suit upgraded to evening wear with a blue bow tie and cummerbund.

The bell chimed once more, and Klara Schulz appeared in the doorway, dressed in full plate armor, with a surcoat of blue and silver silk over the top. She progressed down the room, between the two lines of her Knights. As she did, they drew and raised their swords, forming arches of steel for her to pass through. She stopped in front of Kowal, and the two old enemies stood facing each other in shared solemnity.

"Over the years, many great rulers have crowned Grand Masters of the Knights of the Hinterland." Kowal raised his voice so that it filled the room, rich and melodious, the voice of a man used to an audience. "Kings, emperors, popes. Although that tradition broke in recent centuries, the things it represented remain. The honor of the Order. Its place in protecting us from the monsters that lurk in the shadows at the edges of our world. The dream of a better world.

"There are no kings in America, no emperors, no pope. The old world of rigid hierarchies has fallen away, and our nation is a symbol of that renewal. In America, it would be as fitting for you to be crowned by a farmer as by a CEO because we are all equal in principle and law."

He turned, lifted the crown from the pedestal, and held it up for the whole room to see.

"I don't do this as your ruler, as your leader, as someone to whom you should bow. In the traditional ceremony, the new Grand Master would kneel in homage, but today you stand tall. I am here—we are all here—to honor you as an equal. Equal in strength, in wisdom, in courage. Equal in the fight against those things that hurt the innocent and threaten to tear our world apart.

"We live in difficult times. The power of magic is growing in this world, and with it, the threat that magic can represent in the wrong hands. Yours are the right hands, and it will be our honor, from now on, to fight beside you."

"Drive back the darkness," the Knights chanted, and some of the Silver Griffins joined in. "Lift the light. Hunt down the monsters. For the glory of God and a better world."

Harold Kowal reached up and placed the crown on Klara Schulz's head.

As he stepped back, the crown started to glow. Power radiated from the gems around its outer surface. It gleamed from the sharp peaks. It flowed down through Schulz until every inch of her shone with an inner light and the room filled with magic.

Lucy clapped, and soon everyone joined in. The room filled with applause, then cheers and whistles. Glasses *clinked* against each other in celebration. Throughout, the Knights stood at attention, solemn and alert. After a few minutes, Kowal waved a hand and silence fell again.

Schulz reached up and took the crown from her head. She held it in front of her, staring as if she couldn't quite believe what was happening. Slowly, the light emanating from her faded, though some remnant of it remained, like sunlight reflected off the surface of a still pool, granting warmth and light to all around.

She held the crown out to Kowal.

"I return our crown to the care of the Silver Griffins and of the mundane authorities with whom they work," she said. "Share it with the world as you see fit and as is safe. May it serve as a beacon and an inspiration for all.

When the Order needs it again, we will come for it." She swallowed. "I fear that will be all too soon."

Kowal took the crown and placed it solemnly back on the pedestal. Then he extended his hand to Schulz.

"Grand Master," he said.

"Director." She took his hand, and the two old rivals, representatives of groups that had so often fought each other in the past, shook on a new peace.

There was more applause and a series of champagne toasts. With the coronation over, the Knights relaxed, in as much as any of them ever did. Some even indulged in refreshments and chatted with the other guests. Others lurked in the corners of the room, wary and watchful.

Maria, a glass of champagne in each hand, walked up to Ellis. She handed him one of the glasses.

"Thank you kindly." He took the glass. "This takes me back. Don't reckon we've shared champagne since…"

"Since our wedding night, the last time we celebrated. It was all downhill from there."

"Bad idea, it turns out."

"*Si*. But with the best of intentions. You are a good man, Ellis. We were a shitty couple."

Ellis grinned and held up his glass. "Here's to shitty couples and to finding something better after."

At the edge of the crowd, Jackie walked up to her Uncle Harold. Despite the presence of a ready audience, he wasn't holding court. Instead, he stood silent, occasionally sipping his drink as he watched the other guests.

"A lesson for you, little Jack-Jack," he said. "You have to pay attention at moments like this. Take a quiet pause to drink it all in."

"Shouldn't you be mingling, entertaining people with stories about past glories and the history of the Griffins?"

"Soon, this will be one of those stories. I want to remember every second." He smiled at her. "I'm headed back to D.C. in the morning, but I wondered if I might visit again soon? I really enjoyed it this time."

"Of course! I've enjoyed it too." Jackie hugged him. "Next time, if you're here on a secret mission, let me know from the start, okay?"

"Very well, if I must."

On the other side of the room, Lucy nervously approached Grand Master Klara Schulz. She didn't know what she wanted to say or if she would have a chance to say it, with so many important people trying to occupy Schulz's time, but she felt the need to acknowledge what no one else had said.

As she came closer, Schulz raised a hand, silencing the wizard who was talking to her. "Excuse me," Schulz said, "but I wish to talk with this remarkable young warrior alone."

Schulz nodded at Lucy, who followed her out of the room, down the corridor, and onto the museum's grounds.

Schulz looked up at the night sky, and her eyes shone like the stars.

"Remarkable, isn't it?" she said. "The wonders He has given us. We have so little time to treasure it in, but if we can preserve some part for the future, we reach a little farther into eternity."

"How long do you have left?" Lucy asked.

Schulz shrugged.

"Two years, maybe three." She smiled at Lucy. "I'm not afraid. My body may pass, but God will hold me forever."

"You believe that?"

"Don't you?"

"I don't know. I know that it will be a shame to lose you."

"We're only returning to Germany," Schulz said as if that was what they had been discussing all along. She pulled a business card from inside her armor and handed it to Lucy. "Here, if you ever need to reach me again, or the Grand Master who follows. I hope that next time we meet as friends. If not, we will at least make it a quick fight so we can get back to the real work."

She reached up as if to straighten her hair, and for a second Lucy saw a crown there, one made of magic, one that could never be set aside or displayed in a museum.

"I am glad that I lived to see a Grand Master crowned," Schulz said. "Not because it was me, but because we needed it. Sometimes, leadership is the burden we must bear to see a better world. I think you will bear that burden too."

"Perhaps." Lucy shrugged. "I have other things in my life. I don't want to lose the time I need to treasure them."

"Wisely said." Schulz glanced at the stars once more, then walked back inside.

Lucy looked up at those stars. They were beautiful, but they didn't draw her attention like they did Schulz's. Some people found wonder in infinity, but for her, it was closer to the ground.

She pulled out her phone and brought up a picture, one of the ones she and Charlie had included in their new display. It was the whole family on a hiking trail outside L.A., arms around each other as they smiled at the camera. A simple image, but something to treasure. The people she most loved in the world, together, safe, and happy. A simple moment in her personal history, preserved for eternity.

According to Andy Warhol, art is anything you can get away with. But can magical artists get away with magical art coming to life in Los Angeles? That's a big mistake and Lucy Heron and the Silver Griffins need to put a stop to it before too many humans discover magic is real in _OGRES AND MOM_.

Chicken Pot Pie (old school)

This is the best chicken pot pie I've ever had but it's not for the faint of heart. There's no 'lite' version. If you're gonna try this one, you have to be all in, but it's worth it. I promise. And remember that biscuit recipe from the last book? You'll need it for this recipe. But if you're in a hurry, you can use the canned, just don't tell my relatives. If you have the time, make the biscuits and set some aside to eat by themselves.

Also worth noting, I'm not a big fan of cooked peas and carrots in pot pies and love this recipe because it's low on vegetables (someone tell Michael). The chicken is the only star.

Make this one a night where you need some comfort food and put on your sweatpants. After a couple of servings, you may need them, but you'll still thank me.

Preheat oven to 450 degrees Fahrenheit.

Ingredients:

- 4 lb. chicken roaster (or turkey)
- 1 T salt
- 2 stalks celery
- 1 bay leaf
- 14 peeled small white onions

Those Biscuits

- 7 T butter
- 7 T flour
- 1 c full-fat milk or light cream
- 2 c chicken broth
- Dash of salt and a speck of pepper
- Dash of mace
- ½ t Worcestershire sauce
- 2 T sherry
- Pinch dried tarragon

Cook the chicken in a large kettle or Dutch oven with the salt, celery, bay leaf and enough boiling water to cover the chicken halfway. Simmer covered for about 1 ½ hours or until a fork can be easily inserted in a leg. Add the onions in the last half hour. Replenish boiling water when needed.

Take the chicken and onions from the broth and cool. Save the broth and skim off the fat as it cools. Strain it.

Make the biscuit dough and cut biscuits ½ inch thick and chill. (You can also use a premade pie crust and put on top and bottom if you prefer)

Melt the 7 T butter and add flour while stirring till

smooth. Slowly stir in milk and 2 cups of the saved and strained chicken broth. Cook until thickened, stirring frequently. Add salt to taste and rest of ingredients except chicken and onions.

Remove any skin and bones from chicken and cut into large cubes. Arrange with the onions in a greased casserole dish or deep pie pan. Pour the sauce over it and top with the chilled biscuits. Brush the biscuits with a little of the milk (or cream) and bake for 20 to 25 minutes or until golden brown. Makes about 6 servings. Enjoy (and it's even better as warmed up leftovers)

Get sneak peeks, exclusive giveaways, behind the scenes content, and more. PLUS you'll be notified of special **one day only fan pricing** on new releases.

Sign up today to get free stories.

Visit: https://marthacarr.com/read-free-stories/

So, cancer is back, or it was. In the middle of a couple of other health thingamabobs – an hiatal hernia and a thyroidectomy, cancer popped up. Same old, same old. Melanoma again, but presenting in a new way.

Fun fact. Turns out melanoma is the trickster of cancers and can appear in ways that look alarming – like 4th stage on the surface alarming – and turn out to be only stage one. Fun times.

Surgery – the third one in six weeks – was last week, so at least that's behind me. But there's still a few things left to ponder and one of them is what went right and what would I like to do differently?

There were a lot of doctors from a lot of specialties talking at me at once with a lot of information. Gastroenterologist, endocrinologist, oncologist. Interesting point – each medical tangle was discovered separately and each new one was slightly more serious than the previous till we landed on the bingo card. Cancer.

Friends were doing their best to help me wade through

all the info but at some point that became overwhelming. Not enough people were asking me, what do I want, and instead were offering what they thought was best.

Certain illnesses do that to well-meaning people with cancer at the top of that list. And this is the 5th time I've had melanoma, which may have ramped up everyone else's fear. However, that made it harder for me to find support and hear myself think. Particularly because after each surgery I was mentally and physically more exhausted.

Eventually, I was able to figure out the one or two people who were more willing to listen and sort things out. It made all the difference and helped lower my stress and made this whole adventure about me instead of others' expectations.

What do you want? It's the most powerful question there is. It's also a simple tool to help me keep my life on track. Whenever I find myself getting overwhelmed, it may take me a few moments, but eventually I remember, take a deep breath and ask again. What is the thing I want most here?

That helps me to see which options take me in that direction.

It also can help when other people are offering their two-cents worth and none of it matches. Not answering the phone every time it rings also helps.

Finally, a good friend said, "There's more than one way to do this. Whatever you choose that's the one that will be blessed."

(I realize I've stepped out onto a spiritual limb, but it's where I live most of the time and these author notes are about getting to know me...)

That was what I needed to be reminded of. To not shrink my faith down to one narrow choice like this was a game show. It got easier to trust myself and take what I like from all the advice and leave the rest.

Trust is another necessary ingredient to being able to answer that question – *what do I want?* Courage to step out and forge my own path can sometimes be another.

Getting down to what I wanted to do also helped me make a decision and get back to life. Peace found me again and suddenly my entire day wasn't all about cancer or surgery. It was a fuller picture and helped me stay present for all of it – joy included - no matter what maelstrom is going on around me. More adventures to follow.

AUTHOR NOTES - MICHAEL ANDERLE
MAY 28, 2021

Thank you for not only reading this story but our author's notes as well.

GPT-3 (and 2)

So, if you have heard about deep learning and big data, you might have discovered something called GPT-3** (Description from Wikipedia at the end). I am using an older version (GPT-2) to play with because I'm not special enough to have access to the Beta. They will come to regret that…sniff sniff.

(They will absolutely not regret that decision. I'm fantasizing here.)

Since this is one of the toys I'm playing with, I'm going to bore many of you with my fun related to this technology and stories.

One of the bigger issues (sometimes) for me as an author is what the hell to write about in my author notes. Therefore, I have chosen to play with this technology here.

Two birds, one stone.

Below you will find the phrase (in bold) that I provided to the GPT-2 Engine and the resulting text it spat back. I have NOT edited or changed the results (although I might have rejected the first effort and clicked the button to try again.)

I have two (2) tests for this book:

This is so much fun…and so *painful*…that I decided to see what might happen if you put a cookie, a witch, and an SUV together. Sound familiar?

The young witch drove her SUV around the corner, stopping behind a large tree to block anyone from seeing her. Grabbing her tall black hat, she snagged the little oak switch she commonly used for the same purpose and leaned over to snip off the hanging bough. The current lit up the white. She grabbed a lit candle and held it up to it, letting it dance a gentle path over the blackened wood. A sizzle ensued as the water did its magic. Her hair frizzed in the dry heat and sweat dripped down her back. When the candle had burned away to the nub she leaned in close and inhaled the sweet, chemical scent of the wood. I turned to head for the exit and walked past the large stone knight head on…

Ok… That was confusing. Let's try this again.

The young witch drove her SUV around the corner, stopping behind a large tree to block anyone from seeing her. Grabbing her tall black hat, she snagged the little oak switch she commonly used for the event and lifted it onto her hat.

"Well, y 'all!" she declared with false cheerfulness, "Who's ready to draw on Sunday? Come on out!"

Raven smiled, her heart beginning to hurt as she saw the number of faces from across the village in front of her.

She had made a promise to herself to only draw with those who'd found themselves here through the luck of the draw. There was no way she could find it in her heart to draw for just anybody. As much as she appreciated drawing for the cause, she could...

I'M NOT AFRAID...YET.

The second version included dialogue, which is a help for authors like me. I'm more character-motivated, so I can riff off of dialogue a lot more easily than I can an action scene. The dialogue provides me grounding in the character, and my mind pops up ideas much more quickly.

Anyway, that's something I'm playing with as an author and publisher—considering how we can use some of the new technology to provide new experiences with our characters for...well, everyone.

Ad Aeternitatem,

Michael Anderle

**Here is the definition from Wikipedia:

Generative Pre-trained Transformer 3 (GPT-3) is an autoregressive language model that uses deep learning to produce human-like text. It is the third-generation language prediction model in the GPT-n series (and the successor to GPT-2) created by OpenAI, a San Francisco-based artificial intelligence research laboratory.[2] GPT-3's full version has a capacity of 175 billion machine learning parameters. GPT-3, which was introduced in May 2020 and was in beta testing as of July 2020,[3] is part of a trend in natural language processing (NLP) systems of pre-trained language representations.[1] Before the release of GPT-3, the largest language model was Microsoft's Turing NLG, introduced in February 2020, with a capacity of 17 billion parameters - less than a tenth of GPT-3's.[4]

The quality of the text generated by GPT-3 is so high that it is difficult to distinguish from that written by a human, which has both benefits and risks.[4] Thirty-one OpenAI researchers and engineers presented the original May 28, 2020 paper introducing GPT-3. In their paper, they warned of GPT-3's potential dangers and called for research to mitigate risk.[1]:34 David Chalmers, an Australian philosopher, described GPT-3 as "one of the most interesting and important AI systems ever produced." [5]

Solve a murder, save her mother, and stop the apocalypse?

What would you do when elves ask you to investigate a prince's murder and you didn't even know elves, or magic, was real?

Meet Leira Berens, Austin homicide detective who's good at what she does – track down the bad guys and lock them away.

Which is why the elves want her to solve this murder – fast. It's not just about tracking down the killer and bringing them to justice. It's about saving the world!

If you're looking for a heroine who prefers fighting to flirting, check out The Leira Chronicles today!

AVAILABLE ON AMAZON AND IN KINDLE UNLIMITED!

CONNECT WITH THE AUTHORS

Martha Carr Social

Website: http://www.marthacarr.com

Facebook: https://www.facebook.com/
groups/MarthaCarrFans/

Michael Anderle Social

Website: http://lmbpn.com

Email List: http://lmbpn.com/email/

Social Media:

https://www.facebook.com/LMBPNPublishing

https://twitter.com/MichaelAnderle

https://www.instagram.com/lmbpn_publishing/

https://www.bookbub.com/authors/michael-anderle

www.ingramcontent.com/pod-product-compliance
Lightning Source LLC
Chambersburg PA
CBHW050512110726
47899CB00005B/1425